An
Inconvenient
Letter

OTHER BOOKS BY JULIE WRIGHT

Regency Romance

A Captain for Caroline Gray

Windsong Manor

Contemporary Romance

Lies Jane Austen Told Me

Lies, Love, and Breakfast at Tiffany's

Glass Slippers, Ever After, and Me

Contemporary Young Adult

Swimming in a Sea of Stars

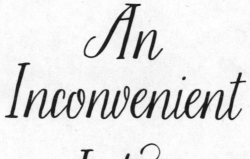

An Inconvenient Letter

PROPER ROMANCE

JULIE WRIGHT

SHADOW
MOUNTAIN
PUBLISHING

Library of Congress Cataloging-in-Publication Data
Names: Wright, Julie, 1972– author.
Title: An inconvenient letter / Julie Wright.
Other titles: Proper romance.
Description: Salt Lake City : Shadow Mountain, [2024] | Series: Proper romance | Summary: "Complications arise when Marietta's secret love letters are accidentally found by the wrong man."— Provided by publisher.
Identifiers: LCCN 2023032363 | ISBN 9781639932306 (trade paperback) | ISBN 9781649332479 (ebook)
Subjects: LCSH: Love-letters—Fiction. | Courtship—Fiction. | Nineteenth century, setting. | England, setting. | BISAC: FICTION / Romance / Historical / Regency | LCGFT: Historical fiction. | Romance fiction.
Classification: LCC PS3623.R55 I53 2024 | DDC 813/.6—dc23/eng/20230807
LC record available at https://lccn.loc.gov/2023032363

Printed in the United States of America
Lake Book Manufacturing, LLC, Melrose Park, IL

10 9 8 7 6 5 4 3 2 1

To unrequited love—
You saved me the hassle of inevitable breakups.

And to True Love—
You saved me.

Chapter One

To love a boy without him knowing when one is, herself, merely a girl is not a shameful endeavor. But society expects the girl to grow out of such sentiments, to swallow them down as she would her morning eggs, and to move on with her life.

Sadly, at seventeen years, Marietta Stone had grown up but had not grown *out* of her admiration of a certain boy.

"I'm forbidden to see you," she said aloud as she wrote the words in her letter. She continued without speaking again for fear that her mother's maid would be passing in the hall and overhear and tell her mother that she had become addled in the brain.

> *Yet I see you clearly in my mind's eye: your golden hair like wheat ready for harvest, your blue eyes as clear as the snow melting into the river. I hear your laugh and know we are sharing a joke that only we two comprehend.*

She smirked at that line. In truth, Frederick Nathaniel Finch had only ever laughed at his sister's expense, or hers, as the case often was. Frederick was her best friend's brother, and Etta had been in love with him for as long as she could remember. Well, perhaps not *that* long, since she *did* remember him as a rather rotten young boy with a propensity to tease, but it had been several years since he'd stretched out into a man who could be called tall, and his laughing eyes filled her with delight every time she saw them.

She hadn't seen him in over a year—not since before the Great Catastrophe of the Season. Not her season, but her sister's.

Her older sister, Anne, had been adorned in beautiful gowns, her hair swept up into elaborate braids and pinned with the lovely hairpins passed down from the girls' grandmother. Anne had trained for her debut into society her entire life. She spoke softly but with confidence. She walked as if floating. She could converse with a member of the nobility without humiliating herself.

Surely everything would be perfect.

But the season had decidedly *not* been perfect.

It had been a Great Catastrophe. Etta's mother and sister had returned from London with reputations bruised and confidence in tatters. Mama had thundered and stormed and forbidden them to associate with the Finch family. Etta had not seen Frederick, or even her friend Lucy Finch, since. They were not allowed to so much as throw a stone in the direction of the Finch property.

This was why she had to write Frederick letters, although she would not have seen him even without her mother's admonition to avoid his family.

At the time of the Great Catastrophe, Frederick Finch had been in France. She needed to forget him. She wrote the letters to accomplish just that. She reasoned that if she put all her feelings to paper, they would no longer be trapped between the beatings of her heart, and she could focus on her upcoming season.

Etta sighed and returned to her letter.

> *Do you remember when you had decided to build a fort with your cousin Gerard, and you declared no silly girl should ever enter? But then you couldn't see how to fit the boards in the tree branches so that you could nail them down properly and required my help to work it all*

out, and then Gerard insisted you had to let me in the
fort since it was I who had built it? He said that I was
not at all a silly girl, and you looked at me like he just
might be right. I think of that look sometimes and wish
I could see it in you now. Heavens, I wish I could see
you no matter what way you looked at me.

Etta stopped writing long enough to gaze out the window, though in truth she saw nothing beyond the panes of glass. She bit her lip and dipped her pen in the ink. Her life had become so much lonelier since she'd been banned from the company of her friend and her friend's brother.

She put her pen to paper again.

Soon I will be in London, dancing at balls and
being introduced into society. It is my dearest wish that
you be one of the gentleman callers presenting me with
a posy. I long for you to see me as more than your sister's
dearest friend, as more than a little girl.

Alas, chances are that you will stay away from
London during my season the way you did last season.
I will likely be engaged before I see you again. Since we
are not to be, it is time for me to bid you adieu. I must
put away these childish fantasies. I will, instead, focus
my efforts on discovering a relationship grounded in re-
ality, not fancy. My time in London will be a chance
to create myself anew and find a man who will notice
my presence and miss me in my absence. Since you have
never done either, this will be my last letter to you. I
will not think of the name Frederick Finch again.

Yours no longer, M

Etta folded the letter before dripping red wax at the overlap and stamping the image of a rose into it. She turned the paper over and was addressing it to Mr. Frederick Finch when her door opened.

Etta, worried it was her mother, stuffed the envelope in her desk drawer, slammed it shut, and turned to see who the interloper might be. "Anne! You gave me a fright."

Anne stopped and tilted her head slightly, making her lovely golden curls fall to the side elegantly. "What are you doing, Etta?"

Etta stood and moved away from the desk. "I am worrying about my season." That was true enough.

Anne frowned and slumped her almost perpetually straight shoulders. "You shouldn't worry, exactly, but you must be careful. You would not want a repetition of my catastrophe." Anne's face paled at the memory.

"Your time in London was not entirely awful, Anne," Etta said.

Anne sighed. "You only say so because you weren't there. It was discussed in every gossip column in every paper." She paused, collecting herself, and then delivered the message she had originally intended to convey.

"Mama wishes us to work on our embroidery. She feels you need the practice."

As if the mention of her mother had reminded her of her posture, Anne straightened again. Etta did too. Both girls had a habit of squaring their shoulders when their mother was nearby.

The pair moved together down the stairs and to the drawing room, where they sat on the blue settee.

Anne continued their conversation from earlier. "You will need to be above reproach in all things while you're in London, Etta. No slipping into discussions regarding husbandry or estate management like you did last night at the Goodmans' musicale. The men do not like us inserting ourselves into their conversations."

"Papa does not mind."

"But Mama does. And so do all the other mothers. You must be, in every way, presentable when you go to London."

"Why do I need to be presentable?" Etta asked with a smirk. "The point of having an impressive dowry is to make me presentable with no effort on my part."

Anne laughed but grew serious and said, "After my Great Catastrophe, you will have to tread more carefully than any other young lady, dowry or no. You see, the dowry did not save me from censure. It won't save you either."

Etta set her embroidery aside. She gave Anne's hand a gentle squeeze. "You exaggerate the catastrophe. Mama says that you had many callers and received many lovely bouquets. She says there is no reason to feel apprehension."

Anne shook her head and appeared to be determined to focus on the needlework in her own lap. "And what good were any of the callers or flowers? Or the wasted hours of fussing with my hair and gowns, pinching my cheeks to obtain a rosy glow, and then smiling until my cheeks hurt worse than from pinching them? I returned home with nothing more than a scandal."

To call the event that had occurred a scandal seemed strong to Etta, but she had not witnessed it. Etta still did not understand why she and Anne were to share in the shame that should have belonged to their mother.

Her mother held the whole of the Finch family responsible for Anne's failure to secure a husband. Etta was secretly glad the events had happened to Anne and not to her—but not because she wished her sister ill. She loved Anne more than she could bear. But while her mother would forgive any perceived failing in her sister, she did not love Etta nearly so well. In some twisted way, her mother held Etta accountable for events that had nothing to do with her. Etta hadn't even been present in London. However, her mother felt that Etta's friendship with Lucy Finch was enough to merit blame. This led to many reminders that Etta was a disappointment.

"I have worked tirelessly for a successful outcome for you two girls. I do believe you will waste my efforts, Marietta!" Mrs. Stone had said on more than one occasion.

On those occasions, Etta escaped to her father's study, where Papa made her feel intelligent and wanted by discussing whatever matter of business he was currently engaged in.

Anne squeezed Etta's hand, pulling her back to their conversation. "I am glad I will not be returning alone. I will have you at my side."

"Of course. There is nowhere else I would rather be."

It was true, even if Anne made Etta appear positively plain when they were seen together.

Anne truly was the loveliest girl in all the world, with hair that shone like gold and sapphire eyes that were contemplative and full. She and Etta were, in many ways, a study of opposites. Where Anne's hair was golden, Etta's was a dark reddish-brown, and Etta's eyes were hazel to Anne's blue. Anne's beauty shone like the midday sun, whereas Etta's was more like the twilight.

But for all Anne's beauty, accomplishments, and charms, her shy demeanor made her a perfect fit for the quiet of the country. She preferred to keep her own company. She preferred music to conversation. She preferred the gardens over a ballroom.

Etta felt a sigh deep in her bones.

It was wrong that her mother had turned her and her sister into rivals of sorts, especially when Etta wanted nothing more than Anne's happiness. She smiled at her sister. It wasn't Anne's fault that their mother was less than enthusiastic regarding Etta's upcoming season, despite having had a year to consider a plan of action to guarantee success. Mama had always been a woman who planned, who took action.

"I thank you, Anne, for trying to assuage my concerns. I'm sure London will be lovely."

"It will be made all the lovelier because we will be together," Anne said. She had abandoned her needlework. "We will be quite formidable together. Do you not agree?"

"Of course!" Etta said. "The men will be swooning at our feet from the moment of our arrival."

"Men swooning . . . the very idea." Anne shook her head.

"They very well may, dear Anne, for you."

"Oh!" Anne let go of Etta's hand so she could give a playful smack to Etta's arm. "For you as well! You'll see! It will all be perfect because we will be together."

Before Etta could agree, or disagree, as she felt inclined to do, their mother entered the drawing room. Both girls immediately picked up their embroidery and resumed their efforts as if they had never stopped.

Mama stared down at them over her perfect, straight nose. She had classic Roman features, which she took great pride in.

Etta felt that her mother went to bizarre extremes to keep her beauty unaffected by the years. She always carried a sharp odor from the many creams she applied to maintain her appearance.

Mrs. Stone narrowed her eyes at the girls as though trying to discern what mischief her daughters were up to. When she could see nothing out of place, she smoothed her skirts over her thin frame and sat. As was usual of late, she was clearly disappointed to find herself in the irksome company of her youngest daughter.

Marietta could hardly see why. It was not as though dire circumstances required her parents to marry off their daughters with any speed. Her father made many good investments, and that, along with the income brought in from the tenants working her father's land, meant their finances were in order, as were their good names—aside from the Great Catastrophe. There was no ill health or entail that plagued their father. All was well enough, with or without husbands.

Still, her mother felt personally affronted by Marietta's love of business and estate management and her inclination to follow her father everywhere he went. She took even greater offense over the lack of ladylike accomplishments that would make Etta a desirable wife.

Mrs. Stone also took it quite personally that her eldest daughter had failed to marry when several girls of her same age from the neighborhood were now happily situated, and one was even expecting her first child. Mama's competitive nature strained comprehension. Etta knew her mother did not like placing all her hopes of a successful season on her younger daughter, whose prospects were much less glowing than Anne's.

"Marietta." Her mother's stern voice pulled Etta out of her private musings.

"Yes, Mama?"

"Did you write your Aunt Sophia as I requested? I know you were tending to other correspondence when I asked you, but I'm well aware of how easily distracted you become. If your aunt could arrange a few invitations for us, it will be just the thing."

Her mother could not ask for favors from her sister-in-law herself since the two women had never got on very well. Etta was always made to send any correspondence on behalf of her mother.

"I did finish my letter to Aunt Sophia. It's on my desk right now waiting to go out. I did not become distracted by my other letters."

Etta took a deep breath and held it as if holding air in her lungs would somehow take the sting from her mother's insult. She found she did so often when her mother was nearby. She worried one day she would have to hold her air so long that she would forget to breathe out again and faint dead away.

Mrs. Stone didn't bother to respond, instead turning her attention to Anne to discuss London's dress and milliners' shops, which they would simply have to visit as soon as they arrived in town, for the local establishments would not have the latest styles and varieties that were available in town.

Her mother enjoyed the idea of dressing up Anne, though she merely tolerated the thought of dressing up Etta.

Anne was patient with the conversation, though she was clearly not in thrall over the many delights such a shopping excursion would create for her Mama.

Etta felt similarly to her sister. Why must they shop? Did they not already have sufficient hats and gloves and dresses?

Well, perhaps her mother did not have so many now as she once did, but that was a topic no one was allowed to mention. The loss of her mother's favorite ball gown coincided with the loss of Anne's attention from several eligible young men.

Worse, the Great Catastrophe of the Season had meant the loss of Etta's best friend as well, though no one else seemed to worry over that detail.

"New gloves will be lovely, Mama. Do you not agree, Etta?" Anne said in an obvious attempt to bring her sister into the conversation.

Before Etta could respond, their mother turned her hawkish gaze on her youngest daughter. "Why don't you fetch your letters and give them to Greene to post, Marietta?"

"Of course, Mama." Etta laid her needlework to the side and was about to stand when her sister hurried to her feet.

"There's no reason to trouble yourself, Etta. I need to send some of my own. I'll fetch the letters, Mama."

Before her mother or Etta could protest, Anne was gone in a swish of pale rose-colored skirts.

"You've been frightening her again by making her recount the misery of her season, haven't you, Marietta?"

Etta felt her cheeks warm. "I don't think so, Mama. I truly believe she is looking forward to the season." At least, Etta imagined Anne might be looking forward to it, although Anne's every comment regarding the whole adventure was filled with determined cheerfulness rather than *actual* cheerfulness.

Could it be Etta *had* frightened Anne by asking for further information? She didn't see how, but Etta hadn't been there, so how could she understand the mortification? She'd only heard the stories of the rather epic conflict that had transpired between her mother and her best friend's mother and the way potential suitors had scattered like a flock of birds from the trees.

Her mother's sharp gaze cut into Etta's thoughts. "After last night's disaster with the musicale, I have been thinking."

Disaster was far too strong a word to describe events. Etta had merely offered the opinion that people who worked land should have the same voice as those who owned land when it came to voting. True, she had been stared at with a great degree of shock for inserting herself into the conversation, but she would not go as far as to call it a disaster.

As if reading Etta's mind, Mama said, "It *was* a great disaster. And it made me consider our position—*Anne's* position. And I know your father felt it would be fine for you to come out, but I've decided that it is best to postpone your season until your sister is suitably settled in a marriage of her own."

"Postpone? You mean for me to stay home from London?"

"So you *do* agree. I am so glad to find you thinking sensibly for once."

Etta had not agreed to anything. She wanted to go to London. She wanted her season. She wanted to find someone who loved her so she could make a home of her own, one where she would not have her every step criticized. "But Mama . . ." What? What could she say?

"It is a balm to me that you understand how important this season is for your sister, as it will allow her to create ties to families of importance. If you were both competing for the affection of suitors, it would detract from Anne's potential. But if Anne can stand in her own light a little longer, it will give her a second chance. I am so glad that you understand how your presence would be a distraction from your sister's goals. I know you would not want to ruin your sister's happiness with your propensity to offer opinions on affairs that do not concern ladies. We certainly do not need another Great Catastrophe. I am so pleased we are in agreement."

Mrs. Stone brushed off her skirts as if there might be some errant crumb or dust particle that needed sweeping away. Then she stood and left the room.

Etta sucked in a breath and held it but let it out slowly when her vision began to darken with spots.

She glanced around the room to see all the items that reminded her of the way her mother had tried to coax some sort of achievement from her. Her gaze fell on the pianoforte that she had never truly mastered except to plunk out cringingly off-key tunes but that her sister managed to play well enough to bring tears of joy and awe to her listeners. Etta next looked upon the several framed paintings that Anne had created for their proud parents, and then on the embroidery both she and her sister had been working on. Anne's had perfect, even stitches while her own showed hasty and less-than-perfect ones. Finally, Etta gazed toward the ivory draperies swept back from the double doors to the garden where she could not even manage to grow the herbs or flowers her mother had insisted to be so easy to care for that any simpleton could achieve the task.

The flowers had all died. The herbs had dried up into pathetic little sticks well before any leaves had appeared on them.

Etta's father had never worried over those things. He always said she had a strong head for household management, which, in his opinion, was the most important of the ladylike skills, and that those other endeavors were not nearly as vital. Her mother, however, disagreed.

"I am useless," Etta said aloud to the room around her. "Entirely useless."

She wandered the house aimlessly for a time before she realized there was no solace to be found anywhere. Her feet, of their own accord, carried her in the direction of her bedchamber, as if sensing that she needed the solace of her desk and the correspondence she had been keeping with several of her aunts.

Her Aunt Sophia, in particular, had written just the day before, answering Etta's questions regarding animal husbandry. The letter had been warm and friendly and complimentary and *kind*—not scornful of Etta's interest in the affairs of business.

Etta *needed* kind at that exact moment. She opened her bedroom door so quickly that she frightened Jillian, a maid close to Etta's own age.

"The room's not quite done up yet, miss."

"Leave it, please. I need a moment to myself at present."

Jillian bobbed and vacated the room.

Etta groaned and sank to the chair in front of her desk. She loved the desk because, although it had only the one drawer, the drawer was brilliantly concealed so that few even knew it existed.

Thinking on that small drawer that ran the length of the bottom of the desk forced Etta's gaze downward to something out of place—something she'd known to be out of place as soon as she'd sat but had not had the presence of mind to understand until that very moment.

The drawer was not entirely closed.

Etta frowned. She always closed it, lest people of little discretion decided to help themselves to her private thoughts. People like her mother.

She held her breath and slid the drawer fully open. They were gone.

Her letters . . . the letters she'd written but should *not* have written were no longer sitting together in a tidy pile of paper and ink and inappropriate emotions.

She gasped and covered her mouth with one hand while the other frantically scattered the other papers within the drawer to see if she'd merely covered them with some other correspondence.

Then Etta stood, threw back the chair violently enough to upend it altogether, and dragged the drawer entirely from the desk. She overturned its contents to the floor and fell to her knees to sift through the wreckage.

"No! No. No, no, no, no!" They were well and truly gone.

Anne knocked on the door and entered at that moment but fell back when she saw what could only have appeared to be a mad frenzy.

"Etta! What is all this? Are you unwell? Are you hurt?"

Etta scrambled to her feet, feeling as though her skirts were a devil's trap at that exact moment. "Anne! Anne, when you came in here not long ago to find Aunt's letter, did you open this drawer?"

Anne tried to fall back at the crazed pleading, but Etta had already formed a tight grip on Anne's arms. Too tight, if the wince in Anne's face and the squirm of those arms within Etta's grip were to be read correctly.

"No!" Anne declared. "It was already open when I came to collect Aunt's letter."

"Already open? How could it be already open? I always close it. Always."

"Well, it did appear that you had tried to close it, as one end was tucked in much farther than the other."

Etta thought frantically. That *was* possible. She had been summoned downstairs quite abruptly. Sometimes the drawer's edges did not glide in as smoothly as she would have wanted, and she often had to jostle the drawer before it closed. She had not jostled it earlier. She was sure of that much.

"Did anything look out of place?"

Anne glanced at the contents that had been spilled all over the floor. "You mean like now?"

Etta wanted to growl at her sister. "There were three letters. Did you see them?"

"Of course I saw them. I'm not blind, Etta."

"Where are they?"

Her sister rolled her lovely pale blue eyes in a way that would have made their mother scowl. "I sent them off, of course."

"No." Etta released her sister as if she'd been burned and shook her head as if she could shake the horrible truth away from herself. "You could not have done such a thing. They were not properly addressed."

"Yes, they were. Quite properly."

It was too hot in the room. Or perhaps it was too cold. Etta brought a hand to her mouth and closed her eyes while she tried to think her way out of the predicament her sister had created for her. But there was no way out. The most terrible, wretched, mortifying thing that could possibly have happened had happened.

The letters were mailed.

And there was nothing Etta could do about that fact. She was ruined.

Chapter Two

Gerard Hartwell studied his cousin, feeling irritated with himself for the jealousies that sprang up in him. Frederick, fair-haired and equally fair-tempered, had not experienced a moment of worry regarding his future, whereas Gerard had nothing but worries. He allowed himself to brood a moment longer before he heard the commotion of the dogs scaring the birds out of the hedgerow. He squinted his eye and took aim up to the sky that had all but disappeared behind the mass fluttering of feathers. He fired his weapon.

"You missed." Frederick grinned wickedly, his nose red with the frigid air. "So many targets, and you didn't hit one of them."

"Yes. Thank you. I am well aware." Gerard lowered his weapon and frowned at the now clear blue expanse. "It seems I am missing a great many things of late." He handed his gun to Frederick's gamekeeper and awaited one that had been freshly loaded.

When it was handed to him, he didn't bother lifting it.

Frederick eyed him. "Don't be so wretchedly *wretched*, man. You aren't killing any birds, but you are managing to kill my mood."

Gerard looked away, not wanting to meet his cousin's eye. "It is easy to have an elevated mood when life has handed you ease and good fortune. I suppose that is what makes it so difficult for you to have compassion for the ill-fated."

"Are you referring to yourself? Do you want me to hang my head at the incredible injustices done you? You, who are well-connected and handsome, if chatter from the ladies is to be believed, though I think they exaggerate quite a lot."

"You forgot poor."

Frederick shrugged. "What is poverty to a man who can marry away such a defect?"

"To be forced to marry for money certainly limits my prospects for happiness."

The noise that erupted from Frederick's mouth could only be described as a scoffing sort of bray. "Don't tell me that you had planned to make a love match." When Gerard did not respond, Frederick's scoff turned into a full laugh. "You *had* planned on such a thing. Well, cousin . . . I'm not quite certain what to say regarding such news. Have you already had your eye on some unsuspecting girl? Do I know her? She's obviously not a woman of wealth, or you would have wooed her already to save your own skin and, apparently, your heart. Is she pretty, then? Do you think she would fancy me?"

At that, Gerard punched his cousin in the arm hard enough to make Frederick rub the offended spot.

Frederick scowled and dropped his hand immediately when he realized he'd been caught showing weakness for massaging feeling back into his arm.

"There's no reason for violence, Gerard. It's not as if I am the one who spent your inheritance at every hazard table in every gaming hell London has to offer."

Why did Freddie always speak so plainly? Gerard had never had a good relationship with his father. His father had been everything snapping and cruel when he'd had too much to drink. And he'd often had too much to drink. There had once been the hope that when his father passed, Gerard and his mother would finally be free from the ill effects of his father's impropriety. It was Gerard's fondest wish that his mother would be able to live the rest of her life peaceably. She was a

kind woman with a generous heart. He owed her everything for helping to mold him into the man he was.

But his father had managed to infect them with his bad choices
even after his passing. If Gerard could only get his feet under him, he
could stop his mother from ever feeling the pain of this hurt. Gerard
narrowed his eyes at his cousin. "Are you trying to make me feel worse?"

"No, but I am trying to make you see reason. Your life is not over.
You are not some disgraced nobody. So you've lost your fortune—"

"And my lands, if I don't find a way to pay the debts," Gerard
interrupted.

"Yes. And that. But if you marry quickly to a lady of means, those
debts are not entirely insurmountable."

"How do I explain to a woman why she must marry me quickly?
What self-respecting woman would enter such an arrangement?"

"There are many women of fortune with less than fortunate ap-
pearances who would happily wed you tomorrow if it meant they
would actually marry."

"Freddie, I truly hate it when you remind me what a cad you are."

His cousin acknowledged the truth of the insult with a shrug. "If
I thought you had a prospect of that kind that could guarantee me a
fairly quick repayment, I would loan you the money until the banns
were read and the deed was done."

Gerard gripped the barrel of the gun he held and considered.
He might be able to save his estate with such a quick injection of
funds. "You mean to say that were I to enter into a relationship with a
woman who had a sizable enough dowry, you would give me a loan?"

"On the spot."

"What's stopping you from loaning me the money now and trust-
ing I'll pay you back?"

Frederick laughed as if Gerard had made some sort of joke. "No
man is willing to invest in something without assurances."

"You don't think I would pay the loan back?" The insult to Gerard
hurt worse than his poverty. A raven cawed in the distance as if laughing along with Freddie over Gerard's hope.

"I do think you would *want* to pay me back. But, cousin . . . want and capability are not the same thing. You need not fret, however. You need only find a young lady with a father of stable means who would be giving his daughter a modest dowry, and the loan is yours."

Gerard huffed. "Oh yes. There are so many of those options available to me that my problems are now solved. I thank you for your service."

"Sarcasm is not one of your strengths. In all seriousness, you could woo Miss Anne Stone. She's pretty, and her father has been very generous with his daughters. And her reputation is slightly damaged, which makes her desperate enough to overlook even your faults."

"Anne Stone? From the family your mother has declared to be the absolute worst sort? The family your sister has been forbidden to even think about?"

"That silly squabble between mothers is nothing to us men. Stop looking so sullen. Really, you do have a tendency to grumble and brood over the smallest of things."

Gerard rolled his shoulder and hefted the gun, grateful for the distraction it provided. "Oh yes. Smallest of things. We're only discussing my future. Trivial, really. Before I decide to despise you, let's return to discussing a pheasant dinner." He fired, and missed, again.

"With the luck you seem to be having, there will only be biscuits and beans to eat." Freddie lifted his own gun, his eye squinted, his finger ready to pull the trigger.

That Freddie missed as well gave Gerard a small amount of satisfaction. "I do believe you mean with the luck *you* seem to be having, Freddie."

Freddie did not argue the point, as neither of them had managed to show they had any skill in the sport that day.

Gerard was glad to have taken off the black crepe armband. The time of official mourning for his father had passed, but he felt that until he had the estate turned around, he would always be in mourning. If Freddie hadn't been gracious enough to allow Gerard and his mother to basically live at his house, there would have been no way

Gerard could hide his poverty from his mother. As it was, keeping such a secret had become a terrible burden. His mother bordered on occasional silliness, but she was astute enough to know the truth if he wasn't excessively careful to keep it from her. "I do wish I had some means of recovering quickly. I do not know how long I can keep the terrible truth from my mother," Gerard said softly, considering all the ways it would be easier to find a wife and accept his cousin's offer.

Gerard rubbed at his temple, as if he could massage away the headache of it all. "But I worry my lands may never recover from the neglect and ill-usage of my father. The last seven months have proven I cannot keep tenants. As soon as their contracts are fulfilled, they refuse to sign new ones. They up and move away to places where they can be guaranteed fair treatment and housing that is free of leaky roofs and rodents. They do not trust me to be a better man than the one who raised me. I am glad you will not loan me money without assurances, for I may never be able to repay you. And I will not have that on my conscience. I will not be like my father."

Freddie looked sorry to be saying what he was about to say. "Then you must heed my advice and marry. And soon."

"Yes. I suppose I must." The words tasted like ash on Gerard's tongue. The two cousins turned away from each other and the somber mood they had created and returned to the matter of shooting. In the end, they did manage to bring home four large pheasants, which was more than enough.

Later that night, when the family had joined together for the evening meal, Gerard's mother smoothed her hands over the black dress she wore and sent a sly smile to her sister. The two women were practically identical to one another in looks, though not exactly in disposition.

Gerard's mother was plump and good-humored, quick with a smile, and always ready to smooth over tensions that might arise among any group of people. Gerard felt certain her easy manner had made her life with her husband much more bearable. His aunt, who was also plump, was more prone to jealousies and grudges. It always struck him as baffling that the two of them got on as well as they did.

Proof of that oneness of mind was that his mother's sly smile was returned by her sister. Gerard tensed in an effort to withstand the upcoming storm of their conspiring.

"I had a thought, Gerard," his mother said.

Whenever she started with some variation of that phrase, Gerard wished that she spent less time with her thoughts.

"Yes," Mrs. Hartwell continued. "A thought that I think will be quite agreeable to everyone involved."

Gerard sincerely doubted it. And if the pained expression his cousin shared with him was any indication, Freddie also doubted it.

"My dearest and oldest friend, Frances Bates, you remember her? Well, her daughter has grown to be quite lovely."

The hair on the back of Gerard's neck stood on end. *No*. His mother could not be serious. "You are not referring to Miss Abigail Bates?" He phrased the question in such a way because no one could possibly refer to Abigail Bates as lovely. He supposed her appearance was well enough, if one cared too deeply regarding such things, though her cheeks were unnaturally red, as if she spent hours pinching them each day. But it was not her appearance that repelled Gerard so completely. Rather, it was the way she laughed at everything, believing the entire world to be made up of diversions. He felt certain that if he told her his father had recently passed away, she would likely explode with great guffaws, as if in response to the most hilarious joke imaginable.

Being that Abigail was the daughter of his mother's oldest and dearest friend, Gerard had often been thrown into her path, starting from when they were both under the care of their nurses. He had no good memories of any moment when Abigail Bates had been present except one, and that was because his cousin Lucy and the Stone girls had been there.

"The very same!" His mother replied with obvious delight that he mentioned her friend's daughter by name. Why she acted surprised he remembered Abigail baffled him when she refused to allow him the luxury of forgetting the woman.

"She will be in London this season, and I thought how lovely it would be for us to see each other. Perhaps you could call on her to take her for a ride in the curricle."

"I sold the curricle, Mother." In truth, Gerard had sold a great many things from their property in town. If he could not find a way to make an item useful for the purpose of retaining his lands in the country, then he had no need of it. When his father died, his mother had fallen into a state of fragility that left him managing affairs that the mistress of a house usually handled. He was glad for it now since it meant his mother had no idea how dire their circumstances actually were.

"You sold the curricle?" His mother appeared wounded by the very idea. "But what will I tell Miss Bates when we arrive this season and have no curricle?"

"I do not know what you will tell her when *you* arrive this season. But for my part, I will not be in town for the season."

No news within all of England could have shaken his mother to the degree that his absence from the season did at that moment. "But that's impossible!" She all but wailed the sentiment. "How will you ever court Frances's daughter if you are away from town?"

"That *is* the quandary, is it not? I suppose some other fellow shall have the privilege."

"But what is so terribly important that you would neglect your responsibility to your poor mother?"

Gerard ground his teeth together. She could not see that his actions were all about keeping her from poverty. She could not see that he would have to work, engage in actual physical labor, to bring his lands to the standard that would attract tenants worth having. She could not see because he chose not to tell her the extent of it.

"I will be seeing to the estate, Mother. I will be seeing to the duties left to me by my father." No truer words had ever been said. His father had left him the mess that surrounded him on all sides, and he would do what he could to put it to rights again.

"But the steward and all the servants will do that."

All of the servants would not, for the simple reason that there were so few left. Most of them had been casualties of his father's habits and the resulting poverty. Gerard could simply not afford to keep them. Though for some of them, even if he could, he would not. Several of those in his father's employ had been skimming money from the estate. He had no way to prove it, but when Grady, his father's steward, and he had gone over all the accounts, Grady agreed that such theft was more than simply possible; it was quite likely. Gerard's father had not allowed Grady to fire people who produced problems on his estate. The man was delighted to see that the son was not at all like the father. Between Grady and Gerard's efforts, they had trimmed the fat considerably.

Gerard could not rely on him too heavily for he did not wish to have the man quit simply because too much had been placed upon his shoulders. While Grady still oversaw many responsibilities, such as collecting the rents from those remaining tenants and overseeing the harvesting and livestock, Gerard would not ask Grady to split rails for fences so that the livestock did not trespass into the crops. He would not ask Grady to patch roofs or do any of the other tasks that would, no doubt, leave calluses on hands that were used to being smooth.

He would do those things himself—as much as he was able.

But Gerard could not tell his mother such details. She would be thrown into a fit of histrionics upon learning that her son was doing hard labor. She would want to know why he wasn't paying someone else to do such work, and when she learned that there was no money to pay for help, she would have even more questions for him. If he mentioned his plans for the season, she would push him into marrying Miss Abigail Bates. Such a marriage was the easy solution—one that his cousin wanted him to choose. His father would certainly have chosen such a course had it been available to him.

Gerard had grown tired of people more committed to easy solutions than to correct solutions. He shook his head. He would not be so imprudent.

"Are you contradicting me?" his mother asked.

"What? Oh. No, Mother. I was only thinking of some matters that would require my attention after dinner."

"I thought we would all play cards together tonight. You plan to rush off?"

Gerard truly loved his mother, but he sometimes wondered if the years had been unkind to her mind, because she was not the strong, vibrant woman he had once known. Had his father's straying and excesses led to the dimming of her mind? Or had that simply been the natural work of years and age? Gerard did not know. But he was determined to set to rights all the many wrongs in their lives so that his mother might live out the rest of her life in relative comfort.

"I am sorry, Mother. But I need to return to Hartwell Hall tonight. Business is a thing that waits for no one."

"It waited for your father often enough. He didn't see a need to tend to business in the evenings."

Freddie shot Gerard a look of compassion that only fueled the agitation in Gerard's chest. He smiled for his mother. "Truer words have never been said. I will try to return quickly."

Though Gerard's estate in the neighboring county was not far from his cousin's, it was far enough that his mother experienced difficulty in traveling it over and over. Since her husband had died, she spent most of her time with her sister. Gerard found the situation to his advantage, because he'd had to reduce the size of his domestic staff. He'd kept them for the duration of their contracts and was quite glad to see that none of those had been for longer than a year. As each servant had reached the end of his or her contract, Gerard had quietly given him or her notice along with a reference letter that would allow for new employment opportunities.

His mother would surely perceive the quieter, more subdued state of the manor and be horrified. There was not the constant polishing and sweeping and dusting as there had been before.

Gerard was glad Mrs. Hartwell didn't invite her sister to stay at their place for a change of scenery. Since his aunt greatly loved her home and commanding those within it, she found she didn't much care to leave without a compelling reason. Gerard's mother was, for now, safe from learning that her house and grounds staff were barely enough to keep the manor running adequately.

Maybe marrying wasn't such a terrible idea.

Maybe he would better serve his estate by quickly finding a young lady of adequate fortune and marrying without delay.

An image of Abigail Bates flashed in his mind. No. That would never do for him.

After dinner that night, as he rode his horse to his own estate, Gerard continued to muse over the idea of marrying. He rode alone because he'd temporarily excused his valet, Wilson, from the hardships he had placed on himself. There was no one to dress for or impress when he was at Hartwell Hall. He could shine his own boots and brush his own clothes if he needed to.

Besides, not bringing Wilson meant not being obligated to stop at an inn to sleep for the night. He had no spare coin for such frivolities. He kept a bedroll tied to the saddle and would sleep when he became too weary to keep his seat.

The constant back-and-forth travel was wearying, but if Gerard stayed away from his cousin's estate for too long, his mother might decide to return home. He was fairly certain his mother would accompany his aunt and Frederick's sisters when they went to London for the season.

That would give him until the season's end to repair all that his father had broken in their lives. It would be enough time.

At least he hoped so.

Things had to be better by then. If they weren't, what would he do? Marry Miss Abigail Bates even though he felt ill at the mere thought of her? No. He resolved, once again, that he would never stoop to the inferior situation of being shackled to a woman he could not, in any way, esteem. Blast but he hated that he had to continually talk himself out of such blatant stupidity.

The ride to Hartwell Hall was uneventful. Though he'd only slept an hour or so on the road, it had been enough to see him safely to his door. He entered the house and thought of the bed that awaited him upstairs, a bed he could not visit no matter how fatigued he was.

There was work to be done, and time could not be squandered in the same way his inheritance had.

Gerard handed off the remaining pheasant to be given to those left in his employ and hurried to change into clothing suitable for the day's activities. Once outside, he took a deep breath and began tugging on his father's old riding gloves.

"You've returned, Mr. Hartwell."

He glanced up from the gloves to see his steward, Mr. Grady. "Yes. I'll have two days before they'll require my presence again at Rosemary Manor. Let's make the most of it."

"Of course, sir." Grady nodded and led the way to the stables where fresh horses were waiting.

Initially, Gerard had no idea how much he would come to appreciate Grady, not only for the man's knowledge and intelligence but for his loyalty and for his desire to see things returned to their former glory. Grady had managed to convince tenants who were determined to leave at the ends of their contracts to stay and try one more year. Of course, he had done it with the promise that improvements would be made to the houses, barns, and fences.

Slowly, Gerard had been making good on that promise. He even found he didn't mind the work all that much as it gave him somewhere to direct his frustration and anger. For every nail hammered into a fence or a roof, *he* felt improved as well.

The work wasn't easy. It was dirty and unforgiving. When he hit his thumb with the hammer and let fly words he was glad no one was present to overhear, he wondered again if maybe marrying wasn't the better way out of his predicament.

His mind conjured up the image of Miss Abigail Bates, her pinched-too-hard cheeks, and her scornful laugh.

He shook off the pain in his hand and began hammering again. He was discovering that thinking of that particular lady certainly made it easier to choose the better path.

Chapter Three

"You're angry with me," Anne said after a moment of watching Etta take deep gulping breaths while she paced around the mess in the middle of the room and muttered, "No. No, no, no," over and over.

"I'm not angry," Etta said through clenched teeth.

"You sound angry."

"I'm not angry." Etta schooled her voice and tone so she sounded kinder.

"You act angry."

Etta unclenched her fists and stopped pacing. "I am not angry," she said again.

"You look angry."

Etta tried to smile but gave up. "All right, then. Fine. I *am* angry. How could you have mailed those letters? Who asked you to rummage through my desk and touch things that were not yours to touch?" Just moments before she had noticed the opened drawer, Etta had been foolish enough to worry over not going to London. Now she felt glad she wasn't going, for surely the recipient of those letters would be unlikely to keep the contents to himself.

Frederick Finch was not a discreet man.

"I'm sorry, Etta. I was only trying to help." Anne looked like she might cry, which softened some of Etta's anger. Not all. But some.

"The only way to help now would be if you could find a way to retrieve those letters before they are ever read." Etta said this to prove that any help was useless, as the task was impossible, but as she spoke, she realized there was a flicker of possibility amidst the impossibility.

"We must leave," she said.

"Leave? Why? Leave for where?"

"We are to pay a visit to Lucy."

Anne had already begun to move to the door, eager as always to rectify any error she may have made. But she stopped when she heard where they were going.

"But we cannot. You know Mama has declared we are to have nothing to do with that family. You, yourself, even said that Mrs. Finch was—"

"Yes. I know what I said." Etta swept up her pelisse and motioned her sister to the door. "I will explain on the way to Rosemary Manor."

"Mama will never let us go to the Finch's house." Anne said this several times as Etta retrieved Anne's pelisse as well. "After what happened in London," Anne continued, "she has determined to loathe their entire family forever. She has said so herself on many occasions."

This was all true enough.

What had happened was that a young man of wealth and title, Lord Lansbury, Earl of Lansbury, had become fairly fond of Anne during her season in London. He had danced with her at every ball they both attended. He had walked with her in the park and called on her several times. She had grown rather fond of him as well. Anne, with her mother's encouragement, had allowed herself to become convinced that Lord Lansbury would be making her an offer of marriage before too long. He had admired her exceedingly.

Anne and her mother knew it.

According to Mrs. Stone, a marriage was inevitable. But she did not account for Etta's friend Lucy, who was also experiencing her first season. Lucy had imagined Lord Lansbury to be in love with *her* and believed that he planned to offer for her hand. And while it was true that Lord Lansbury had also danced with Lucy at every ball, had paid her a few calls, and even walked with her in the park, there was no real evidence that he preferred Lucy over Anne. At least, that's what Etta's mother said of the matter, making Etta believe the man had been very sly in his attentions with the two women—else they would have known of the other and perhaps been more guarded in their own feelings.

Anne and Mrs. Stone did not realize that Lucy had formed any sort of attachment beyond the natural interest that comes when dealing with a member of the peerage. Therefore, when Mama confided in Mrs. Finch the feelings that were developing between her eldest daughter and Lord Lansbury, she had assumed her neighbor would rejoice with her.

Mrs. Finch did not rejoice.

Mrs. Finch had, instead, shrilled a noise so awful that it called the attention of everyone within hearing distance. And then Mrs. Finch had thrown a full glass of bright red punch into Mama's face in the middle of the Leeson's ball. Everyone witnessed the scene of Mrs. Finch frothing over with resentment and Mama doused in red liquid that dripped down her face and the front of what had been an exquisite golden ball gown with pearls sewn into the bodice.

The dress had been ruined.

But so had Lucy's and Anne's reputations.

For who would want to align themselves with two young women who had such vulgar mothers? It was a blight on their family names.

Both Lucy and Anne returned to their homes fairly disgraced and much talked of in all social circles. They had even been abused in the society columns of several papers.

To say Anne had been hurt at the injustice of her reputation would be an understatement, but Anne's disappointment was nothing to her mother's. And Etta was the one who was punished for the situation, as she was denied access to her friend Miss Finch and partially blamed for the entire event since she had dared to be friends with Lucy in the first place. Etta missed Lucy. And Anne, compassionate as she was, hated for her younger sister to be forlorn.

"There is no need to tell Mama where we are going," Etta told her sister.

"You want me to lie?" Anne's eyes grew larger even as Etta herded her down the stairs.

"Of course not. I want you to be silent while we walk out of the house." She put her finger to her lips and dragged and pushed at her sister until they were out of doors. The gray, brisk weather did nothing to reduce Etta's determination.

"Why are we going to Lucy's?" Anne asked once they were on the graveled walk, and she cast a longing look back toward her own home.

"Surely you saw where the letters were going when you posted them." Etta gave Anne's hand a gentle tug to keep her from thinking of turning back.

"I hadn't really paid that much attention. I only saw that they were addressed."

"You didn't notice? You truly missed noticing Frederick Finch's name?"

"I saw the name Finch and supposed it was to Lucy. I only gave the letters a cursory glance."

Etta blew out an irritated breath. "Anne, where was your head when you were poking about my desk this morning?"

Her older sister's cheeks turned a lovely pink shade that Etta was certain she would have found adorable if she didn't feel so cross. But instead of answering Etta's question, she drew back her shoulders.

"Don't put this all on me. Why on earth would you be sending letters to Frederick Finch? It's most unseemly, Etta. What could you be thinking to begin such correspondence with a man with whom you have no understanding and to whom our mother has declared to be no friend to us after what happened?"

Etta's eyes fluttered briefly closed as she considered the mortifying truth. But there was no reason to hide it from her sister now, not when she so desperately needed Anne's help. Her own cheeks warmed despite the chilly air until she felt certain they were far more deeply stained than her sister's had been.

"It helps me clear my thoughts. After the Finch's Christmas party two years past, Frederick had been so kind to me that I thought . . . I imagined that perhaps he cared for me. I'm afraid I've been able to think of little else since."

Anne came to a halt in the middle of the road. "You must be teasing. Please tell me you're not serious. You didn't."

Etta's insides knotted and twisted. "I'm afraid I did. You know I've always thought well of Lucy's brother. He has always been so kind and helpful to me and to our family. I thought perhaps he felt the same about me . . ."

"You said all this in the letters?"

"Yes. And quite a bit more, I'm afraid."

"Why? Why would you write such things?" Anne's eyes could not possibly become any wider underneath her pink-trimmed bonnet brim.

Etta snatched at a budding leaf from a tree they were passing and yanked it from the branch in frustration. "Unrequited love can be a tricky thing. As I said, writing it out clears my head. No. It clears my *heart*. It frees me from agonizing over what cannot be."

"That is ridiculous. To write letters like that where anyone could find them, anyone could see . . ."

"But no one was supposed to see. They were for my private musings." Etta released the bud to the ground and felt guilty for taking out her irritation on a poor tree.

"How private could you have meant them to be when you took the time to address them?"

Her sister made an excellent argument. Etta did not recall addressing them.

"Etta!" Anne almost shouted to bring Etta back to the moment. "I posted *all* of them. How is such a thing to be undone?"

"With haste, Anne. With haste." Etta began walking faster. "Will you help me?"

Even as she stumbled to keep up with Etta's long stride, Anne looked around as if searching for some instrument that would aid

them, but finding nothing of use out in nature, her eyes finally landed
again on Etta's.

"Of course I'll help you, but Etta . . . how? The chances of the
Finch's butler letting us inside are not encouraging enough to consider."

"We must try. We must appear conciliatory."

"If you had wanted to seem eager to make amends, then perhaps
you should have brought along some sort of gift or offering. Cook
made a lovely tart. We could have brought it with us."

Etta cursed the lateness of Anne's brilliant thought. A gift would
have been just the thing, but they could do nothing for it now, could
they? Etta glanced along the hedgerow. "What do you think of a bouquet? Lucy loves flowers. Perhaps . . ."

"Yes," Anne agreed instantly. "That will be perfect. Except it's a bit
frosty for flowers, don't you think?"

"Well, yes. But we will be vigilant in our search."

They stepped off the road, Anne careful to keep her skirts from
the dirt and damp and Etta too determined to accomplish the task
quickly to give heed to dirt. Far worse things were in store for her if
she did not gain access to the Finch household.

All things considered, she made quick work of picking a rather
varied and sizable bouquet for the girl who had once been her closest
confidante and friend. The white snowdrops and the dusty pink blossoms of the hyacinths were lovely. She broke the ends of the stems to
make them even and tidy, knowing Mrs. Finch abhorred anything
that was not tidy, and pushed through the grasses back to the road,
where she shook off her skirts, straightened her bonnet, and gripped
the bouquet with determination. She hastily pulled the ribbon from
her bonnet and used it to tie the stems together.

Anne took a bit longer to set herself to rights, but soon they were
walking quickly again. Rosemary Manor was a good distance away,
and they took the road rather than the trails that joined the two properties together. But the weather was not so awful to make it impossible, and the walk was easy enough since they hadn't had any rain

recently. Etta used to take the trails to Rosemary Manor nearly every day before everything had gone so terribly wrong—before London and mothers and suitors and punch.

The two sisters walked in frantic silence. Etta could only guess what Anne might be thinking. Their mother would not approve of them calling on a family that had been declared to be their greatest enemy. She would approve even less of Etta writing letters to Frederick Finch. Such a thing would be far more damaging to her reputation than punch spilled over the front of a gown. Such a thing could be damaging to Anne as well.

Etta was sure that Anne had considered this likelihood too. Etta had put them in this awful situation, and she was determined to put an end to it as quickly as possible. She hastened her steps, but when she and Anne arrived at the door of Rosemary Manor, she realized that she wished for a little more time to collect herself.

"Well . . ." Anne prompted. "Aren't you going to knock?"

Etta smoothed her skirts, straightened her spine, and rapped the great, brass ring door knocker against the wooden door. The sound thundered and echoed ominously, making Etta wish with all her heart that she might give up this scheme and retrieve the knock before anyone came to answer it.

She could not turn to flee because there was nowhere to run quickly enough to avoid being caught. And knocking on a door and then running away was ridiculous behavior for a grown woman.

The Finch's butler, Gibbs, answered. If he felt surprised to see two of the Stone ladies standing there, he did himself credit by not showing as much.

"Yes?" he asked.

"Yes. Hello. I am—we are—here to call on Miss Lucy, if she is available. We've brought her flowers to cheer her afternoon."

"Flowers? For Miss Lucy?"

"Yes. Will you let her know we're here, please?" Etta needed to be bold. He would turn her away if Lucy asked him to, but until then, he would not leave two ladies standing on the front step.

He took their bonnets and pelisses and showed them to the library, likely because Lucy was already in the drawing room and he didn't want to catch her unawares by such an unexpected visit.

Anne paced by the shelves and wrung her hands. "They're sure to tell us to leave. Our visit will not be welcomed, Etta. And what will we do if they *do* tell us to leave? How will we ever retrieve the letters?"

"The tray where the post is kept is by the stairs. Perhaps you can create some sort of distraction to allow me to slip away and check the tray."

"Distraction?" Anne shook her head and held her hands out wide. "What sort of distraction could I possibly create?"

"You could pretend to swoon?"

Anne shook her head. "You haven't given this any thought, have you?"

"What time have I had? I should never have been in this situation, Anne."

Anne hung her head. "I'm sorry, Etta. This is my fault."

That response was not at all what Etta had been trying to provoke. She did not want her sister's guilt.

"If I hadn't written the letters, we would not be in this position. This is my fault. And I will amend it. Do you trust that I can?"

"I trust you always, Etta."

Etta did not deserve such devotion, but she was glad of it just the same. Before she could consider any further sort of planning beyond a feigned swoon, the library door opened.

Etta expected to see Gibbs, but what she saw instead was a blur of bright yellow flying at her. It was Lucy, not looking cross but with eyes full of tears and a trembling smile set upon her mouth. Her arms wrapped around Etta, crushing the bouquet between them.

She wept into Etta's neck. "I can't believe you're really here, standing in my home."

"With flowers," Anne said, likely intending to be helpful.

"With flowers?" Lucy pulled away, her brilliant blue eyes awash with the shedding of tears. Her gaze turned to the flowers that had become rather sad from being smashed. Lucy's yellow day dress had some slight green markings from the flower stems, but she seemed not to notice. "Oh, they are lovely."

She directed Gibbs to put the flowers in water for her and then led Anne and Etta to the drawing room where they all might sit and visit for a while. Etta glanced at the green marks on the front of Lucy's dress and hoped the dress wasn't ruined. It would be a tragedy to have two dresses ruined in the breaking and possible remaking of their friendship.

Lucy rang a bell, and when her housekeeper, Mrs. Davis, entered, she gave directions that a tray was to be brought in immediately for her dear friends.

In truth, Etta had no idea what to make of such a production. She had harbored only a faint hope that Lucy would allow them into her home, but for her to welcome them and be so thoroughly attentive was unexpected in every way.

"I am so glad you are here—both of you!" Lucy exclaimed. "I had come to believe that our two families would be locked in an endless quarrel over our mothers' behavior. You cannot know how many times I have written you both a letter to apologize. But I could never bring myself to send any of them."

"Yes," Etta said. "Letter writing may not be the best way to mend these wounds."

Anne shot her sister a look of complete horror as Etta hinted at their reasons for visiting, but Etta ignored it. They were in the house. They had not been thrust out. She felt mostly certain of attaining her aim in retrieving the letters.

That her old friend felt remorse over the incident in London, that she seemed to be seeking reconciliation, was a subject of fascination to Etta. She had not realized how lonely her life had become until that moment when she suddenly had her friend again. The details of the friendship were murky, to be sure, but possibility existed in a space where it had not previously. The shift in their relationship was a thing to marvel at.

"I am sorry as well," Etta said, feeling that she ought to have given such an apology much sooner. "But we cannot hold ourselves responsible for the impropriety of our mothers. Let us be friends again."

She put out her hand to Lucy, which Lucy took and squeezed with fervor.

"I am so very glad you are here." Lucy dabbed her handkerchief at her eyes, which had grown moist again.

Anne frowned at Etta and nodded her head toward the door as if she could will Etta to her feet and on to the task they'd come to accomplish.

"Oh dear!" Etta said. "I do believe I left my parasol in the library. Would you mind if I went and fetched it?"

"Why did Gibbs not take it from you when you arrived? I will speak to him about that." Lucy's hand reached for the bell as she said, "But for now, he will retrieve it for you."

Etta stood. "Oh no. No need to trouble anyone else. I'll be but a moment, if you don't mind."

Lucy's hand went back to her lap, covering one of the green streaks. "We have so much to discuss that any delay feels inconvenient, but I can wait a little longer. We have waited this long, after all."

"Yes. You can both discuss any upcoming plans for the season." Etta hurried to leave the room before anyone said or did anything that might hinder her from her task.

She had letters to claim, and she had no intention of leaving Rosemary Manor until she had done so.

Chapter Four

Gerard felt the exhaustion in his bones. Every step his horse took toward his cousin's home felt as though it extended his journey rather than shortened it; such was the delirium in his mind.

He'd made progress on the estate. Not excellent progress but progress just the same. His work would be faster were it not for the many days of cold weather. Numb fingers complicated the process. He'd managed to salvage one more relationship with his tenants, and he'd managed to repair a fence to keep the livestock out of the west field. He'd experienced a setback, however, when one of the tenants he had been sure would choose to stay chose instead to leave by the month's end when the contract was up.

That tenant had been a wonderful example of hard work and tenacity. He had produced crops that yielded a profit for both the Hartwell estate and for the tenant personally, even in years when it seemed the weather was entirely against him. But he'd been made promises regarding water that Gerard's father had not fulfilled, and he did not trust the son to be anything more than the father had been. Losing this tenant was a serious blow indeed. How was Gerard to make his lands profitable when the best and most productive people did not have faith in him to turn things around?

Could he turn things around?

Gerard wasn't entirely certain he could continue as he was—with little sleep and only eating when he resided at his cousin's house. He tried not to eat anything while at Hartwell Hall. It felt wrong to do so when he knew those in his employ were tightening their own belts and rationing food as best they could.

He would make it right by them. He would.

But something must change. How would Gerard maintain the livelihoods of these people who depended on him if he were dead? His cousin's offer continued to parade through his thoughts. But to marry a woman for her money? He did not believe his conscience could bear such an immoral path.

He hated how his mind vacillated back and forth in such a manner. But how moral was it if he did not take an eligible option when lives were at stake?

He sighed and wished for his cousin's house, where there would be a warm bed and a hot meal.

Gerard's dilemma perplexed him greatly. He felt guilty for keeping the state of their affairs from his mother and for his insistence that she stay at Rosemary Manor with her sister and the accompanying comforts. He felt guilty every time he left her, for to deceive was not in his disposition. But he felt guiltier still when he left Hartwell Hall, because there was work still requiring his attention, staff who needed to be fed and given assurances of their positions, and tenants who deserved to know someone was paying attention to their needs. Yet there he was, heading to a warm bed and a hot meal.

He would not return to his cousin's if it were not for his need to keep his mother appeased. His presence every few days placated her into extending her stay. As deep as the fatigue ran in his bones, his gratitude for his cousin ran even deeper. Frederick allowed him to come and go. Frederick put up with his mother's antics. Frederick knew of all his troubles and offered unbiased advice, and though Gerard did not always take the advice, he was still glad to receive it.

"Exhausted." He said the word out loud as if somehow vocalizing the deep fatigue would lessen it.

It didn't.

Finally, Rosemary Manor came into view. Gerard dismounted his horse and left him with a groom to be cooled, brushed, watered, and fed. Gerard then approached the house through the back entrance of the large French doors in the library. That was a place he was sure not to run into his mother. He felt unequal to her energies at present.

Exiting the library carefully, he checked the main hall for any signs of his mother, his aunt, or his cousin Lucy. He was about to make his escape to the staircase when he saw someone entirely unexpected: Miss Marietta Stone.

Curious. What could Marietta Stone possibly be doing at Rosemary Manor? Gerard was all but certain that his aunt had banished the entire Stone family for the affront to Lucy in London—not that he truly understood that situation in its entirety. He felt convinced that the story he had received from his aunt was biased in his young cousin's favor. According to rumor, the elder Miss Stone had stolen all of Lucy's hopes and dreams by trying to flirt with Lucy's prospective intended.

Gerard, for one, was glad that Lucy's prospects had been damaged if it meant she would not align herself with that wretched Lord Lansbury. The man was an insufferable cad. Lucy deserved better.

Intrigued by the sudden appearance of Miss Stone and the way she seemed to be skulking away from the drawing room, Gerard watched her undetected. Her pale blue dress and slippered feet made a swishing, snicking sound as she moved. Her auburn hair hanging in ringlets that fell out of a twist at the back of her head and her lithe figure made him think of a time when they'd both been small and she'd been climbing trees.

Her hair had been hanging in her face in stringy, leaf-filled clumps. Her dress had been torn. Her golden-brown eyes had been filled with curiosity and fire. They'd spied a baby bird on the ground, and she'd climbed down to rescue the small creature. She'd climbed the tree again to place the bird back in its nest, even though he'd protested that the bird's mother would reject it once a human had laid hands on it. She'd scoffed at the notion and gone ahead with her plan anyway. Then they had both sat together on the thick branch to see what would happen. Etta had been gratified, and more than a little smug, that the mother fed that fallen bird the same as she did the others.

Miss Stone had smelled like the honeysuckle that grew near the trees, and she'd raced him back to the house, where her mother scolded her quite severely for getting her dress dirty and not behaving like a lady. Her mother had told her that no man would want such a wild thing for a wife. At the time, Gerard had scarcely understood why any man would choose to marry at all, but he figured a man could do worse than a girl who climbed trees. Not him, of course. For at the age of seven, he had already determined to never marry. But for someone who didn't mind such things as girls and ribbons and dancing, Etta would do, he thought.

Etta no longer looked like a girl who climbed trees. Pity.

She went to the staircase and looked up as if checking to see if anyone was coming down. She then momentarily disappeared through the open doorway to a set of stairs that led down to the kitchens. Had she gone downstairs? Gerard couldn't tell, so he quietly slipped out of the library and toward the place he had seen her last.

He had to flatten himself against a wall near some statuary when Etta reappeared and went back to the staircase going up. With one final glance in that direction, she reached toward the table where a silver tray sat.

The tray was almost always there, and from experience, Gerard knew it was usually where the day's mail waited to be picked up and delivered to various members of the family when they arrived home from their daily activities.

He edged closer, curious as to why Miss Stone would be surreptitiously handling his cousins' mail. Unable to come up with a logical reason, he stepped out into the middle of the hall. "What exactly are you doing?"

Miss Stone inhaled sharply enough to inform him that he'd

startled her, and the letters that had been in her hand fluttered to the floor.

Gerard hurried to her side and moved to pick up the letters for her, as gentility demanded anytime a lady dropped something, but he found himself taken by surprise when she fell to her own knees and snatched up two of the letters before he could reach them. Perhaps he'd been wrong to think she'd outgrown climbing trees. He'd only been able to retrieve one of the letters before he held out his hand to her so that he might help her back to her feet. Etta accepted the proffered hand, but when Gerard let go, she smiled rather charmingly and turned her palm up. "Will you please hand me my letter?"

He almost did as she directed, thinking he must have been mistaken regarding the family's mail being on that tray, but as he held out the letter to place it in her grasp, he spied the address. In a clear, elegant hand was his cousin's name, Frederick Finch. Gerard pulled his hand back.

Etta's eyes widened as he did so, and she let out a sound of dismay, which was decidedly irregular.

"Sir, I ask again. Please return my property to me."

Rather than inspiring him to do as she requested, her tone made Gerard hold the letter more tightly in his grip and pull it close to him so that she might not take it. He couldn't say exactly why he felt she might actually try such a thing. It was a ridiculous notion, but not one so ridiculous that he ignored it. He'd always believed he possessed good instincts. And she was, after all, the girl who tore dresses while climbing trees.

"No," he said.

"I beg your pardon?" Miss Stone's hazel eyes flashed in irritation at his answer.

If he was being honest with himself, he felt a little surprised as well. But not enough to change his response. "No. I think not."

Her smile dropped into a tight line. "Give that letter back. It's mine." Her voice was low and dangerously close to threatening, which was certainly not ladylike. Her mother would scold her were she nearby. He'd always thought her mother to be extraordinarily prim.

Gerard very much wanted to laugh at the way Etta showed no fear of him. She was not anything like the demure young ladies he'd grown used to meeting whenever Frederick insisted he go to a ball or a dinner party. Her behavior was exactly that which he'd remembered from their childhood—charmingly unafraid. She was still the little girl she had always been. He could almost smell honeysuckle in the air.

"As I said, I think not. It is addressed to my cousin, plain as day, and I am not about to hand over his private mail to his neighbor."

If the tightening of her mouth and the reddening of her cheeks were any indications, his response made her furious.

"But that *plain-as-day* address is written in my hand, and that is my seal in the wax, so ownership started with me, and, as he has not yet had the chance to see the letter, I am still its first and rightful owner. Hand it over. Now. Please." She likely added the "please" hoping that it would remind him of nice social behavior, but she certainly didn't sound nice or socially behaved as she said it.

"Hm." Gerard took a leisurely walk in a circle around her. With each step, his mind furiously worked to puzzle out the mystery of the moment. "What, I wonder, could be in this missive that would have your face so red and your eyes so terribly desperate? Is it a declaration that you've decided to shred his mother's dresses for the injustice done to your mother in London? Or perhaps you've sent a bill to cover the cost of your own mother's lovely gown that was surely ruined?"

Etta watched him warily, reminding him of an animal caught in a trap and wild to escape. "Or perhaps it is more sinister in nature. Perhaps you've challenged him to a duel over your family's honor."

"A duel!" She scoffed.

"Stranger things have happened," Gerard said with a shrug.

"I really don't believe they have. And could you please stop circling me like a vulture? You're making me dizzy."

He allowed that he very well might be making her dizzy and

obliged her request. "So no to the duel then. . . . Perhaps this letter contains a confession."

Miss Stone stiffened with that guess, which made him think he'd hit the mark. "I know. Perhaps you've confessed to poisoning his dog."

She blinked, clearly not expecting such an idea to be put before her.

"Poisoning his dog?" she said coolly. "What could ever bring you to imagine such a thing?"

Gerard shrugged again. "Sport is acting a bit sickly lately. Frederick mentioned it the other morning. *Did* you poison his dog?" He eyed her with a look of open suspicion.

"Of course not! What kind of devil could you think me to be?"

"Ah well. Please don't be upset. I do not think you a devil at all. But if it is none of these things, then it must be a declaration of love."

Miss Stone almost gasped. Her mouth fell open but closed again as she swallowed her astonishment and straightened her spine. She held out her hand. "Please return my letter to me. It was sent by mistake, and you surely could not be so cruel as to wish harm upon me."

But Gerard did not hand over the letter. Instead, he tapped it into the palm of his other hand and circled the room some more. He was beginning to make *himself* quite dizzy as he circled and tracked her from the corner of his eye. He was fairly certain that if he tried to leave the room with her letter, she would tackle him before he could cross the threshold, regardless of what such an attack would do to her reputation.

With each rotation, several ideas settled into place at once, rolling into one magnificent idea. It was reckless. Foolish. Absolutely not appropriate. He blamed his fatigue.

But the idea, once formed, became more solid in his mind with every passing tick of the large clock in the hallway. If the letter truly contained some sort of declaration of her affection for Frederick, she would be sorely heartbroken by the reality that Frederick was not the marrying sort. Not yet. Maybe not ever. Poor girl.

While Freddie had lost his father not long before Gerard had lost his, the difference between the cousins was that Uncle Finch had not left Freddie in a financial disaster. There was fortune enough to last him for the rest of his life and beyond, which meant he had the opportunity to be quite choosy when selecting a wife. As much as Gerard loved Frederick, he knew his cousin would not choose a neighbor girl whose family had been part of public ridicule—not even considering the hypocrisy that Freddie's own family had been embroiled in that humiliation.

His cousin wanted a beauty, a woman who had fashionable female accomplishments so that he might display them to his guests at dinner parties. Aside from appearance, His cousin wanted a woman to hang on his arm and his every word. Gerard had a strong suspicion that Miss Stone did not fit that requirement. In short, Freddie wanted a woman who would allow him to be admired more than he already was. He did not want to be the one doing the admiring.

Miss Stone deserved better. The girl who had saved a baby bird deserved to be appreciated and cherished by her husband. Freddie would thrash her feelings quite irreparably.

With such thoughts in his head, Gerard remembered that Freddie had mentioned Etta's sister, Anne, the other morning.

Anne had always been a good friend to Gerard, even if she hadn't been as involved in their play as Etta. The Stone girls each had a sizeable dowry, enough to solve his problems. And he wouldn't be only marrying for money with Anne. He would be marrying for friendship. A man could do worse than friendship.

Gerard's gaze flicked from Etta's hand, where two letters were gripped tightly, to the letter in his own hand. Three letters seemed to indicate quite a lot of confessing on her part, which would suit Frederick well enough since he enjoyed the admiration of others. But if Miss Stone hoped for Frederick to return her affections, she would be disappointed. This made Gerard's plan to approach this situation one of heroism. If Etta were to have any chance with his cousin, she would need his interference. If nothing else, he could offer sympathy that might perhaps ease the pain of her inevitable rejection.

And if he might benefit from it as well, what of that? He had always liked Etta. She'd been a spirited child. And she would make an amiable sister-in-law and a charming, playful aunt to his future children.

He stopped pacing and stood before her. "I have a proposition for you, Miss Stone."

She narrowed her eyes at him. "Why does such a statement from you cause me a significant amount of anxiety?"

"Do you think you know enough of me to imagine me capable of justifying such anxieties?"

She lifted her chin. "You led me into a great deal of mischief as a child."

"That is not true at all. Most of our misdeeds were your idea. Well . . ." he amended his statement. "Actually, they were Freddie's, but you were a willing accomplice."

She went on as if not hearing him. "If our childhood is not enough to speak to your character, Lucy has had a great deal to say regarding you as a grown man."

"I'm sure she has. But a cousin who was raised as practically a sister always has her own prejudices. You shouldn't listen to rumor. You must know people have a great deal to say regarding your family this past year. Surely it isn't all true."

Miss Stone had the good sense to blush. "Of course not," she said softly, ducking her chin back down. "You can't believe everything you hear. Those rumors have made for a very trying year."

"I completely understand the sentiment of having had a trying year."

She sighed and shifted slightly as if trying to view him better. "You said you had a proposition for me, Mr. Hartwell?"

He was glad she brought the conversation back to the matter at hand. "Yes. I will get to that in a moment. But I must ask—and you have my word as a gentleman that this information will be kept in the strictest confidence—do you have feelings for my cousin?"

Her lips pressed together tightly, her eyes leaving his momentarily before she gave a near-imperceptible nod.

"I see," he said, though he suspected that to be the truth. "And do the several letters here with us now contain proof of that affection?"

She nodded again.

What could she have been thinking? To write such correspondence was nothing short of a scandal. She would risk her reputation for a hope?

"You have trusted me with your confidence, Miss Stone, and trust is a thing I do not take lightly. You can rest easy knowing your trust is well placed. I will tell no one, and you can keep your two letters."

Miss Stone opened her mouth in what was sure to be a protest, but Gerard hurried on. "I will keep the third for a short period. At the end of the designated time, I will return the letter unopened to you."

"Why not return it to me now?"

He could not deny the fairness of such a question. He thought quickly. "Because my proposition is really more of a bargain, one that I believe will provide you an advantage as well." Gerard smiled as charmingly as he knew how. "I have many people in my life who are anxious to see me wed."

The woman looked positively horrified. "I am *not* consenting to marriage."

"Of course not. Nor was I asking for your hand. Miss Stone, you would like to catch the interest of my cousin. And I . . . *I* would like to court your sister. If we work together, I believe we can both accomplish our goals."

"Anne." The flat tone of that one name left him no doubt that she found no delight in his proposition.

Chapter Five

Etta was sure she'd heard incorrectly. Mr. Hartwell wanted to court Anne? How would Anne feel being bargained away for a letter? He couldn't be serious.

But when she repeated back his words, he affirmed that she had heard correctly. However, Anne was a quiet, gentle soul. She did not deserve to be placed in the middle of a game played by bored bachelors. The very idea of Anne coming to harm made Etta angry. "Do you find this amusing? Is taunting a person who has been, in every way, forthcoming in response to your rather impertinent questions some sort of sport for you?"

"Of course not!" Gerard appeared to be genuinely surprised that she might accuse him of ridiculing her. "Miss Stone, I assure you I am most sincere. Let me explain. As I said, I have many people in my life who are anxious to see me wed. Your sister is truly graceful. More, she is a friend I can trust. She is everything that any man could hope for in a prospective partner. I would like the chance to see if she and I suit. If we do not, then there is no harm done. But it will allow those anxious to see me wed to believe I am well on my way to such an establishment. It is a matter of the highest importance that I am convincing. Otherwise, I could be ruined."

"Poor dear." Etta could not help but show scorn considering he held her very life in his hands. "And why is that my concern? What does your dilemma have to do with me or my sister?"

"It matters to you because you have admitted to feeling affection for my cousin. And if I know anything about my cousin, it is that he is never satisfied with what is his. He has always wanted to possess the toy in someone else's hands."

"I am not a toy, Mr. Hartwell, and do not appreciate the disrespect you show me by referring to me as such."

"I apologize. Of course you are not. But my cousin . . ." Mr. Hartwell seemed conflicted regarding his words before he said, "I apologize."

Etta let her fingers trace the wax seals on the letters in her hand. If only she'd been faster in picking up the three envelopes. If only she'd not allowed Mr. Hartwell's speaking to her to startle her into such clumsiness, she wouldn't be standing on the marble floors of the Finch household having the most absurd conversation in the history of the English language. "I don't understand."

"If my cousin believes you to be enamored with me, he is far more likely to show an interest in you."

"That's ridiculous. What sort of man finds himself intrigued by a woman courted by another?"

Again, Gerard appeared to be conflicted before he said, "That is a puzzle for you to sort for yourself. But for now, let me assure you that what I have said is accurate. And though you may have somehow gained access to this house today, if my aunt were to have anything to do with it, she'd have you thrown out immediately. What chance would you have with my cousin when his mother will require some time to become used to your presence again? Even if Lucy begged, she is unlikely to change her heart. But if your sister was on my arm as my guest, my aunt could hardly deny your presence."

He made some interesting points.

The most interesting point, however, was retrieving that which was rightfully Etta's, that which Mr. Hartwell seemed determined to keep within his possession. If the contents of that letter were made known, it would ruin all prospects for her future as well as the future of her sister—a thing she could not allow. Besides, what if Anne could be happy with someone like Mr. Hartwell?

Etta had been gone for far too long from the drawing room. Lucy would soon come searching for her, or worse, would send someone to search for her. Etta could not stay and speak nonsense to Mr. Hartwell any further. "I must return to Lucy," she said aloud.

"Certainly you must."

She had hoped for him to be having a lark at her expense, to not mean any real harm and to hand her the letter, but he tucked it into his coat pocket instead.

"Mr. Hartwell, please. These letters were never meant to be sent here. They were sent by accident. Please do not tire me with silliness and games."

"I do not mean to tire you. But you will find I am sincere in my entreaty. There are those who wish me to marry. Your sister is a friend I admire—one who has always listened to you. You could be instrumental in bringing about a good deal of happiness. And my time with you will open my cousin's eyes to your many charms."

"What if they do not open his eyes?" Etta felt immeasurably absurd for asking such a question. What could Mr. Hartwell know of her charms, if she, indeed, had any?

What did it matter? Mr. Hartwell had been right regarding Lucy and Frederick's mother never allowing such an attachment. But she felt intrigued all the same—especially with her mother not allowing her to go to London. Etta deserved this chance to at least try to secure happiness for herself. And perhaps Anne would find happiness as well. If she left such things up to their mother, neither sister was likely to have the lives they deserved.

Etta had to consider she might not have another chance to secure herself a situation that would be amiable. Should she not at least try?

Mr. Hartwell smiled. "My cousin is not always astute."

It took Etta a moment to realize he'd answered her question about Mr. Finch noticing her charms.

Mr. Hartwell continued. "But if he does not notice, then at least you will have the comfort of a certain letter returned to your possession."

She glanced back toward the drawing room and half-turned her body in that direction before she said, "Let me think on it. I will give you a response, but you must let me think on it."

"Of course."

"And you will not open the letter or give it to anyone?"

"You have my word, Miss Stone."

She couldn't say why, but she believed him. She dipped the barest curtsy before placing the two letters she had managed to save into her reticule and hurrying to return to Lucy. When she opened the drawing-room door, her sister was already standing nearby as if she had been blocking the entrance in some way. Lucy's position made it clear that she had been trying to get through.

"Oh, there you are," Lucy said, offering a slight scowl to Anne. "I was on my way to find you. I worried my mother had discovered you were here." The second part was said in a lower tone, likely more to herself than to Etta, but the truth of it and the truth of what Mr. Hartwell had imparted struck her forcibly.

"Here I am," Etta said with a smile that she hoped appeared reassuring but that she felt certain was anything but.

"But your parasol . . . did you not find it?" Lucy asked.

"Pardon, my what?"

"Your *parasol*," Anne said deliberately. "The one you went to the library to find. Did you find what you were looking for?" Anne's subtlety was not a thing to be admired as she nodded her head in the direction of the door. Her behavior could be nothing short of suspicious to even the most naive of people.

"It turns out I did not exactly. But I am satisfied, Anne, that all is well. I must not have brought my parasol at all, for it is not in the library as I had assumed." She turned her attention to Lucy. "My mind has been so distracted lately while preparing for Anne's upcoming season, you see."

"Your season as well." Anne had relaxed considerably and was now moving back toward the tray that had been placed on the table. It was filled with fruits and cakes and tarts. All sweet things that Anne would love to indulge in since their mother was fairly strict when it came to sweets of any kind.

"Not mine, actually. Only yours, Anne. I will not be going to London this season."

Both Anne and Lucy expressed surprise at such news. Anne practically quivered in emotion. "Why not? I have no wish to return alone."

"Mama feels it is best if I wait another year. Besides, you do not wish to be tripping over my sometimes shocking opinions."

Anne wrung her hands lightly, a movement small enough to be unnoticed by anyone who wasn't familiar with her behaviors. "I do not look forward to the season at all. Now I am to go alone?"

"You will be fine," Etta hurried to assure her. "Mama has always said you cannot fail to shine when standing in your own light." Etta felt the pangs of disappointment as she remembered the many times her mother had smiled dotingly at Anne as she said such things and then frowned in Etta's direction. Etta tried to remind herself that she had the benefit of her father letting her follow him around while indulging her many questions. Still, her mother's disdain hurt.

"My light has been significantly dimmed. I truly do not wish to partake in the season's offerings," Anne said. Having once been the subject of public scorn, Anne had every right to feel apprehensive about returning to London, but that she could no longer even glance at the tray of cakes and tarts proved she felt more than simple apprehension.

Lucy looked down at her hands.

To change the somber shift in conversation, Etta crossed to the table and fixed herself a plate with a slice of cake, two tarts, and some cheese and fruit. It was all far more than her twisting stomach could take.

But the other two ladies did not follow her example. Anne looked positively ill, and Lucy looked more penitent than Etta had ever seen.

"Your not wanting to go is due to my mother, isn't it?" Lucy said to Anne in a soft voice filled with dismay. Her hands had stilled on her skirts, and her stance was all but slumped in regret.

"No. Not at all," Anne said. "I didn't enjoy being on display in such a manner the first time. Did you, Lucy?"

"I liked the dancing. And I think I would have liked the socialization better if it hadn't felt like a horrible contest between me and every other woman in London. I don't want to return either."

"Exactly," Anne agreed.

Etta wanted to reassure her friend and her sister. But she had nothing reassuring to add. She would not be going to London. She was relieved that her old friend was open to renewing their friendship and did not want to inflict pain or guilt on Lucy. What had been done between the families had been done. Lucy could not be held responsible for Etta's mother's reaction to a past squabble—even if that reaction was a reason Etta was being kept at home. That fault belonged to Etta's mother.

But she would not say such things aloud. Etta gripped her plate and, with determination, took it to the settee where she sat and popped a grape in her mouth. When she'd swallowed it, she said, "You should both be excited about your prospects. Everything is going to be just fine."

Lucy did not look convinced. Anne continued to look horrified.

Etta ate another grape. What more could she do?

After several rather uncomfortable moments, Lucy prepared her own plate. Anne finally did the same. They both sat and nibbled at their food and sipped at their tea. No one viewing the spectacle would describe the three of them as being lively or interesting. Anne sat, shifting her legs and rearranging the fruit on her plate before she finally set her plate down in favor of her teacup. She wrapped the small cup painted with delicate rosebuds in both hands, likely pulling as much comfort from the action as she did warmth. Anne was perpetually cold and was often scolded by their mother regarding the way she held her teacup. Anne often said that warmth calmed her anxious thoughts.

"I don't really know that I can do this again. Mama was so disappointed last year." Anne's mournful tone tugged at Etta's heart.

"You can," Etta said, trying to be pleasant. "You will. It's a matter of doing what we've been trained to do. You will make new friends and acquaintances and be charming and pleasant."

"And you will not be alone," Lucy said. "I will be there to help in whatever way I can." She peeked a glance at Etta. "It will not be like last time."

Etta had the sinking feeling that her mother would not allow Lucy anywhere near Anne during the season if such interactions could at all be gracefully avoided.

Etta cleared her throat. "There is something you should know. The whole incident last season with the punch saved you both from a very unhappy attachment. Lord Lansbury, who caught your attention and admiration, has been rumored to have trifled with one of his mother's maids. She's had a child since."

"No!" Anne said.

"How do you know such a thing?" Lucy asked.

"Papa was speaking to one of the men from his club, and they told him so. He accidentally mentioned it yesterday when we were walking to the stables together to check on the foal. It's quite the scandal, for Lord Lansbury made no indication that he would help provide for the child."

"When were you going to tell me?" Anne asked.

"Now, apparently. I had meant to tell you earlier, but with all the letter writing, it quite slipped my mind. Etta shot Anne a meaningful look, at which Anne blushed. "The whole incident with Lord Lansbury has been hushed up to whatever degree such a thing can be, and such a rumor, true or not, never does the same sort of damage to a man's reputation as to a woman's—especially when that man is titled, but I thought you both would want to know. The feud between our families should be a celebration, for we all escaped an unfortunate connection."

Lucy put down her plate and said, "Perhaps we could do something to bring our mothers together . . . a dinner party? That would allow them to soften before the season starts."

"Our mothers are both well known for their determination in all things, including their ability to hold on to ill feelings. We have only a fortnight for such scheming." Etta frowned at the intricately patterned rug of green vines as if it were the source of the deep fatigue she always seemed to feel around her mother. "We should have made such a plan months ago for it to have any hope of success."

"I'm glad you told us of Lord Lansbury. I am much relieved. You know . . . I have never wanted a season," Anne said quietly. "Is that wrong to confess? I would have been content to stay home where I belong and have a life that I understand and enjoy. I don't think that's asking too much." Anne's small voice brought an end to the discussion of convincing mothers to spend time in the same room together.

"A season is a source of serious affliction," Lucy said, shaking her head. "Do you think our mothers understand the pressure they place on us?"

"I think they must," Anne said. "They went through it too, after all."

The silence that followed as they considered their own mothers in the same uncertain situation was overbearing, but they all muddled through the discomfort as best they could.

Wanting to find a topic of conversation that was not so depressing, Etta forced a smile on her face, set down her plate, and said, "Did you know my father's prize hound had puppies? One of them, quite the smallest little dog you've ever seen, stole into the kitchen after Cook had set out a cake she'd prepared for my father's birthday. We're not sure how the little scamp managed it, but he found a way to reach up and pull the cake to the ground."

Lucy laughed along with Anne, and she exclaimed, "Oh dear! That poor puppy must not have known what he was getting himself into. Your cook is rather frightening, if our short careers as pie thieves are any indication."

"The woman is positively terrifying! Cook caught the pup with his face covered in confection and wagging his tail as if he were the king himself. It's a wonder she didn't order him drowned on the spot. The shouts coming from the kitchen were enough that even my father stepped out of his study to see what the fuss was all about. It was quite an adventure."

Etta felt pain at such a statement. What adventure could the antics of a clumsy puppy be compared to the adventures she might have had in London? "You should come to see the puppies, Lucy," Etta said to pull herself out of her melancholy. "They have the loveliest floppy ears and are full of great mischief."

Anne's love for the puppies overcame her worries for the moment as she brightened. "Yes! Please do come and see them. There were four in the litter, and watching them trip over those silly ears makes for an entertaining afternoon. If we're lucky, one might dig up Mama's flower bed."

Lucy's eyes misted over even as she laughed. "I am pleased to be invited. Of course I will come."

Etta felt encouraged that everything would be all right. Well, as all right as things could be with her sister so worried, with her letter in the hands of Lucy's cousin, and with Mr. Hartwell making outrageous suggestions for how she might regain ownership of it. How could she offer her sister up like some sort of sacrifice to a man capable of blackmail? But how could she not? She needed her letter, or her sister would be ruined rather than courted. Had she known what the day held in store for her, she might not have risen from her bed.

No.

That was not true at all.

She would have leaped from her bed, retrieved the letters from her desk, and cast them into the fire, where they would be incapable of causing so much mischief.

Except . . . as Lucy laughed at something Anne had said regarding the puppies, Etta felt her heart quite pleased with the workings of the day. She'd had a friend returned to her because of those letters. Perhaps their mothers could be worked on to heal the breach between the families. Perhaps Mr. Hartwell would return her letter to her without making ridiculous demands. Perhaps all would be well.

The thought had no sooner entered her mind when the door to the Finch's drawing room swung open and a voice thundered, "What rumor is this I hear, Lucy?"

Etta shrank back under the weight of Mrs. Finch's fierce gaze. The woman's lips tightened into a thin slash that grew thinner with her every step closer to where the three young ladies sat. Her plump cheeks were sucked in so that her cheekbones had a definition to them that was not usually visible.

She crossed her arms over her chest without once giving Etta relief from her frank and disdainful stare. "So it's true. The Stone girls have dared intrude in the sanctuary of our home with no regard for the respect we are owed."

"Mama—" Lucy started but was immediately interrupted by Mrs. Finch.

"How could you allow these charlatans pretending to be your friends into our home after what happened last year?"

"But Mama, I—"

"This impudent baggage stamped out your every hope for a well-connected, happy future!" Lucy's mother tossed a glare in Anne's direction.

Etta almost made the error of scoffing aloud at the idea that Anne would take anything from anyone. The fact was that Mrs. Finch's furious maneuver with the punch had saved both Anne and Lucy from being drawn into Lord Lansbury's scandal. But Mrs. Finch might not know the particulars, and Etta was certain the woman would not want to hear such rumors from the youngest Stone daughter. Etta was glad she caught herself before making a sound since Mrs. Finch's foul mood had enough fire all on its own to keep it burning brightly.

"And for her to show up here, now, right before the season is to begin! What is your scheme here, girl? Are you here to ruin Lucy's prospects for yet another season?"

"No, Mrs. Finch." Anne looked surprised to be addressed so directly.

"Mama!" Lucy cried out in dismay.

Mrs. Finch flushed slightly, perhaps feeling slightly foolish for speaking with such spite. Then again, perhaps not, because the next thing she did was turn to Etta and snarl, "Possibly you will be the one attempting to sabotage my daughter and steal all her gentleman callers."

Etta was scandalized at the very suggestion. Not that she considered herself as saintly as Anne, but she would never do anything to hurt her friend. "Of course not, Mrs. Finch. I will not even be in London for this season."

Mrs. Finch blinked in evident surprise. She likely would have dropped her mouth open like a drawbridge were it not for her breeding. "Why on earth not? What could your mother possibly be thinking keeping you from your debut?"

The rivalry between Mrs. Finch and Etta's mother was not a secret to anyone in the whole of England—especially not after the whole punch incident, and though Etta understood her mother to be undeserving of her compassion, she felt highly defensive of her at that exact moment. She searched her mind for an answer that would allow her mother to hold her head up high while also allowing Etta the same.

She could think of nothing. Her mother's reasons for keeping Etta home were unfair, but for Mrs. Finch to know of such things when she herself was treating Etta unkindly was too much for Etta to bear.

"I have no inclination to go to London when I have so much here that requires my attention." Etta's breathing felt inadequate as she made the dubious claim. What could require her attention when her mother and her sister would be departing shortly?

Mrs. Finch must have been entertaining the same sorts of thoughts as she raised both her eyebrows and waited for Etta to explain further.

Why, oh why, were Lucy and Anne so fixedly silent through the whole horrid conversation?

"I . . ." Etta glanced at her sister, whose eyes seemed to convey a genuine interest in what excuse Etta could possibly make and still call herself an honest woman. This irritated her, because if Anne hadn't mailed those foolish letters, none of this conversation would have been necessary. Etta's breath hitched. The letters. The confrontation that had happened only a short while ago in the Finch's hall . . .

"I have recently been forming an attachment."

When her words elicited shock from both Lucy and Anne and a rather indelicate snort of disbelief from Mrs. Finch, Etta hurried to add, "Though there certainly is no agreement or understanding between us at this time . . ."

She faded off, unable to believe what she had allowed herself to speak.

Lucy asked, "How is this possible?"

Though Anne did not say the words out loud, her expression conveyed a much stronger sort of astonishment.

"Yes, well, I am sorry; I did mean to tell you. It's one of the many reasons I wanted to see you today."

What was she doing? Why could she not stop talking, especially since Anne appeared more horrified with Etta's every word? Anne knew that no one was calling on Etta. No one had sent flowers or paid visits or anything of the kind. The only man who took an interest in Etta's life was her father.

"Well?" Lucy said. "Do not keep me in suspense. Pray, tell me who this suitor might be so that I may be delighted with you, for you blush so much right now that I am certain he is quite dear to you."

Etta could well believe she was blushing. Her cheeks felt like they'd been lit aflame. It was with extreme regret that Etta had to complete the falsehood. How had she become so entangled?

"*Suitor* is much too strong a word. We are only friends, you see . . . at present. The name of the man in question is dear to you, I am sure. It is your own cousin, Mr. Gerard Hartwell."

Chapter Six

Gerard had slept a great deal of the day away and awoke at Rosemary Manor in a fair amount of physical pain due to the lifting of fence poles and pounding of nails he'd done while he'd been home. His valet, Wilson, seemed out of sorts as he set out the hot water for shaving. Gerard's mother insisted he arrive at dinner cleanly shaved. But Wilson attended his duties in so agitated a manner that Gerard finally stopped him.

"What is it that has you behaving as though hellhounds are about to come crashing through the door at any moment? Honestly, Wilson, I'm not entirely sure I trust you to be steady enough to bring a blade to my jaw."

"I'm sorry, sir. But things are happening in the household of which you might not be aware."

Gerard frowned. "Has someone taken ill?"

"Not quite, sir. Some rumors have circulated regarding you that have caused your aunt and mother a great deal of fretting, if their maids are to be believed."

So. His mother and aunt knew of his poverty. He wondered how they could have found out the truth, but what did it matter? The point was they *had* found it out. "That is unfortunate," he said. "I had hoped to keep my circumstances private for a while longer yet."

"Forgive me, sir, but the rumors are true?"

"Ah, Wilson, I appreciate the jest, but you know they are true enough."

Wilson's graying eyebrows drew together. His mouth opened as if he meant to argue the point, but he closed it again and leaned Gerard's head back so he could begin the shave. "Of course, sir."

Wilson's final comment was an agreement, though it felt like something else. Gerard did not know what to make of the conversation. Wilson knew of his financial situation. Indeed, Wilson knew all of Gerard's private affairs. So why did he act hurt, as though he had been left out of pertinent information? Wilson was normally such a practical and efficient man. Gerard did not have time to contemplate the feelings of his valet, not when there was the matter of his mother and aunt. They would likely have much to say regarding his wretched state of finances. He felt the shame of not being able to preserve his mother's dignity. She must be horrified to have learned of her poverty.

There were benefits to his family's discovery of his situation, however. Gerard need no longer hide. He could come and go from Hartwell Hall as necessary rather than traveling back and forth almost every other day, wearing him to a shadow of his former self.

He found he was actually quite relieved to no longer bear the burden of his situation alone and was able to enjoy the soothing warmth of the frothy lather on his face as Wilson prepared him to be shaved.

Wilson remained aloof and professional as he continued to ready Gerard for dinner. His valet was as crisp as the starched cravats held out for Gerard to choose from. Something bothered the man.

"Wilson?"

"Yes, sir?"

"Are you cross with me for some reason?"

Wilson's ear tips turned pink. "Cross with you, sir? Why would I ever be cross with you?"

"Right. Of course. I'm sorry I mentioned anything. You just seem slightly miffed. Are you unwell? Would you like some time to yourself?" He couldn't see how Wilson would require such a thing when he'd had the last few days to himself, but he was willing to grant it if the man needed it.

"No, sir." Wilson's whole face had reddened.

Gerard decided not to continue the questioning. He truly liked Wilson and had no wish to cause him unease. Wilson did try harder to hide his obvious irritation with Gerard, and Gerard endeavored to not notice.

It made for an awkward hour while Wilson readied him for dinner, but Gerard endured it since he knew he still had to face the scrutiny of his mother and aunt. At least Frederick had already known about Gerard's financial disarray and could defend his actions in hiding the unhappy truth.

The two women would likely again bring up the option of Miss Bates as a marriage partner. Gerard shuddered. What if they insisted on it? That thought made him think of his encounter with Etta. It had been a surprise to see her, but certainly not an unwelcome one. If she agreed to help him, Etta could very well be his sister-in-law soon enough. He enjoyed the idea of courting the elder Miss Stone. He had always liked her. She was beautiful and intelligent. Gentle and quiet. He wondered what she thought of him.

Gerard then remembered he had left Etta's letter in the pocket of his coat. He removed it and tucked it into his dinner coat pocket. He would need to hide it somewhere safe so that Wilson didn't find it and try to give it back to Frederick since it was he to whom the letter was addressed.

He should return the letter to Etta. It would be the gentlemanly thing to do. Blackmail was certainly not the act of a gentleman.

But Frederick wasn't wrong when he said marriage offered him a solution to set his estate to rights. The Stone girls were well situated financially. Their father had seen to their care and comfort in a most responsible manner.

If only Gerard's own father had done the same for him. If only his father had cared enough to carve out a small piece of his life and set it aside from his selfish pursuits so that his wife and son had their futures seen to. Gerard hated considering that his father had gambled their lives away and then had the nerve to up and die on them, thus avoiding the consequences of his own actions.

And now Gerard was left chasing down shillings to repair all that his father had broken. He stopped before exiting his room and forced himself to relax. He had to stop moping. He could not spend his time wishing for things that were not to be.

He headed toward the dining room to face the music that was sure to hit many flat notes.

When he entered the dining room, all gazes turned on him. The eyes that met his held varying expressions. His mother was, understandably, openly furious. But that his aunt was equal in her fury was a surprise. He would have imagined she would feel some pity for him and his circumstances. Lucy appeared to be delighted. And Frederick looked at Gerard as if he had never laid eyes on him before.

What was amiss?

It wasn't as though it were his fault that his father had left the family in such dire circumstances. And why was Lucy staring at him as if he were a great source of diversion? When had poverty become amusing?

"What is it?" he finally asked.

"Perhaps we should all sit?" Frederick said as he waved a hand to the set dining table. "We can discuss the matter at hand while we eat."

They all sat. And though the footmen served the creamy mushroom soup into their bowls, no one lifted a spoon to partake.

"Well then," Gerard said. "You all clearly have opinions on my circumstances. Let us be out with them so that we might eat without this rather awful apprehension."

Frederick dismissed the footmen.

Surprisingly, as soon as the room was cleared from all unwanted ears, Gerard's aunt spoke first. "How could you have done this?"

He could see her side of things to some degree. He had intruded on her love for her sister by allowing her to think they were just visiting when, in reality, his cousin and aunt were supporting them with food and comforts he could not provide.

"I am truly sorry to have trespassed on your kindness, Aunt. I do hope you will forgive the intrusion." He hoped he conveyed his deep regret well enough, but he thought that perhaps he hadn't, because her expression had gone from merely angry to thunderous.

His mother spoke next. "How could you do this to Lucy, your own cousin, who has been like a sister to you for your whole life?"

His thoughts stumbled to a stop. "What has Lucy to do with any of my affairs?"

The table erupted into a chorus of dismay. He heard Frederick mutter something that sounded suspiciously like, "Oh, now he's done it."

But done what?

"Truly, it should not matter to Lucy. I mean no offense, Lucy, of course," Gerard said.

Lucy smiled warmly. "No offense taken, Gerard. And for the record, I want you to know you have my warmest support."

That caused him to frown slightly. What kind of support could she give to him in such circumstances?

"I do not give mine," his aunt said, her tone frostier than the darkest winter night.

"Mother, please—" Frederick began but was interrupted immediately.

"There is no amount of pleading that can excuse his betrayal of this family," she said.

"I do not see my position as one of betrayal, Aunt Lucinda. I have acted to the best of my moral understanding. One cannot deny the dictates of one's responsibilities."

"Your responsibility is to this family, Gerard," his mother said.

"Yes," he agreed with fervor. "Yes. Exactly. And it is of this family that I have been chiefly thinking."

"No." His mother's voice was shrill and her cheeks splotched with red. "I do not believe that your secrets are kept with a desire to protect us." His mother thumped the table with her fist, a thing which Gerard felt certain he had never seen her do in the whole of his life. The force of her action sent tremors enough through the table to cause the crystal and silver to make clinking noises. "Secrets are damaging little demons."

His aunt harrumphed an agreement. Lucy hid a delighted laugh behind her hand.

Frederick's curious stares were unnerving to Gerard. His cousin also appeared exhausted, as though he'd been harassed for information for many hours, which he probably had been. There were few secrets between the two men, and his mother and aunt knew it. They'd likely cornered Frederick and badgered him into sharing information.

"Is she the reason you refuse to call on my friend's daughter?" Mrs. Hartwell asked.

They had all gone mad. Every last one of them. "Mother," Gerard said, "my current situation is but one of many reasons I will not call on Miss Bates. The others, I'm afraid, quite eclipse the one. Wait . . ."

Suddenly, all the words his mother had said finally settled into his brain. She had asked, "Is she the reason?"

She.

"Let us begin at the beginning," Gerard suggested. "What is it that has you all howling at my heels like wolves?"

"I'm not howling," Lucy said brightly, but her smile dimmed under her mother's withering stare.

"We received a visitor today," Frederick supplied, "a young lady who is known to us all but to whom you are apparently far better acquainted?"

Gerard shook his head, hoping that Frederick might offer more clues than that.

"Marietta Stone came to visit with her sister this afternoon," Lucy said.

"Yes." Gerard felt as though he were trying to see a picture while staring at it through a thick black cloth. "I saw her in the hall." And then he began to worry. Had his family discovered the letters? Had she dropped one of them somewhere? But even if she had, what would that have to do with him?

"Yes." Mrs. Finch fixed her narrowed gaze on her nephew.

He felt he now knew what a hat felt like when it was stuck through with a pin. He could not have moved while under that gaze if he had tried. But he would never have tried. His aunt was a formidable woman.

"Yes," she continued. "And she was filled with all sorts of insightful information."

"Well, I have always thought her to be an insightful girl," Gerard said carefully. Had she told them all that he'd tried to blackmail her into helping him with her sister?

"So you don't deny it? You are courting Miss Stone, the sister of your cousin Lucy's sworn enemy?" his mother asked.

That was not at all what he had expected to hear.

Etta had told them he was courting Anne? Already? Without talking to him? He felt suddenly more nervous. What did Anne think of that? Had Etta spoken to her already?

"I wouldn't exactly say that I am courting anyone just yet. Merely that—"

"Don't be sly, cousin," Lucy said. "It is my opinion that you and Etta shall make a fine couple."

He was about to thank Lucy for being so forward-thinking when her words sunk in. Etta?

Etta had told them he was courting her?

No.

No, no, no. Etta was still a girl. He had no wish to even consider that prospect.

"She *is* a pretty little thing," Freddie said slowly, as though the thought had only just occurred to him.

"Well, I suppose she is, but—"

"And wonderful in every way," Lucy agreed.

"I don't doubt that, but . . ."

But what? What could he say to any of this?

Etta had told all his relations that he was courting her? What had happened to her insistence that she needed some time to think? And how had she become the love interest and not her sister? Had he not been clear? She had not even given him the courtesy to warn him that she might say yes to his scheme. And she hadn't said yes to *his* scheme. She'd begun an entirely new scheme, and she had surely not hinted that he would have to face such an interrogation.

Gerard glanced at Frederick. Perhaps Etta's affection for him ran deeper than he had believed. It was Freddie's fault that Gerard had ended up with the wrong sister. If Etta hadn't written him, then none of this mess would be happening.

His mother must have grown impatient waiting for him to respond, because she prompted him with another question. "Do you deny it?"

"Well, I . . . No, Mother. I do not deny it." Indeed, at this point, how could he?

"Miss Etta Stone?" Frederick said incredulously. "And you never thought to tell me?"

"I didn't think you would approve?" Gerard hadn't meant the comment to sound like a question, but creating fiction from nothing had proven to be quite a lot of work. Gerard felt his face heat with the many falsehoods he was now spinning. He had always prided himself on the fact that his word was a thing of value, but now here he was bandying the truth about like it was a shuttlecock in a game of battledore.

Frederick's glance slid to his mother before he said, "Even when we spoke earlier, you did not tell me."

It occurred to Gerard that this rumor was the reason for Wilson's earlier frustration. The man had thought that Gerard was endeavoring to court the younger Miss Stone without telling him. And now Frederick was unhappy for the same reason.

"Well, what have you to say for yourself?" Frederick asked.

Gerard squared himself to the task. "To be clear, Etta and I are just good friends at present. We are not officially courting by any stretch. I do not wish to bring harm to the family; I know all here have very strong opinions against the Stone sisters. But I have always admired them *both* for their strength and elegance."

There. All of that was true to some degree or another. And, he hoped, it left the door open for him to court the elder Miss Stone. Let his family make what they would of all those truths strung together.

"But the Stone sisters are Lucy's enemy." His aunt's clipped words left no confusion as to her feelings regarding the matter.

"Mama . . ." Lucy's tone was one of tired frustration. "I've told you how I welcome the renewal of my friendship with Anne and Etta, and I am glad for you, Gerard. Etta seems to be quite taken with you."

He knew what Lucy said regarding Etta liking him was as false as his courting the woman, especially considering the letter she'd written to Frederick.

"Thank you, Lucy. I appreciate your support. I would appreciate it if you all could offer me some support in this. Feelings are not to be dictated by the whims of familial politics. The heart cannot help where it feels most at home."

Lucy sighed as if she'd heard some great romantic verse and then, finally, took the lead and picked up her spoon to eat the soup that had surely gone cold during the strange interview.

Gerard had been right to get the discussion out of the way, for everyone followed Lucy's example and began to sip at the soup, though his aunt and mother ate with the frustrated energy of women who were not quite done waging war.

The rest of the meal's courses were a terse sort of affair, where his aunt stabbed at him on one side and his mother jabbed at him from the other. But all in all, he had fared well enough.

None of them, aside from Frederick, knew of his financial woes. His mother's honor remained hers to keep for the time being.

Frederick lifted his glass and drank it dry before settling it back onto the table. "I did say earlier that you were pleasant enough to recommend you to a lady of circumstance, and so you are. I do wish you would have told me of this when we spoke, for I feel a bit monstrous for putting you off the way I did."

"No need to be concerned, Freddie. You cannot help what you do not know." *And what I myself did not know . . .* he thought.

"Well. I can act based on what I do know, and I feel a great deal better informed at present than I was earlier. We'll continue our discussion after dinner."

Gerard knew what Frederick wanted to discuss. The idea made him more nervous than relieved.

Dinner was cleared away, and the two gentlemen retreated to Frederick's study so they could talk without the prying ears of staff members, aunts, and mothers.

"Miss Etta Stone. What a lark, cousin," Frederick said after he'd fixed himself a drink.

"I do not consider her a lark, Freddie." Granted, he hadn't thought of Etta in any way except as Lucy's childhood friend.

Freddie sat down, put his feet up on his desk, and lounged back in his chair. "Interesting. If she is not a mere diversion, do you plan to marry her?"

"I do not know. Not yet. I am only friends with Etta at this point."

"I'm hurt you didn't tell me sooner, Gerard." Frederick pursed his lips into a pout that was almost humorous.

"Are you truly hurt or just vexed that a thing happened without your knowing of it?"

"I would suppose both. But truly, a Stone girl?"

"Does she pose a problem?"

"You mean other than my mother despising her family for that whole botched-up business of marrying off Lucy last year? I can see no problem with her at all."

"You're behaving rather cryptically when you obviously have some opinion."

Freddie put down his feet and sat up straight in his chair. "I do. Don't I always? The Stone ladies were given generous dowries, so you know I approve . . . I just wondered how such a thing could have begun. She's not even out yet."

Gerard hated to repeat the falsehoods he'd been forced into this evening, so he tried to stick to the truth as closely as he could, relying on stringing many truths together the way he had earlier. "I know how your mother feels about the Stone family, but I have fond memories of spending time with both Stone sisters while I visited here during the summers. If you'll recall, they were almost always here." He made sure to mention both sisters so he could reasonably switch from pretending to court Etta to actually courting Anne.

Gerard continued. "With Aunt Lucinda still so cross about Lucy's season, it seemed better to not bring up the Stone ladies if it could be avoided."

Frederick laughed. "You have always been the cautious, methodical one. How your father managed to raise one such as you when he was so entirely opposite is a quandary. But this is a quandary I quite enjoy. You remind me that morality mustn't be boring. We should invite your lady and her sister to dinner. I'll invite a couple of friends so numbers are even. My mother can hardly object. What say you?"

Gerard gave a smile that he tried to put feeling behind. "That sounds like a marvelous idea."

A great deal of unease settled into his soul. How was he to pull off acting out some sort of fondness for Etta? He'd never been good at pretending. And he wasn't yet certain that the lady in question could convincingly pretend to care about him either. How could she when he had a letter that said she was in love with Freddie? He needed to speak with Miss Stone as soon as possible.

Chapter Seven

"Why would you tell such a lie?"

That was the question Anne had demanded Etta answer as soon as they had found themselves alone and walking back to their home.

Etta had avoided answering a dozen different ways, and by the time they'd arrived at their front door, her sister had withdrawn into hurt silence. The pair usually discussed everything, sharing a lucky intimacy of close sisterhood that other girls of the neighborhood envied—not only in age but in legitimate friendship. Anne had even been aware of Etta's infatuation with Frederick Finch. That Etta was keeping her reason for fabricating an entire courtship from her was a thing Anne could not, apparently, abide.

Before the last hour, Etta would have said that keeping secrets was a thing she could not abide either.

How much an hour changed everything.

As the day progressed, Etta expected Anne to confront her again, but Anne did not.

Though Anne clearly harbored wounded feelings over Etta's falsehood—for surely the declaration that Mr. Hartwell was courting her *had* to be a falsehood in Anne's eyes—and though Anne clearly felt betrayed over Etta's inability to explain herself, Anne had not mentioned the incident to their mother. Anne had not spoken much at all at dinner and had retired to her room early. Mr. Stone was away for the evening on business, leaving Etta alone with her mother in the dining room.

"What happened today, Marietta?" Mrs. Stone's iron gaze pinned her to her chair and denied her the one thing she wanted more than anything, which was to flee to her bedchamber to reflect on all the events of the day and to make sense of them, if only in her head.

Etta tried to keep her features smooth to hide her guilt. But no matter what her face betrayed, her insides felt soaked in shame. "We went to visit Lucy."

The slightest flare of her mother's nostrils was the only indication that her mother was furious at this news. "I might have guessed, with poor Anne looking so distressed. Have we not taken enough abuse at the hands of the Finch family? Must you place your sister in a situation designed to make Anne recall horrible events?"

"The sermon in church on Sunday was on reconciliation. I wish to do right by our neighbors. What better way than to forgive them and reforge the friendship stronger? Besides, it's not as though Lucy was the one who—" She cut off at a sharp look from her mother.

"I did not think it necessary to forbid you from entering into association with that family, Etta, but I was apparently mistaken."

Etta fiddled with her spoon and glanced around. Her mother's scrutiny flicked to the spoon, and Etta put it down and placed her hand in her lap. She returned her gaze to the table. "I'm sorry, Mama." It was better to apologize, though Etta was not sorry. And she felt grateful that she had not been forbidden, because now it was done, and her mother could not change the course of the situation. Etta had won her friend back.

"I am glad you see the error of your ways," her mother said. "Happily, it is not a completely unforgivable mistake. You are, from this moment, forbidden to enter the Finch household or to speak to any member of their household again."

Etta's gaze darted up to her mother's face. Surely she could not be serious, not now when the truce had already been declared. "But Mama—"

Her mother's eyes narrowed. "Did you not hear me, Marietta? I will not have our good name made ridiculous by that family any more. They've been the cause of far too much mischief to trust them to keep themselves in check. You would not want them to hurt your sister's chances for happiness, would you?"

Etta's gaze returned to the table so that her mother would not see the tears forming. "Of course not, Mama. But won't it appear strange for us to return to a feud that has been reconciled? Will it not be the cause for much gossip?"

"I forbid it, Marietta."

And that was that.

Mrs. Stone returned to her pudding, taking her time, drawing out the minutes before the footman could clear the table and go below-stairs, before Etta would be released to return to her room to fret over this unforeseen catastrophe.

How would she ever retrieve her letter from Mr. Hartwell if she were not allowed to speak to the man's family? How would she ever explain to him why she had told such a ridiculous lie to all his relations and convince him to go along with it?

If her mother thought the Finch family posed some sort of ficti-tious danger to them, she would certainly be surprised by how much of a danger they posed in reality. If Lucy's brother received Etta's letter, no one in Etta's family would be able to show their faces in society again.

Her poor father. What would he say?

When Etta was at last released to her rooms, she felt as though she might wear a hole in her blue rug from all the pacing and that she might rub her skin raw from all her hand-wringing, but pacing and hand-wringing did her no good, for she could not see a solution to her current dilemma. Her mother was simply not the sort of woman to be dismissed or disobeyed.

The next day, Etta awoke to Anne's voice, which was a surprise, as

Anne usually slept in while Etta normally awoke early. She could only account for this break in their typical routine to her staying up half the night fretting.

"Etta, get up. Oh, do get up!"

Etta would have turned away from her sister, but the next words from Anne's mouth were, "Mr. Hartwell is here. And he is asking to see you."

Etta sat up quickly and threw her legs over the side of the bed. "Does Mama know?"

"I don't think so. Not yet. But why is he here? Has he really been courting you, and you've not told me?"

If anything, Anne looked to be far more hurt over this revelation than when she thought her sister was simply making up stories and not telling her why.

Etta noted Anne's appearance, which was tidy and ready for the day. She ran her fingers through her hair and felt her sister's words sink in. Mr. Hartwell was downstairs and waiting for her. She needed to get dressed.

"Fetch O'Brien! I require help. Quickly!"

But as she turned to repeat her orders to her sister, she found O'Brien already waiting. O'Brien was her mother's personal maid, but when it came to preparing the younger ladies of the household for any sort of event, she tended to them as well. Apparently, a gentleman caller counted as an event.

She did not bother to ask how O'Brien knew to help her that morning. If the rumor that a man had come to ask after Etta had reached the staff, how long would it take to reach her mother, who might have Gerard thrown out, all before Etta could wrestle her arms into the sleeves of her day dress? But if O'Brien was there at Anne's request, there still might be time to reach Mr. Hartwell before her mother did.

O'Brien seemed to understand the importance of speed and had Etta washed, dressed, combed, and pinned before Etta had had the chance to become wholly panicked. She raced down the stairs with

Anne not far behind. She was glad Anne recognized her need for someone to be in the same room while Etta greeted her guest.

She had to stop at the drawing-room doors, catch her breath, and collect herself before entering the room with a serenity at odds with the rapidity of her pulse.

Mr. Hartwell smiled uncertainly at her as she entered. She frowned as she noticed that his tall frame and broad shoulders seemed to fill up the space in a way that made her very aware of him. She shoved the thought away, wondering how it could enter her head in the first place. This was her old friend! His dark hair fell over his forehead as he bowed. Etta and Anne both dropped a curtsy, though Anne's curtsy was deep enough to be meant for royalty.

Gerard shoved the dark lock back in a motion that made him seem nervous. His hair had always been darker than Frederick's, whose hair was the color of sunlight reflecting off of water. But when had Gerard Hartwell's hair become *so* dark? It made for a lovely contrast against his ice-blue eyes that were almost identical in color to Mr. Finch's and Lucy's.

Gerard cast a furtive glance toward Anne. "Miss Stone." He then leveled a look at Etta. "And Miss Etta. It is a lovely morning, and I thought perhaps you and your sister might accompany me on a walk."

"Yes, I thank you," Etta replied. The faster they got him out of the house and away from her mother's notice, the better.

Anne nodded her agreement to the scheme but didn't seem particularly happy about it.

"Allow me to get my pelisse and bonnet." Etta flashed a smile and hurried out. Anne went with her and whispered, "How did you make this happen? How is he really here? I thought you were lying before when you mentioned him to the whole of the Finch household."

"Fetch your things. We'll talk later." Etta almost told her sister to be quick, but Anne already realized the necessity. The young ladies rejoined Mr. Hartwell in the drawing room and led the way out the side door to the gardens. A bird flew down from the red-leafed trees and passed in front of the stone path they took, and Mr. Hartwell smiled. "A grey wagtail."

"A what?" Etta asked.

"That bird there." Gerard pointed to where it had flown up into a tree that had lost nearly all its leaves. The bird stared as if it meant to keep a close watch on them all. "It's a grey wagtail."

Etta's thoughts felt thick and muddy with apprehension. Mr. Hartwell appeared to expect some sort of recognition from her.

"You don't remember?" he asked.

"I'm not certain what it is I should remember," she confessed as she glanced behind to see that her sister had the presence of mind to stay back far enough to allow them a private conversation.

"Many years ago, we rescued a baby bird together."

Etta blinked into the bright light of the morning and tried to think of what he could possibly mean.

"You don't remember," Gerard said again. She shook her head.

"Well, I was not so much a part of the saving as you were, since I told you the mother bird would reject her baby if you touched it, but you told me I was wrong and put the bird back in its nest. If memory serves, Miss Stone, it was a grey wagtail."

She shook her head and lowered her voice. "I'm sorry. That is all very interesting, but I must ask. Did you bring my letter?"

"Bring your letter? Of course not. And did you truly ask me that before apologizing for changing the terms of our agreement? My mother, aunt, and cousins had me besieged in the dining room last night. I had not a single inkling of what they were going on about regarding my betrayal of the family. It turns out you told the lot of them that I was courting you."

She flushed hot. Why did she think she required her pelisse when it was so very warm outside? "I panicked."

"Panicked." Mr. Hartwell's flat tone did not suggest he felt any sympathy.

"Have you never panicked before and said the most wrong thing possible?"

He didn't answer, which Etta took to mean that he had not.

"Well, I did. I don't normally. But yesterday was such a trying day, and . . . well, it just came out."

They'd moved past the hedgerow and were coming to the edge of the wooded area. She glanced back to be certain that Anne had stayed with them but that she had also remained outside of hearing distance.

"But that isn't what we discussed at all." Mr. Hartwell also looked back at Anne and lowered his voice. "You were to allow me the chance to court Anne, not you. You're a—" He looked at her and faltered, as if he'd tripped on his thoughts. "Well, you're a child still, and—"

"Child?" Etta realized she'd said that much louder than she had intended and had to drop her voice as well. "I, a child?"

"Yes. You. Child. You're my little cousin's best friend."

"Look at me. Do I look like a child?"

Gerard was suddenly staring out across the woods as if deliberately trying to avoid looking at her. "Full-grown women don't climb trees."

"How would you know what full-grown women do?" she countered. "You're barely three years older than I. By your reckoning, you're just out of leading strings. Mr. Hartwell, I am of marrying age."

His eyes snapped back to hers. "But surely you don't want to marry me?"

She stopped short. "Of course not!"

"So why tell my relations we are on the way to a betrothal? It looks quite scandalous. What chaperone can vouch for us?"

Etta took a deep breath. The morning walk in the woods would have been beautiful if she hadn't felt so jumbled. "Let us calm ourselves. We can reason this through and perhaps still achieve our goals. We can go on as friends spending time together. Anne can come along. That will give you the chance to get to know her. Perhaps you can invite Mr. Finch so that he might find something of worth in me. We can still make your original plan work. We can simply act flirtatious for a short duration and then gravitate to our actual interests and tell our relations that we are simply friends and nothing more."

Gerard leaned closer to her and asked, "How did this happen, Etta?"

His leaning in had allowed her to catch a breath of his scent. It was not unpleasant. He smelled like pine and wind, which was an absurd thought, because what did she truly believe wind smelled like? She wasn't sure, but whatever it was, Mr. Hartwell carried it on his person in an uncomfortably delicious way. She pushed those thoughts aside. Why could she not keep her wits about her this morning?

"Let me explain and apologize. After I'd gone back to Lucy and Anne in the Finch's drawing room, Mrs. Finch entered with fury and terror. She accused me of sabotaging Lucy's chances in London. I wanted only to calm her and assuage her concerns, so I told her I would not be in London. And when she asked why not, she did so with such an air of . . . oh, I don't know. Superiority.

My mother and Mrs. Finch have long been in some strange sort of competition with one another—so much like the Montagues and Capulets that there are days I dream of poisoning myself just to be free from hearing more of their quarrels. And truly I didn't want to admit to Mrs. Finch that my mother had already informed me that I am not presentable enough to enjoy a season in the traditional sense. I froze and told her the only thing that came to mind. Which—"

Mr. Hartwell held up a hand to stop Etta. "Your mother said you're not presentable?" His eyes and jaw had been tight since they had begun this discussion, but now his features softened into something sympathetic, which felt worse somehow.

Etta nodded and shrugged as if it were no matter. "She has always said so." She turned back toward the trail and began walking again.

Gerard reached out and touched her arm. "I'm sorry, Etta." He looked sorry.

"It is I who should apologize for lying to your relations in such a manner."

"There's no need. I think you've created a plausible story for both of us, one that will allow us to reach our individual aims. It would seem we have an agreement. For that, I thank you. So you may rest easy, and you may stop strangling your gloves."

She loosened her grip on the gloves. She'd grabbed them but hadn't had the time to put them on in her hurry to rush Mr. Hartwell out of her home. "You thank me? Why? You surely do not enjoy spreading falsehoods to your own family."

"No. Not at all. But here we are. Because you started the rumor, I was left with no choice but to continue the ruse. If I'm being honest, your fabrication saved me from an inconvenient arrangement."

Etta raised her eyebrows at him.

Gerard nodded. "My mother wishes me to marry the daughter of her friend. I fear my mother's choice of woman is not the sort I want by my side for the rest of my life."

They fell into silence as she considered that. Etta's mother had paraded several unacceptable men past her sister during her time in London. Anne had recounted how betrayed she felt as their mother had been a bit forceful in trying to bend Anne's resolve against some of them, especially those men who frightened her. She confided she worried for her safety as she peered into a few of those wolfish eyes. Anne had said she felt relief that Lord Lansbury was acceptable. But then, he hadn't really been acceptable.

Mr. Hartwell broke the silence. "We should discuss the terms of our arrangement, our expectations of one another."

Etta felt uncomfortable with the necessity of their nearness. What must Anne think of them bending their heads together like a pair of lovers? Why must he smell pleasant enough to distract her? "How did any of this come to be?" she murmured, only realizing she'd spoken aloud when he answered her.

"You wrote a letter. Or, rather, several letters. And then you lied to my family."

She narrowed her eyes, hoping it chilled him the same way it did her when her mother made the same expression. "You're a bit of a scoundrel." She frowned as she realized she had said a decidedly impolite thing.

"Well, yes. One must have a reputation, mustn't they?"

Her frown deepened. "You like that reputation? "

"I would not exactly call it a reputation, I suppose, since as far as I am aware, you're the only one who has ever called me such, but a man must begin somewhere."

She stopped and faced him. "This isn't amusing, Mr. Hartwell."

"No. It isn't." But his lip twitched, and his eyes spoke of deep amusement.

Etta scoffed and began walking again, rounding the bend in the wood to the small lake just west of her home. Anne's footsteps clipped closer together, as if she'd had to hurry to keep them in her view.

"What terms do you mean?" Etta asked.

"You have a right to expect an ending to this arrangement, as do I. We cannot detain each other forever."

"That is true. So how will we know if we've achieved our purposes?"

"Let us consider your purposes first. If my cousin declares himself to you, then, obviously, I will step aside. I would never stand in the way of your happiness, Etta."

He said the last without any hint of insincerity.

"And what of your happiness?" she asked. "How do we determine when we've solved your dilemma?"

"I meant it when I said I must marry. I have always admired your sister. She's steady and generous of heart. We were always friends. I would like to see if we are compatible enough to make a marriage work."

Etta's conscience pricked again. Anne deserved more than to be a pawn in a game. "What if Anne doesn't like you or choose you?"

Mr. Hartwell smiled and shook his head. "You really do think me a scoundrel, don't you? If she doesn't choose me, then I shall have to seek elsewhere."

"Will you give me my letter back even if she doesn't choose you?"

"Of course."

Etta stopped where the path came closest to the water's edge and looked out over the lake, watching the sunlight skitter from one ripple to another. "Let us put an expiration date on our bargain."

"Agreed," he said. "If, in two months' time, we have no hope of obtaining our own goals, all we need do is ask the other to be released."

Etta's brow creased. "But how does one simply stop a courtship? How will we end such a charade?"

"Amicably, of course. We would not want our prospects bruised. We will make certain that the whole of England is aware that we esteem each other greatly but are not destined for marriage. We will end as we've begun: as friends."

"Are we friends, Mr. Hartwell?"

He put his hands in his pockets and rocked back on his heels. "Well, I had thought so until you felt it necessary to question it. Can a fact that must be questioned truly be a fact?"

Anne had paused a short distance from where they stood. She looked awkward and curious as she watched them.

Etta lowered her voice further. "I have not the mind for philosophy this morning. I will leave you to ponder over the details of facts and questions."

He studied her. She could feel his eyes on her but would not look up to meet his gaze. She focused all the harder on the water.

"Why did you write letters that could damage your reputation?" he asked.

The question was quiet, curious. She knew the difference between a curious question and a cruel question. She lifted her shoulders in a helpless sort of shrug. "I hardly know," she answered. "I suppose I found the activity cathartic. Almost medicinal, if one could call an exercise of that sort such a thing. Truly, the letters were never meant to be mailed. They were never to go any farther than the drawer in my desk. I likely should have burned them the moment they were penned. I don't know why I didn't."

"Well, why you did or did not burn them is a question I will ask at a different time." Gerard lowered his voice further and leaned in so much that Etta almost had to step back to avoid an intimacy that might seem improper. "So what say you?" he asked.

She felt his gaze on her again, and this time she could not help but look up to meet it. He continued to speak.

"You save me from the wretched familial duty of marrying the daughter of my mother's oldest and dearest friend and allow me the chance to get to know your sister better, and I will allow you to form an attachment to my cousin. And if that doesn't work, at least I will save you from the uncomfortable dealings that come from your rather odd form of medicinal letter writing." His lip twitched at the word medicinal, making her insides twist with irritation.

"What say I? As you've explained, I've already committed us to the scheme. I do not believe we have any choice at this point."

"Shall we shake on it then? Make it official?" Gerard's lips curved upward as if he understood that his suggestion that they touch fluttered her insides with nerves. But how could he understand when she did not?

She thrust out her hand. He took it in his own and squeezed. She was surprised to have her fingers enveloped by rough calluses. He was not wearing gloves either. She had never known a gentleman's hands to be anything but smooth and soft. Her father's hands were almost smoother than her mother's. It was the same with her uncles and any of the gentlemen she had observed. She did not mind the unfamiliar way Mr. Hartwell's hands felt. There was character in those hands, stories she found herself curious to know.

"My aunt and mother want to invite you to dinner," he said.

Alarmed by such news, Etta yanked her hand free. "No. I'm sorry, but that cannot happen."

Likely noticing the change in Etta's mood, Anne rushed to her sister's side. "Is something the matter?" she asked.

"I've been asked to dine with Mr. Hartwell's family."

"I'm afraid I do not see how that is a problem," the gentleman said.

Anne appeared to share Mr. Hartwell's confusion.

Etta felt foolish admitting the truth out loud and so she turned away from Mr. Hartwell and faced Anne directly. "Mama has forbidden me to have any contact with the Finch family. I am never to set foot inside their home again. I am never to speak to any of them." She did not so much as peek at Mr. Hartwell when she added, "I do believe that means you as well."

"That's ludicrous!" Mr. Hartwell exclaimed. "What reason could she possibly give to rationalize such silliness?"

Anne answered for her. "Mrs. Finch and Mama do not get on at all. It's a matter of pride, I think for both of them, to despise one another the way they do. There is no rational reason behind irrational behavior."

It was the most Etta had ever heard Anne say to someone outside her own family.

Perhaps Anne's willingness to speak to Mr. Hartwell meant she held some regard for him.

"But surely if you explain to her . . ." Gerard began, but Anne was shaking her head before he could finish his thought.

"Mama will not tolerate having things explained to her; even less so if Etta does the explaining."

"But she's your mother." His voice was disbelieving. "Isn't that the whole occupation of a mother? To listen to her young even when they prattle to distraction?"

"Not all mothers," Etta whispered. Anne tossed her a sympathetic glance.

"Well, that is ridiculous." Mr. Hartwell huffed and glanced back toward the house as if he might be able to see it through the trees. "No. This will not do at all. Never fear." He lifted Etta's hand and bowed over it. "I have a remedy."

"Wait. What remedy could you possibly have to change such animosity?" She wasn't sure if she meant animosity from her mother to Mrs. Finch or from her mother to her, but Anne nodded her agreement that no such remedy existed, for either circumstance.

"Leave it to me," Gerard said. "Trust me. You shall dine with my family tomorrow evening. You both shall." He bowed over Etta's hand and then Anne's. "I trust you need no assistance to return to the house?"

They agreed that they did not.

"Then I shall send a formal invitation with further information later this afternoon, but now, if you'll both excuse me, I have work to do."

Gerard turned to leave, but before he could go, Etta stopped him by placing a hand on his arm. "How does that story end, Mr. Hartwell? The story with the bird. I remember climbing trees with you, but I truly do not remember the bird. Did the mother reject it?"

"No, Miss Stone. She accepted her baby bird entirely."

Chapter Eight

Gerard felt fairly giddy regarding the change in his fortunes. His cousin would probably loan him the money he needed, and he possibly had the chance to court a girl he had always been friends with. Granted, "probably" and "possibly" were not exactly proof of his luck changing, but they gave hope that hadn't existed before. So when Gerard knocked on Miss Stone's front door and requested to meet with her father, he felt downright confident.

By the time he'd been shown to Mr. Stone's study, he was almost jubilant.

It wasn't until Mr. Stone, with a scowl deep enough to be called severe, entered the study that Gerard felt he had cause for worry. The man's eyebrows were one scrunched line of gray, wiry hairs. The corners of his mouth had turned down so low that it appeared as though the burden to prove the theory of gravity rested solely on his shoulders.

"Mr. Hartwell," Mr. Stone said.

Gerard was certain his name had never before sounded like a devil's curse. He forced himself to smile and extend his hand. "Mr. Stone. I appreciate you for being willing to meet with me, unannounced as I am."

Though Mr. Stone grunted a noise that expressed irritation, he accepted Gerard's proffered hand. "Sit. Please." Mr. Stone gestured toward a large chair in front of a rather imposing desk.

Gerard sat. "It seems you know why I'm here, sir." Things were already uncomfortable. How much worse would it be to get right to the point?

Mr. Stone sat in the chair at his desk. "While I do not know the particulars, Mrs. Stone has given me enough of an earful regarding my daughter visiting the Finch family that your sudden appearance provides me with a few suspicions. Rather than sport with my patience by expecting me to guess the nature of your visit, perhaps you will do me the honor to explain it fully."

The man then closed his mouth and waited for Gerard to speak.

The situation was not at all playing out as Gerard had envisioned. He had thought Mr. Stone would recognize the absurdity of two neighbor women caught in a Montague and Capulet type of war, as Etta had described it. He had thought they would chuckle over it together as gentlemen. And then Mr. Stone would clap him on the shoulder and invite him to go out fishing with him or some such thing.

He had not anticipated an interview with a disapproving father. He sat up straighter. It would be best to keep to the truth as much as possible. Lying to a woman's father was the fastest way to end up in an early grave.

"Well, sir, I have long been friends with your daughters." He mentioned both women since he didn't want to seem a cad when he ended up with Anne. "And though I am aware of the history between your family and my relations, I happened to cross paths with Miss Etta and was immediately, and forcibly, reminded of how much I enjoyed spending time with her and the elder Miss Stone. I asked permission to call on Miss Etta to see if perhaps we could have something more than friendship, and she granted that permission. Possibly we are only dear friends, but we wanted the chance to discover if we are more.

"With our friendship thus renewed, my mother and my aunt requested that she join my family for dinner. Of course, we would love for the elder Miss Stone to join us as well. But Miss Stone and Miss Etta have informed me that they are not able to respond favorably to this request due to restrictions placed on them."

Gerard paused there, feeling he'd gone on for quite long enough. Surely the rest was obvious, but when Etta's father continued looking at him as though he was contemplating having Gerard thrown out, Gerard decided that he would need to finish. "And so, I have come with the hope of gaining your permission for your daughters to attend dinner with my family."

The whole situation was marvelously ridiculous. If Freddie had been allowed to overhear any of it, he would have laughed himself silly.

Mr. Stone remained silent, but Gerard had decided that he was done speaking. He'd asked his question, and he would not let this man intimidate him into jabbering on like some tot still in leading strings. If the man insisted upon stern silence, then Gerard would let him have it.

"You say you have long admired my Marietta?"

The words after so long a silence nearly jolted Gerard out of his senses. He felt a pang of guilt that he wasn't being exactly truthful. He *did* admire Etta, but she was not the object of his hopes. He wanted to appear as stoic and unruffled as Etta's father. "We've been friends since we were children. Both your daughters often played with my cousin Lucy. I regularly visited that household, spending many of my summers there."

"And you feel this acquaintance has somehow earned you the right to move against her mother's wishes?"

"Yes, sir. N-no, sir." The room was far too warm and his cravat tied far too tightly.

"Well? Which is it?"

"Yes, sir. I feel that the time I might spend together with your daughters can only be healing for our two families."

Mr. Stone harrumphed. "You say that because you do not understand the way of these things. But I give you credit, boy. The fact that you are here asking for such exceptions to the ruling of mothers proves you have either a good deal of fortitude or a great deal of stupidity.

Either way, I will allow this dinner if my daughters choose to go. Etta is, after all, the one who must bear the force of her mother's wrath. As her mother's favorite, Anne will feel little of the storm. Etta is a strong young woman. She knows her own mind. We shall see if *she* admires *you* in the way you say you have long admired her. Bear in mind, while Anne might be her mother's favorite, Etta is mine. I will not have her trifled with. I will not have *either* of my daughters trifled with. Do you understand?"

"Perfectly, sir." All the confidence Gerard had found through the course of the past day vanished. Though he'd been certain that Etta felt true desperation to get her letter back and perhaps even enough love for Freddie to be willing to do whatever it took to gain his interest, could he imagine she felt enough to willingly face down her mother alone? Clearly, her father would not stand with her in this matter, though he would not stand *against* her either. How was it so many people managed to botch up the whole business of being family so thoroughly?

The interview was clearly at an end. Etta's father had turned his attention to the paperwork on his desk. But Gerard would not leave until he knew exactly how it would be with Etta. He did not want her to face her mother's wrath alone.

"Will you tell Mrs. Stone that you have given your permission for your daughters to come to dinner, or shall I do it?"

Mr. Stone's eyebrows shot up into his receding hairline. And then he laughed out loud. "You must truly love her if you have the courage to face the lion in his den, or study, as it may be. Fine. Have it your way. I will inform Mrs. Stone that I've given my permission. That will be all."

Mr. Stone's head bowed over his paperwork once more.

Gerard stood and straightened his coat. "Thank you for meeting with me, sir."

Mr. Stone harrumphed again. "See if you thank me after her mother hears of this."

"Not particularly encouraging," Gerard thought as he vacated the premises.

When Gerard arrived back at his cousin's, he made use of Freddie's ink and paper and sent a formal invitation. He hoped Etta's father was a man of his word since he felt she would require her father's support to be allowed to step outside her house. Lucy entered her brother's study and peered over Gerard's shoulder. "What are you doing?"

"Inviting the Stone sisters to dinner."

"Oh!" Lucy sat in the chair across from him. She bit her lip. "I do hope they can come."

"I feel there will be no obstacle, and I believe they shall both be in attendance."

"Oh."

He placed the pen back in the ink pot. "You are still worried."

"Do you think my mother will treat them kindly?"

Gerard made a "tsk" noise. "Why is it that any of us must wonder whether our mothers will behave themselves? Should it not be the other way around?"

Lucy nodded and sighed. "Mother has invited several others for dinner as well. I worry she has some mischievous motive in enlarging the party."

"It will likely be better for us to have a larger party. It helps us all to remember our manners."

Lucy did not appear convinced, but she did not say anything further on the matter. She sighed some more, as if she found the very act of breathing to be too difficult to manage.

Anxiety settled its tight grip on Gerard's chest, making his own breathing erratic.

"This is ridiculous," he thought. "How can a simple dinner cause so much distress?"

But as dinnertime neared and Freddie insisted upon making inappropriate jests, and his mother snapped, his aunt snarled, and Lucy continued with her long, worried sighs, Gerard began to believe he might be the only sane member of his relations.

When the first of the dinner guests arrived a good half hour earlier than necessary, Gerard recognized how grossly he had underestimated his aunt and mother.

"You remember my dear friend Francis Bates, her son Mr. Harold Bates, and her daughter Miss Abigail Bates, don't you Gerard?" Mrs. Hartwell asked.

"How could I forget?" he responded. Though Harold had been much older and hadn't spent the same sort of time with him as a child, Abigail had constantly been thrown in his path. Gerard bowed over Miss Bates's hand, which smelled faintly of something moldering, as if she'd let her gloves get wet but didn't hang them properly to dry. "How do you do, Miss Bates?" he asked, not entirely certain his determination to be polite hid the growl in his throat well enough.

"Quite well, sir." Her gaze fixed on him as she looked up through her eyelashes. Her cheeks were as red as he'd remembered, and the laugh that followed her report of being well, though such a report did not merit any such response, reminded him of why he worked to avoid spending time with the daughter of his mother's favorite friend. "And how are you this fine evening?" she asked with another laugh.

"Please don't," he thought. "Please do not trouble yourself with coquetry."

But trouble herself she did. Miss Bates suggested they sit where they would be more comfortable as they waited for the other guests to arrive. Gerard had no choice but to agree to sit with her, for to do anything else would be rude.

"What has brought you to our part of the country?" he asked.

"Your mother sent my mother an invitation to come and stay a few days to rest and refresh ourselves as we traveled to London for the season," she answered.

A few days? Gerard shot a withering glance in the direction of the older ladies as they talked. His mother beamed at him and his aunt smirked. For his part, he called Freddie over to sit with them.

Freddie pretended not to hear and instead engaged Harold in conversation regarding hunting dogs, but Lucy noticed his distress and joined her cousin and Miss Bates where they sat. After some oddly timed laughter as Lucy tried to navigate a conversation, Lucy, fully apprehending what the presence of Miss Bates meant, tried a different topic. "Tonight should be quite splendid," she remarked. "Two of my dearest and oldest friends will be joining us for dinner."

"It is such a comfort to spend time with dear friends," Miss Bates said with a giggle. "Do I know them?"

"Why, yes. I believe you do know them. They are Miss Anne and Miss Marietta Stone."

Miss Bates let out an indelicate guffaw. "The Stone girls? Are you quite serious? Miss Anne Stone? The same woman you despise so much that your mother doused her mother in punch last year for having infringed on your relationship with Lord Lansbury?"

Lucy's face, which had been open and welcoming, immediately became closed off as she paled and parted her lips to reply. When she only stammered something incoherent, Gerard cut into the conversation. "Gossip, Miss Bates, is unattractive in a lady, would you not agree?" He didn't wait for an answer but instead said, "I am sure you do agree, which is why you will sympathize when I tell you the sad business of rather untrue rumors regarding my cousin, her dear friend, and their mothers. I do not understand why people feel it necessary to report on information of which they have no intimate knowledge. Nothing could be further from the truth than to say that Miss Finch despises Miss Stone. The unfortunate incident of my aunt spilling her punch was hardly worth mentioning until it was made famous through sensationalized facts."

Miss Bates nodded quickly, completely abandoning the gossip she had just employed to make sport of the young ladies in question just moments before. "Oh, I do agree, Mr. Hartwell. It is strange how so many pay heed to gossip. I certainly never would, since so often the facts are materially inaccurate."

Gerard smiled as though they were commiserating together over the sad state of mankind. "Yes," he said. "The friendship between my cousin and the Stone sisters is a thing unshakeable. Isn't that what you've always called it, Lucy?"

"Yes," Lucy said, finally finding her voice. "Unshakeable."

She offered him a grateful smile. He hoped Miss Bates would doubt the rumor enough to perhaps put a stop to its spread should it be brought to her attention again in the future. He felt only a twinge of regret for his stretch of honesty. He had not lied exactly, though he had not been completely forthcoming either. But he would have been willing to tell an outright bouncer if it meant being able to restore his cousin's comfort.

He glanced at Miss Bates but had to look away almost immediately when he realized she was peering at him through her eyelashes again. "Really, Mother?" he thought. How could such an off-putting woman be the best match his mother could see for him? He would have scolded his mother right then and there were he not in company and were it not for the fact that the Stone sisters entered the room at that very moment.

"Ah," he said, standing. "Lucy, your friend and her sister have arrived. We should be gracious hosts and greet them."

"You need not be gracious, Mr. Hartwell," Miss Bates said quickly. "You may stay here with me. For they are your cousin's guests, not yours."

"That is not true tonight." He corrected Miss Bates with as much kindness as he could muster. No reason to insult his mother's friends. "I extended the invitation for this evening's dinner. So, you see, they are my particular guests for the evening, and it would not do to neglect those who are here at my request." He made a bow and retreated as quickly as possible from where Miss Bates sat.

He ignored the way his aunt and mother tightened their lips and narrowed their eyes at him as he passed them to greet the sisters. He had always thought that his father was the only member of his family for whom any shame should be felt, but he now knew he'd been wrong to make such assumptions. He felt wholly mortified by his aunt and mother and their willingness to snub guests.

They did not rise to greet the two young women. The greeting offered to the sisters was the barest of nods and tightest of smiles in the directions of the doorway in which the young women lingered. Such rude behavior was entirely unacceptable. Gerard had not treated Miss Bates with such neglect. Undoubtedly, the two matrons would both have scolded him for days, if not months, if he had been so offensive. He brushed aside his irritation with his mother and gave a determined smile to the newest arrivals for the evening.

"It is lovely to see you both," he said. He bowed over both of their hands. Etta appeared nervous, but she had a smile for him.

Anne watched him with open curiosity in her blue eyes. How hard would it be for her to like him if she thought he was interested in Etta?

"I began to worry you might not come." He released Anne's hand with a pang of regret.

"I do not know how you managed this," Etta murmured through barely parted lips.

He was sure she meant that she did not know how he'd managed to convince her mother to allow her to attend the dinner. He would have answered except that Lucy, who had allowed his greeting to be first, now took her turn at welcoming her guests for dinner.

"Dearest, Etta!" Lucy exclaimed. "I am so pleased you are here, and you as well, dear Anne. You both are very welcome this evening."

Anne cast a look to where his mother sat in deep discussion with Mrs. Bates. Her expression was one of doubt at their being welcome at all.

"We are still awaiting the arrival of Mr. and Mrs. Boris and their sons to even out the numbers," Lucy said as she all but dragged the two sisters deeper into the room.

Gerard's cousin announced the two young ladies to Miss Bates, who did not deserve such attention, as far as he was concerned. Since the greetings were made without any ill consequences, Gerard was able to relax slightly. He remained near Anne's side, feeling all the luck that was his in having her present. Regardless of scheming, silly mothers, he stood by a woman who had been a friend to him since childhood. Her gentle temperament, along with their friendship, made him feel certain they would make a good match. Perhaps this was the first of many such moments when he would have the opportunity to stand near her.

"It is lovely to be able to reacquaint ourselves socially, Miss Stone." Gerard smiled at her, hoping to encourage her to speak to him since she seemed startled to be addressed directly.

"Yes. I am glad to see you taking an interest in Etta. It is proof of your very good taste."

That wasn't exactly the sort of comment he'd been looking for. "Er, well. I have fond memories of spending time with *both* of you while we were younger. You remember all the adventures we had, do you not?"

"Yes. Though I seem to recall Etta shared far more involvement than I since I was often reading."

This was, again, not exactly the response he'd hoped to hear. "Your studiousness was always a thing I admired in you. You have an earnest, sincere disposition."

Anne's eyebrows drew together, and she peeked at Etta as if she wasn't sure why Gerard was speaking to her and not to her younger sister.

He was struggling to find something else to say that might make his actions seem normal and pleasant when he heard Freddie's voice. "Well, if it isn't Miss Marietta Stone. My, but it's been an age since I saw you last." Freddie bowed low over Etta's hand and pressed a kiss to her knuckles in a way that was far more familiar than strictly required.

While a pretty blush bloomed in Etta's cheeks from his cousin's attention to her, heat of an entirely different nature filled Gerard.

Gerard had not been exaggerating when he'd said that his cousin was never satisfied with what was his. Freddie had always wanted to possess the toy in someone else's hands. His current interest in Etta had nothing to do with the woman herself and everything to do with Gerard. The fact that Freddie's attention to Etta likely irked his mother would also have been a delightful inducement to Freddie.

How Freddie could pay a woman such notice when he believed Gerard was interested in her would have completely confused Gerard had he not already understood his cousin's character.

For the first time in his life, Gerard truly did not like his cousin. He couldn't understand why Etta did.

He was unable to dwell too long on his newfound dislike because the Boris family arrived just then. Though the Stone girls were not given proper attention from his mother and aunt, the Boris family was acknowledged with effusions of great joy.

When dinner was announced, Gerard looked to claim Etta to escort her to the table, but he found that Freddie had already tucked her hand into the crook of his arm. "Mother asked that I escort Miss Etta."

Of course. His aunt and mother were scheming to keep him away from Etta. As the hostess, his aunt had the discretion to alter such arrangements—especially when the party was fairly evenly matched in rank. That suited Gerard just fine, and he glanced up to claim Etta's sister. "Sorry, cousin. Joseph has already claimed that honor." Freddie cast an apologetic glance at something behind Gerard, who turned and found his mother and Miss Bates approaching.

Gerard was left with no choice but to offer his arm to Miss Bates and to grit his teeth as his cousin walked ahead with Etta, who smiled entirely too widely for him. "Etta," he thought, "you're no foolish girl. Why would you give your smiles to my cad of a cousin?" Worse, the lady he was truly aiming for was on the arm of Mr. Boris, who was a nice-enough fellow, but still . . . worst of all, he was saddled with Miss Bates, who was laughing when nothing had been said to merit humor.

Chapter Nine

Etta glanced back nervously at Gerard, who was preoccupied with his mother and Miss Bates. She'd not been exactly surprised at the barely perceptible acknowledgment from Mrs. Finch and Mrs. Hartwell, but she had been surprised at the rather frigid reception she'd received when Lucy presented them to Miss Bates. The woman seemed familiar to Etta, though she couldn't account for why. The Boris family had all been introduced properly. Of course, those introductions had been made by Mr. Finch, who seemed entirely ignorant of the simmering tempers underneath the polite smiles on his mother's and aunt's faces.

The politics of their families had never been more keenly felt.

Yet she now had her hand tucked in the crook of Frederick's arm. A small thrill filled her at his notice of her. Her cheeks burned as she thought of the unrecovered letter she'd written, a letter in which she had hoped for just such a moment as this.

"And what causes such a pretty blush?" Mr. Finch asked.

"Oh!" Etta likely blushed the more at having him point out the stain in her cheeks. "It is only that the room is rather warm." Was the room warm? She couldn't say for certain that it felt warm to anyone else, but she may as well have been striding through a blazing fire.

"Is it?" Mr. Finch grinned as if knowing her true reason for discomfort. She turned her face lest her cheeks burn any hotter in his full view.

He chuckled low. "So, I hear my cousin has formed quite an attachment to you."

"N—" Etta shut her mouth with a click of her teeth. She was about to deny any such attachment, but wasn't that why she had been invited? Wasn't that the part she must play to have her letter returned to her? "Yes." The word escaped her mouth much too firmly and much too quickly after her initial misstep. "Well, we are good friends. Yes. And I suppose we are exploring the possibility of more, but truly, at the moment, we are only friends." How many times would she have to repeat that? It was her own fault after blundering into telling everyone Gerard was calling on her.

When Mr. Finch chuckled again, she felt all the perverseness of her situation: to be delirious with affection for one man while pretending to be so for another was entirely outside of her character.

"How did you and my cousin become reacquainted after all this time, especially when Lucy had been so severely banned from your presence?"

Etta glanced to where Mrs. Finch and Mrs. Hartwell were entering the dining room to see if Frederick had spoken loudly enough to be heard, but they appeared to be wrapped in their own conversations too thoroughly to have concerned themselves with hers.

"Mr. Hartwell and I have always been friends, since we were children. You know. You were there."

"Yes. But so have you always been friends with Lucy and myself, yet we have not seen a single hair of your head since last year."

Etta scoffed at that, knowing he was baiting her as he had done for as long as she could remember. "I do not believe Mr. Hartwell was under such strict instruction to avoid me."

"Lucky devil."

"Do you think him lucky?"

Mr. Finch's lips curved upward in a smooth, slow smile as his eyes traveled the length of her. "Can you doubt your own beauty, Etta?"

She released a small gasp of surprise to hear her nickname on his lips. Having grown up together, they, of course, had developed the habit of speaking without the necessary formalities when they were together, but for him to do so in company? What could he mean by such behavior? They were not children any longer. But the warmth that blossomed in her chest over such a silly thing as her name made her feel that perhaps she might still be a child.

And he'd called her beautiful. Or he had at least implied that he believed her to have beauty. Such compliments were normally saved for her sister. Etta merely smiled since she could not think of any proper response.

She found herself happily situated next to Mr. Finch at the table. Though she was Mr. Hartwell's particular guest, she was seated across from him rather than next to him. Mr. Hartwell was seated next to the frigid Miss Bates.

Etta leaned over to Mr. Finch to avoid being overheard. "That woman sitting next to Mr. Hartwell?"

"Jealous?" he asked in return.

"Of course not!" She drew back with a scowl that she had to force from her face immediately. She sighed. She'd long been out of practice on correct conduct.

Frederick gave Etta a lazy grin and whispered, "You are right not to be jealous since my cousin seems to have eyes only for you. Though I do believe his mother and my mother were rather artful in their arrangement of the seating this evening."

"Artful?"

"Yes. I believe my poor aunt had hoped Gerard might take a liking to Miss Bates."

"Oh." The news shouldn't have surprised her since Mrs. Finch and Mrs. Hartwell were already set against her. And it shouldn't have bothered her since she had no romantic inclinations toward Mr. Hartwell, but the news both surprised *and* discomfited her. For Mr. Hartwell's mother to have set up this other woman as a rival of sorts stung.

"You are saying that they prefer this Miss Bates for your cousin over me?"

"Yes, but you can see how very little cause you have for concern. Miss Abigail Bates is a shrewish sort of girl, the very sort that my poor cousin would never consider."

From the way Mr. Hartwell sat at the edge of his chair to avoid being too near Miss Bates, Etta believed what Frederick told her—not that it mattered to her who might catch his fancy, as it had nothing to do with her. But she did not want Anne caught between Gerard and scheming mothers. There was also the concern that if Mrs. Finch and Mrs. Hartwell were so obviously set against her, she would have no chance with Mr. Finch.

"Wait a moment," Etta whispered, lowering her voice to a level that was likely barely audible since she did not wish to alert the lady in question. "Did you say *Abigail* Bates?"

"Yes."

"I've met her before. When we were children. She stayed with your family."

"Yes. She stayed with us on several occasions."

Etta glanced surreptitiously at Miss Bates. "I hardly recognized her."

"A decade does tend to alter one's appearance."

Etta thought about when she'd last seen Miss Bates. She hadn't liked the girl, especially since Abigail had a way of spinning tales to get others into trouble and laughing when people or creatures were hurt. It had been a fortnight of agony when Abigail had stayed at the Finch estate. She wondered if Miss Bates recognized her and whether the woman recalled their last interaction together, when Mr. Finch's dog had followed them to the lake, and Abigail had begun teasing the poor creature. When Etta had tried to protect the animal, she'd accidentally put Abigail off balance and sent her careening backward into the water. Abigail had told the governess that Etta pushed her on purpose because she was jealous that Freddie and Gerard were paying all of their attention to her. It wasn't true, of course, but Etta had not been allowed back to the Finch estate until the week after Abigail had left. Perhaps that was why her introduction to Miss Bates had been so chilly.

From across the table, Mr. Hartwell interrupted Etta's fretful recollections. "How do you like your soup, Miss Stone?" he asked Anne.

Anne blinked in surprise at being singled out. "It is delicious. Thank you."

Etta spoke up since it seemed Anne was not willing to say more. "I agree. I do not believe I have ever had a better Lorraine soup." She turned to the gentleman at her side. "Your cook is to be complimented, Mr. Finch."

He accepted this with a nod.

"I seem to recall it being a favorite of yours," Mr. Hartwell said to her from across the table.

Etta was glad to have something to converse about since she hardly knew what to say to Mr. Finch. "How, pray, could you remember such a thing?"

"You fell ill once while spending the afternoon with Lucy and were much too unwell to return home that night or for the next several nights, come to that. The cook had sent up soups and broths aplenty, but the only one you ate was the Lorraine soup. As you were leaving, you told Lucy you were half-tempted to remain unwell just to see if Cook would send up more of it."

Lucy laughed at Mr. Hartwell's recollection. So did Mr. Finch and Anne and several members of the Boris family.

Miss Bates, for once, did not.

Neither did the women who had apparently been scheming on Miss Bates's behalf.

It was the second time Mr. Hartwell had recalled an incident from their childhood in which he seemed to remember her fondly. Why was it affecting her so much?

"You were certainly paying attention," she said softly. The room suddenly felt warm again. She looked down at her dish and hoped no one noticed her face growing hot once more.

Mr. Hartwell asked the dinner party if they had childhood antics that they fondly looked upon. Several shared memories and experiences. Joseph Boris's story regarding tricking his sister into believing that the horse in the pasture was a dog with long legs was delightfully entertaining.

Mr. Hartwell explored the vaults of their childhood memories, trying again and again to lure Anne into the conversation and using Etta as the bait. He mentioned having loved that Anne was such a great reader that she would settle under a tree somewhere while the rest of them were off adventuring and that when they came back wet and often muddy, he envied her wisdom.

Most of the company laughed while Anne blushed. Etta joined Gerard in his travels through their memories. "Do you recall the time you and Mr. Finch tried to frighten us girls by pretending to be ghosts?"

"Yes!" Lucy hurried to agree. "You had taken several of our finest sheets and cut holes where the eyes were."

"I remember that!" Mr. Finch interjected. "And the scheme mostly worked. Lucy and Miss Stone were quaking in their slippers for fright. But not even a momentary shiver came from Miss Etta. She stood her ground with her hands on her hips like the sternest mama and admonished both of us to remove those sheets at once, for my mother would have us punished for cutting up her sheets like we'd done." Mr. Finch laughed heartily at the memory. "And Mother did exactly that, if I recall accurately . . ."

Mrs. Finch could no longer sustain her animosity in the presence of such mirth. She, too, smiled. "Never have a pair of boys deserved it more. My best linens! Gracious. Such ruin over a silly prank."

"A prank that did not work, I might add," Mr. Hartwell said with admiration in his voice and in the look he swept over Etta. "Our dear Miss Marietta Stone proved quite fearless on many occasions. So much so that I often had to pretend not to feel my fears simply to keep her from making me look the fool."

Mr. Finch grinned. "*I* never had to pretend not to feel my fear."

Mr. Hartwell took that opportunity to poke at his cousin. "Ah, but not because you did not want to look the fool but because you *were* the fool. It was your idea to cut holes in my dear aunt's sheets."

"Was it truly?" Mrs. Finch appeared entirely astonished to hear such news. "He blamed you for the scheme, Gerard!"

"Yes. Well. He did so with my eager support. As I was merely a guest for the summer, it seemed you would perhaps be more lenient with me."

"True, true," his aunt said with a laugh that was again accompanied by all the other dinner guests at the table. Anne did not join in the conversation, however, no matter how Gerard tried to coax her into it, but she seemed pleased by the levity of it all.

Mrs. Finch continued to smile even when Mr. Hartwell returned the story to its primary purpose of praising Etta and Anne.

"Yes," he said. "All that work and punishment for nothing, since Miss Etta refused to be frightened. She even told us that had we been actual ghosts, she still wouldn't have been frightened because she could not imagine any ghost acting so silly."

Etta marveled at how Mr. Hartwell had managed to coax a smile from the woman who seemed to frown at anything that remotely had to do with a member of the Stone family. More, he had used Etta's nickname in the same way Mr. Finch had done earlier.

She acknowledged the reasons for such familiarity. They had all grown up together—had all shared adventures in the woods and by the lake. They had built forts out of fallen branches, used old logs for tables and chairs at pretend teas, and used those same old logs as rather abysmal boats, all of them nearly drowning at one point or another. But Gerard's casual use of her name caused an unexpected fluttering in Etta's middle. She understood why it would cause a stir in her from Mr. Finch, but how had it happened with Mr. Hartwell?

But while Mr. Hartwell had managed to get a smile from his aunt and mother, his continued praise of Etta's courage and Anne's kindness did not bring a smile to Miss Bates. Her mouth flattened into a straight, tight line until it finally curved downward.

Mr. Boris took the opportunity to declare that, though he didn't believe in ghosts, he was prodigiously afraid of them. He then shared a story his great-uncle had told him about an old manor that had been reported to be haunted.

"Many years ago, my aunt spent a month with her cousin in a manor in the north. She said terrible wailings and mutterings could be heard at night, and she was certain the noise came from her brothers, who were always teasing her, so she crept out of her bedchamber one night with the intent of sneaking up on them and frightening them in turn, but what she saw was a thing she said she would never forget: a woman in white floating through the halls while she wrung her hands and wept bitterly—"

"That is utter nonsense," Miss Bates interrupted with a laugh that felt entirely out of place. "Floating through the halls indeed. Your aunt was surely jesting when she told such tales, for there are no such things as ghosts, and people who propagate such nonsense are the worst sorts of society."

Everyone at the dinner table went quiet. Had Miss Bates meant to call Mr. Boris's aunt the worst sort of society, or had she meant Mr. Boris himself? Etta felt a stab of pity for everyone at the table: for poor Mr. Boris, who had been so rudely interrupted, for Mrs. Finch for having her guest abused so, and even for Miss Bates, who had made such a grave social misstep as to render the rest of the dinner guests quite silent.

Etta could not allow the uncomfortable silence to persist, and so she hurried to say, "I do understand your feeling, Miss Bates. But although I do not believe in ghosts either, I find the stories surrounding them to be diverting tales of sometimes caution, sometimes mystery, and sometimes even love. For did your aunt ever tell you, Mr. Boris, what her ghost lady lamented?"

He took a moment to respond, likely wondering if another interruption would take place, but then he finally smiled at Etta and said, "The home was rumored to have been haunted by its previous mistress, who had lost her husband to a tragic carriage accident."

"Ah, there now. See?" Etta asked. "A story of love. What greater tale could be told than one of enduring love? Love that endures is truly the hope of us all."

The tension in the room abated, and those at the table gave their agreement before moving on to other topics.

"Now you've done it," Mr. Finch whispered in her ear.

"Done what?"

"You've gone and given my mother a reason to be glad you are here. I cannot imagine what she will do now since she had been so determined to dislike you and your sister, and here you both are as amiable as anything. And look, see how Miss Bates is now the one under negative scrutiny?"

"You should not delight in her discomfort. Social missteps can happen to anyone."

But Mr. Finch seemed to take as much delight in being scolded by her as he did in Miss Bates sitting awkwardly on the other side of the table.

With dinner at an end, Mrs. Finch stood so that the ladies might retire to the drawing room.

Etta felt a great deal of confusion when both Mr. Finch and Mr. Hartwell watched her go. Mr. Hartwell was playing a part, but Mr. Finch's sudden interest made her feel more insecure than when he'd ignored her for the past few years. She had pined for him then, prayed for his notice, and never received any attention. But now? He seemed incapable of looking away from her.

There was polite conversation for several moments between the ladies. Mrs. Finch had thawed and seemed much more at ease, which was a relief to Etta. All seemed to be going well.

"Aren't you the darling of the evening," Miss Bates whispered after moving to stand near Etta.

"Pardon me?"

"Do not feign innocence, Miss Stone." Her red cheeks were sucked in, and her brown eyes flashed.

"I'm afraid I have no idea what you mean."

Miss Bates procured a glass of sherry from the tray on the table and took a sip before saying, "I think you should know that Mr. Hartwell and I have an arrangement. Therefore, your time spent flirting with him as you've done is really quite useless and a bit vulgar to watch."

Etta could not have been more astonished. She was certain, after watching him sit so much at the edge of his seat and lean away from Miss Bates at such a severe angle that it was a wonder he did not fall from the chair, that Mr. Hartwell had no arrangement at all with the woman.

"Well," Etta said, forcing her lips to curve into her most polite smile, "you certainly need not be worried regarding me if you have an arrangement. I wonder that I've not seen you more often, what with Mr. Hartwell spending so much time with his cousins since his father's passing."

Etta's eyes were drawn to the door where the gentlemen had, at that exact moment, chosen to join the ladies. With her attention diverted, she was not prepared for the gust of furious breath that left Miss Bates's mouth as she tossed the remaining contents of her glass directly into Etta's face. The shock of the liquid hitting her caused her to stumble back as she held out her hands to protect herself from further assault.

Mrs. Hartwell gasped. Lucy's mouth hung open. Anne let out a cry of dismay. Mrs. Boris cried, "What on earth!"

Mrs. Finch said, "Oh, not again." She rolled her eyes toward the ceiling with a decided air of irritation.

"Abigail!" Mrs. Bates said her daughter's name in mixed mortification and admonishment.

Even Miss Bates seemed shocked by what she had done as the sherry dripped down Etta's face and neck.

Mr. Hartwell hurried to Etta's side. He handed her a handkerchief embroidered with his initials. "Are you all right?" Without waiting for her to answer, he turned to Miss Bates. "What could you have been thinking?"

"I . . ."

Etta had once gone to see a traveling carnival with a tiger kept in a rather small cage. The animal swiveled its large head back and forth at all the people who had paid to see it. The trapped look in Miss Bates's eyes reminded Etta of that poor tiger.

"It was an accident," Etta said loudly enough that everyone in the room would hear her. "Her slipper caught on the rug just there." The rug was a good two feet away from where Miss Bates stood, but no one dared argue the point. "I do believe I should find a washbasin to clean up. If you'll excuse me." She dipped a brief curtsy, squared her shoulders, and left the room.

Lucy followed her out. "Oh, Etta! I am so, so very sorry. I cannot believe she did that to you. I am horrified in every possible way."

Etta used Mr. Hartwell's handkerchief to dab at her dress. She couldn't help herself. She started laughing.

"Etta! How can you laugh at a time like this?"

Etta only laughed harder as they made their way to the washbasin in Lucy's bedchamber. "Did you not hear your mother? Oh Lucy, how can you not laugh? Your mother said 'not again,' as if we were all in a habit of tossing drinks in faces. It is too, too much hilarity to contain!"

"I am so sorry though. It makes me all the sorrier knowing my mother has done this very thing to yours. Do you know Anne made excuses for my mother the way you just did for Miss Bates? How can you both make excuses for people who behave so badly toward you?" Having reached the bedchamber, Lucy dipped a hand towel into the basin of water and used it to help Etta clean herself.

"Anne is always generous of heart. As for Miss Bates, I felt such immediate pity. What else could I do? How wretched must her life be to feel so threatened by a woman she has not seen since her schoolroom days? Besides, what good comes from causing a scene?"

Lucy nodded. "I appreciate you saving the evening as well as you could."

Etta grabbed Lucy's hand. "And I appreciate that we've repaired the rift between us and are friends again."

Etta had to scrub at the tears in her eyes so that she might get back to the business of wiping away the sherry from her face, neck, and gown. She hoped her maid would be able to remove the stain for, though the dress was not her favorite, it was one she liked.

When the girls entered the hallway leading to the drawing room, Mr. Hartwell was there waiting for them. "Are you all right?" he asked again.

"All better." Etta felt like laughing again and could not keep the grin from her face.

"Are you laughing?"

"Not any longer," Lucy said. "But she was laughing herself to fits a moment before."

Gerard tossed a look of incredulity in Lucy's direction and then shook his head at Etta. "*What* about the odious actions of Miss Bates could you possibly find humorous? I am of a mind to have her thrown from the house."

"Pray do not be cross with Miss Bates. I am not injured. All is well." It was rather endearing that Mr. Hartwell had rushed to defend her honor.

Lucy moved toward the drawing room, though she waited at the door to enter. It took a second before Etta realized she was allowing her and Gerard a brief moment of private conversation because she imagined them to be lovers. She did not leave them entirely alone lest she cause a scandal.

Mr. Hartwell reached toward Etta's hand but did not quite take it. "Do you know," he said softly. He frowned and started again. "Do you know my favorite part of the whole experience with us pretending to be ghosts all those years ago?"

"I could hardly guess at such a thing, Mr. Hartwell." She glanced past him down the hall at Lucy and wished she had not left them this moment alone. Mr. Hartwell's hand so close to hers and yet not touching hers made it difficult to keep her head clear, though she could not say why this might be.

"It was your compassion," he answered. His eyes stayed on hers in a way that held her transfixed. "You would not have scolded us nearly so much had it not been for your anger with us for frightening Lucy and Anne. You took your sister, though you were younger, wrapped your arms around her, and made soft shushing noises while telling her you would never let anything harm her. It was a thing of beauty, that compassion." He paused, and his gaze seemed to peer into her soul. He seemed surprised at what he saw. "It still is."

"How can you call taking care of a beloved sister beautiful?" Etta had meant the question to come out as a scoff so that she might lighten the mood he'd created, but she found, once she'd asked it, that she truly wanted to know the answer.

"How could I not? Compassion *is* beauty. It is a gift you bestow on everyone, Etta—even when they do not deserve it. Such a quality is truly exquisite. One who could not see such a thing is blind."

She shook her head at Mr. Hartwell, if only to break away from his gaze. "I am sure I do not deserve such compliments."

She needed to escape to the safety of Lucy. Even being in the drawing room where she had so lately been humiliated felt safer than standing in the hall with this man, who suddenly made her feel things she should not feel toward him. They were pretending. Only pretending.

Etta moved as if to pass him, but Gerard's fingers, which had been hovering achingly close, gently wrapped around her own.

"Can you doubt your own value?" Mr. Hartwell asked.

She frowned. Mr. Finch had said a similar thing to her earlier that evening, but for reasons she did not trust herself to explore, the difference in words struck her forcibly.

Beauty and value.

They were not the same thing, no matter what society said.

As her fingers were entangled in Mr. Hartwell's, she felt certain he understood the difference between those words, and yet he had used both to describe her.

"We should return to the drawing room," she said softly, pulling her hand away from his reach.

He nodded. The moment was over. He held out his arm, and she, reluctantly, placed her hand in the crook of it.

They joined Lucy at the door, and the three of them entered the drawing room, where they were met with many curious stares.

Mr. Finch sidled up to her with a smirk on his face. "Well, that was certainly an interesting twist to what had promised to be a dull evening. What on earth happened between you two?"

She knew he wanted to know what had happened between her and Miss Bates, but she looked at Mr. Hartwell before she said, "I hardly know."

Chapter Ten

Gerard all but glared at his mother the next morning when they met in the breakfast room.

She'd never been the sort of woman to lie abed until late in the day, and he was happy to find that no one else in the household had come down yet as it allowed him a moment to speak freely. "Mother, I have never been more disappointed in you."

"Disappointed? In me? Whatever for?" She had the nerve to seem surprised at his declaration.

"You invited Miss Bates and her family to dine here and then to spend a few days? What could you have been thinking?"

"I had to." She'd been fixing herself a cup of tea but stopped to stamp her foot stubbornly, a habit she'd only started once his father had passed. The new mannerism usually made him chuckle, but not today, for he felt entirely too vexed with the woman. "You said you would not go to London for the season. How else was I to give you the opportunity to spend time with her?"

"Why would I need such an opportunity? You already know that I am seeking Miss Etta Stone's favor." He groaned inwardly at his falsehood. He was seeking the elder Miss Stone's favor. Nothing seemed to be working as it should. He'd hardly been able to speak to Anne the whole night. She'd brushed aside his every attempt. Then

there was that moment he'd had with Etta in the hall when he had felt
his emotions make a rather uncomfortable shift. He could not dwell
on that now, however. His mother had to be shown reason. "For your
friend's daughter to fling her drink into the face of a woman I invited
as a guest, well, it's a pity she did not conduct herself in a manner
worthy of her breeding."

"How was I to know she'd waste a perfectly good sherry like that?"
She offered him a smile, likely hoping it would ease his temper. Her
sense of humor usually coaxed him from a mood, but at that moment,
her humor brought him further annoyance.

"Mother! Be serious. I do not know how to apologize to Miss
Stone and her sister. How am I to ever gain her trust again? It was
not easy for her to come here after all that has transpired and with the
strained relationship between her mother and my aunt. And now, *how*
am I to repair this? What are Miss Etta and her sister to think?"

"I am sorry, Gerard." Mrs. Hartwell finally looked penitent,
though she did so far too late. She seated herself at the table, and
Gerard did the same.

"If you're truly sorry, then you will excuse me from any socializing
during the remainder of your friends' stay. I would leave for home
until the Bates family has all gone on to London, except I do not
think it wise to leave the neighborhood after last night's events. I owe
the Stone sisters my attention." Even as he said it, he worried whether
staying away from his own estate was a wise course of action.

He had not seen the quandary of his situation before that moment. To solve his financial distress and save his estate, he was required to engage in the business of courting. But to make certain he
didn't lose the estate in the meantime, he needed to be working. How
was he to accomplish both tasks simultaneously when there was only
one of him?

"I will make excuses and apologies for any of your absences. You
may come and go as you see fit." His mother interrupted his private panic. "I am sorry for my interference, Gerard. After last night's

behavior, no one will fault your absence, at least not anyone in our family."

"Thank you, Mother."

He was spreading preserves on his bread when his mother said, "You know, despite what has happened between the Stone and Finch families, that young woman behaved very prettily last night. Even your aunt said so."

"Thank you, Mother. I quite agree." Etta's response to her attacker was above reproach. Lucy joined them at that moment, followed quickly by Freddie.

"Good morning, family of mine." Freddie accepted the newspaper from the silver tray the footman held out for him and began reading even before bothering with food. It was his way in the morning. Though Freddie seemed buried in whatever news the paper divulged, he said, "I wondered if the Stone ladies might wish to join us on a carriage ride, Gerard. And you as well, Lucy. It's a fine day."

"I think that sounds like a lovely idea." Lucy beamed at her brother for having suggested the scheme.

Since Gerard had no intention of staying anywhere near the house while Miss Bates was yet an occupant, he readily agreed, though he did so while his mother protested that to leave Miss Bates out of the plan was to give a snub that would be detrimental to them all, as it showed very poor breeding.

"Where are you going?" Gerard's aunt walked in as the plans were finalized.

"On a carriage ride with Miss Stone and her sister," Freddie said without looking up from his paper.

Mrs. Finch frowned at her son and then at her daughter. "And you're going as well?" Lucy flushed a few shades of pink. "Well . . . I had been meaning to, Mama."

"And what am I to do with our house guests? You cannot mean for me to entertain them." Mrs. Finch eyed the lot of them.

To Gerard's surprise, his mother stepped in to bear the burden of entertaining the houseguests, which was only fair since she had invited them to stay. "I will order my carriage and take them all out on a tour of the priory ruins. They are lovely in the middle of the afternoon. With any luck, Gerard, Freddie, and Lucy will return before us, and the Bateses will not know they were left out of a different diversion. I do feel it might be the least we can do to make it up to Miss Stone for last night's unfortunate events."

Mrs. Hartwell's face sagged with the distress the memory caused her. She really was the sort of woman who worked hard to ease contention and discord.

Gerard hated to see his mother fretting and worried Mrs. Finch might say something against the Stone sisters and make the whole thing worse, but his aunt merely said, "I really should have served the ratafia instead of the sherry. Perhaps it would have provided some calm to the evening . . ." She trailed off.

Mrs. Hartwell shook her head, checked over her shoulder to be certain no one from the Bates family had arrived for their breakfasts, and said in a quiet voice, "How that girl could do such a thing and not apologize or act penitent in the slightest is troubling. She did not repent to Miss Stone, to you, or to me, though she owed an apology to the whole party. What must the Boris family think?"

Freddie folded down a corner of his newspaper so that he might smirk at Gerard's mother. "They likely think they've never been half so well entertained at any dinner in their lives. They were pleasant people. I do hope we have them again sometime."

Gerard wondered if his aunt had made any apologies to the hostess of the ball where she'd made a similar misstep.

Perhaps.

Perhaps not.

Mrs. Finch might have been thinking the same thing, for she pursed her lips and glanced away. Aunt Lucinda might be more inclined to hold a grudge than his mother, but she was not above her own self-reproach when it occurred to her that she might be in the wrong.

Freddie finally set down his paper and began his breakfast. He ate methodically and scowled after Gerard asked for the fourth time if he were not through yet. "I would be through if you would only stop badgering me."

"I'm not badgering. I'm encouraging you."

Freddie rolled his eyes and began taking slow, deliberate bites, chewing as carefully as if he were nursing a toothache.

His aunt looked at Gerard. "Do give my apologies to Miss Stone when you see her, Gerard. Though I know I do not get on with her mother, I do not mean harm to the young ladies of that family. And I feel wretchedly regarding last night's events."

Gerard stood, unable to watch Freddie methodically chew a bite of egg that could easily have been swallowed whole without chewing at all. "I will tell her, Aunt. And I thank you for your good wishes. I'm off to order the carriage." He hurried to leave lest Miss Bates enter the breakfast room and he be forced to speak with her.

But he did not move quickly enough; he nearly knocked Miss Bates over on his way out.

"Did I hear you say you would be ordering the carriage? Where are we to go, I wonder?" She laughed and gazed up at him with a smile that showed too many teeth. Nothing in her countenance indicated she felt any sort of remorse regarding the previous evening.

Was the woman incapable of feeling, or was she simply so obtuse that she could not understand that what she had done was wrong?

"Miss Bates." He glanced over his shoulder and could see the faces of his family all eyeing him with curiosity—likely wondering how he would handle the question the young lady had put before him.

He decided the truth would be the best policy. Since Miss Bates had a decided dislike for Etta, she was unlikely to have an interest in any activity that might involve that other lady. "We've planned an excursion with Miss Stone and Miss Etta for the afternoon."

If the news gave Miss Bates any sort of unhappiness, she hid it well. "That sounds lovely. I'll want to fetch my bonnet. Will I have time to eat anything before we leave?" And that was that.

For what could he say to discourage her without being the most wretched of humans? He did not want his aunt's reputation to suffer due to her being perceived as inhospitable, especially when he was a guest in her home and when he owed her so much for her many kindnesses to his mother.

He glanced into the breakfast room in time to catch the full effect of Lucy's open-mouthed shock and Freddie's smirk.

He narrowed his eyes at his cousin, whom he held chiefly responsible for the current situation. If Freddie would have hurried with his breakfast rather than make a ridiculous show of the whole thing, they would have all been in the carriage and on their way before Miss Bates had descended the stairs. Gerard turned back to the young lady, giving her the barest of glances before saying, "I imagine you will have time to eat before we leave. Mr. Finch has ensured that such time is available. If you'll excuse me."

Without waiting to see if she excused him or not, he hurried away, feeling intensely disagreeable for having been forced into such a predicament.

How would he explain to Etta and Anne the reason he had allowed that interfering woman to join them? Would the sisters choose not to come due to the newest member of their party? For all he knew, the girls would not be permitted to go with or without the presence of Miss Bates. Their mother might forbid them from leaving the house.

This would have been disappointing before Miss Bates declared her intention to join them, but it would now be catastrophic, for it would mean Gerard would have to endure that lady's company without the balm of seeing Anne.

His scowl must have been deep indeed since Wilson asked him what sort of tempest had been brewed in his teacup that morning.

He tried—and failed—to relax his expression. At least, he believed he failed since Wilson held up a hand as if to keep Gerard from hurting himself in his attempts to appear pleasant. "Never mind, sir. What may I do to assist you?"

Gerard gave quick instructions regarding the coat he wanted to wear. He wished to look his best for Anne and recalled that her favorite color was green. He also requested that a basket of food be prepared so that they all might take refreshment while out.

With the carriage ordered and his favorite green coat procured, Gerard waited outside. His goal of avoiding Miss Bates for as long as possible was not met, as she was the first one out of doors with her bonnet on her head and fastened underneath her chin with a bow.

"Well!" she said with a laugh. "It appears no one else is as excited by this prospect of an outing as we two. This meeting of the minds is something I feel we often share. Do you not agree, Mr. Hartwell?"

He found himself unable to answer, so he made some sort of murmuring noise and drummed his fingers against his thigh as he waited without any degree of patience for his cousins to join him.

When the carriage arrived, Miss Bates held out her hand expectantly as she waited for him to hand her up. He did as expected, trying hard not to frown as she took her time in releasing his hand from her own. "Are you not getting in as well?" she asked.

What sort of devilry was this, wanting to be alone with him in an enclosed space where there was no chaperone?

"No. I prefer to be last in."

When it appeared that she might insist he help her exit the carriage, likely so she could arrange to sit near him, Gerard turned away and said, "I've forgotten my gloves again. I never can seem to recall them. If you'll excuse me, I'll return momentarily."

Momentarily meant he went to Freddie's room after retrieving his gloves. "What the devil could be taking you so long? You've left me alone with a predator."

"Are you calling yourself prey, cousin?" Freddie seemed amused, but then Freddie almost always did.

"Where a scheming woman of that kind is concerned, any man would consider himself prey. I will not go out again until you are with me, and I refuse to sit next to that woman. If, for any reason, she ends up next to me, I swear to you I will leap from the carriage and take my chances with the wheels."

Freddie laughed outright. "You are being a bit dramatic, don't you think? The woman is harmless."

Gerard didn't answer, because he realized he really might be reacting too strongly. Miss Bates had always managed to confuse and irritate him. It was part of the reason he worked to avoid her whenever possible. When his mother mentioned Miss Bates would be attending a particular ball or dinner party, he usually managed to remove himself from those same events.

Freddie took an enormous amount of time worrying over his hair and mused over where they would go in the carriage. "What of Mother's idea of visiting the priory ruins while we're out? The ladies will like exploring them. We can have a basket of food made up for refreshment."

It was a good idea, especially since Gerard had already made arrangements for a basket. He said as much to Freddie, who seemed to be fussing with his hair again. Finally, the man was ready, and the two of them went down together to the carriage. Gerard would have teased Freddie that the kitchen staff readied their sustenance faster than he had done his hair, except that he was in no mood for teasing. He lowered his voice. "You get in first, and you sit next to that woman. You owe me that much for being the reason she's coming with us."

Freddie shrugged and obliged him by getting in first.

When Gerard stepped up into the carriage, he discovered that only Lucy and Freddie were inside. Freddie was sitting next to Lucy.

"What are you doing?" Gerard demanded of his cousin.

Freddie held up his hands as if to show his innocence. "You told me to sit next to the woman inside. There was only one woman. I was doing what you asked."

"You change seats with me right this moment, or I swear I'll—"

A syrupy voice came from outside the carriage. "If you'll take your seat, Mr. Hartwell, the footman can help me up as well." The voice belonged to none other than Miss Bates.

Gerard scowled at his cousins. How dare they sit together and leave him in such a predicament? He sat. Really, what choice did he have?

He moved to the farthest side, thinking that would allow a space between them, but Miss Bates sat in the middle of the seat, as if expecting another guest to join them immediately.

Lucy looked pained. Freddie stifled a laugh. Gerard fumed. Miss Bates commented on the fine weather with a laugh that she did not stifle.

Thus was the mood of the party as they made their way to the Stone estate.

Chapter Eleven

Etta heard the carriage along the drive well before it rounded the bend in the road where trees obscured it from her view. She must have made some sort of noise of surprise when she saw the livery on the carriage door because Anne asked, "Who is it?" while her mother demanded, "Who could it be that has you gawking like a child at the window instead of behaving as the lady I've raised you to be?"

"It's a carriage with the Finch livery."

Her mother sniffed in disdain. "One dinner and now they think they are allowed to trespass on our property? I told you that last night's activities were a terrible idea. I vastly disapprove of your association with these people."

Etta had no response. Neither she nor Anne had divulged the sherry-throwing incident since they were certain their mother would take such an attack personally and return to her original vow to keep the girls from that family.

As it was, it had taken quite a lot to get their mother's permission, if not approval, for the dinner the night previous. Even with her father telling her mother that he felt it a prudent choice to mend the breach, her mother had only been swayed when Etta had said that she was doing it all for Anne's sake.

Her mother had scoffed at such a notion until Etta reminded her that the gossips in London would likely be paying close attention to the behavior of the Finch family toward Anne and her mother. If they perceived any sort of stiffness in conduct, it could reflect poorly on Anne and could diminish her chances, as it could make the whole Stone family seem unforgiving.

Her mother had paused, reconsidered, and then finally agreed. But she hadn't liked it.

Her sour attitude this morning was proof that she disliked it still.

Their butler, Mr. Greene, entered the drawing room and announced Mr. Finch and Mr. Hartwell. The gentlemen were then ushered into the room after bows and curtsies. Mr. Finch had a smirk set upon his lips while Mr. Hartwell looked rather ill at ease.

"Mrs. Stone, it is lovely to see you this morning," Mr. Finch said, his tone all pleasant politeness.

She seemed taken off her guard at his behaving as though there had been nothing amiss between his mother and herself over the past twelve months.

Mr. Hartwell sneaked a glance at Etta as if verifying that she was all right. He then nodded his head slightly in her mother's direction before it occurred to Etta what he was trying to say.

"Mother, may I introduce Mr. Gerard Hartwell? He is Mr. Finch's cousin and has often stayed with the family over the years. Mr. Hartwell, this is my mother, Mrs. Stone."

He bowed again while she inclined her head.

Since she did not appear to have any intention of saying anything, he went ahead as if everything were perfectly normal. "It is an honor to meet you at last, Mrs. Stone. It is no wonder we have not met before, as I was a child for much of my earlier acquaintance with your lovely daughters, and then I went away to school. Since my return, I'm afraid I've not had much time for socialization. It is lovely to rekindle the acquaintance with your daughters."

"Hmm," was the only response she gave in return.

Etta wondered what Mr. Hartwell might do with such an unenthusiastic reply, but Mr. Finch got right to business. "Since it is such a lovely day, we were hoping to have Miss Stone and Miss Etta join us for a carriage ride to the ruins, where we all might take in some fresh air and stretch our legs a bit."

Mrs. Stone stepped to the window to peer out at the carriage waiting for them. "Who else is going? I perceive a woman's hand at the window."

"Ah yes, the hand you see could belong to my sister, Lucy, or it might belong to the daughter of my aunt's friend, Francis Bates. Her family is staying for a few days to refresh themselves on their journey to London for the season."

Etta hoped she'd kept her features smooth once she'd heard who would be joining them on their outing, for the last thing she wanted was to be stuck in a carriage with Miss Bates. Wasn't last night's debacle enough? Did they need to continue meeting socially while that woman remained a guest in their household?

She almost declined the invitation, which would have pleased her mother. But she did not decline, because the truth was that the *actual* last thing she wanted was to have Miss Bates enjoy the triumph of having Mr. Finch and Mr. Hartwell to herself.

"I think such an outing will be just the thing," Etta said. "Anne had only moments before mentioned that she longed to be out of doors for some fresh air."

Anne raised her eyebrows at her, as she had said no such thing. Etta needed to rein in the many falsehoods that were exiting her mouth. She was quickly forming a habit and would become the most infamous liar in history if she did not find a way to bring herself under control again. But in for a penny, in for a pound. She frowned at herself for using a cautionary statement against gambling to justify her behavior.

"Are you sure you wish to come along with us?" Mr. Hartwell asked, likely noticing her frown. "We could go some other time if you would prefer."

She forced a smile back to her lips. "I would not miss this outing for the world. Anne and I will only require a moment to ready ourselves, but we shall be down shortly."

After they exited the drawing room, Anne whispered, "Is it really a good idea to leave them there alone together? Are you not worried that Mama, who is capable of saying any number of things, might fail to keep herself in check? Or are you not worried that one of the gentlemen might say something regarding the whole ordeal with the sherry? Mama will fly into hysterics if she discovers what happened. You know she will. And I do not feel that Mr. Finch is one to be trusted not to share information that amuses him."

They'd made it to the top of the stairs, but Etta paused before continuing to her room. "Why would you think that horrid display last night amused him?"

"He laughed, Etta. To be sure he did not laugh out loud like some braying donkey we know, but he did snicker to himself."

Receiving such news made Etta's stomach feel as though it had sunk into the depths of her slippers. It hurt her in ways entirely unexpected. Mr. Finch had laughed at her? He had laughed at her keen humiliation? Why would he do such a thing when he'd been so kind to her earlier when they were dining together? She had thought that perhaps his attention was a sign of interest, that perhaps Mr. Hartwell had been accurate when he said that an attempt on his part to court her would inspire interest in his cousin, but to hear that he had laughed made her question this.

Anne, not realizing the acute pain Etta was feeling, continued. "It is a pity we cannot ready ourselves in turns so that one of us can stay and make certain that everyone in that room is under the scrutiny of one who could steer the conversation in appropriate directions."

"You needn't worry about Mr. Finch, or Mama, for that matter. Gerard is there. He will see to it that everyone behaves themselves."

"Gerard, is it? You have grown close enough to use Christian names, then?" Her sister grinned as if such news gave her the greatest pleasure.

"No," Etta said with great alarm at having misspoken. Gerard wanted to court Anne, not her. She needed to remember that Anne was his aim. "We have not. I sometimes forget we are not children any longer and must be much more formal now. 'Mr. Hartwell' is what I meant to say."

But even as Etta denied that there was any such closeness between herself and her childhood friend, she wondered at her very different feelings. Only a few days prior, she had not given a single thought to Mr. Hartwell. Now she saw all the ways he was steady and sure. She now believed that were she to fall and reach out her hand, he would be there to take it and not let go. Anne was a lucky woman to have caught his attention.

But how could she feel this way when Mr. Hartwell was the very man who held her letter in his possession and refused to give it back? She shook her head. What could she possibly view as steady and sure about that? The answer was that there was nothing. That Mr. Finch had laughed at her misfortune increased her desperate need to have her letter returned to her possession. She could only imagine how Frederick would laugh at her if he ever read what she had written. But the constant thought of getting her letter back exhausted her. She was tired of this bizarre and irksome subterfuge.

She held out her hands to her mother's maid so that her gloves might be buttoned up and stood still while her pelisse was buttoned over her dress. She was glad she'd chosen to dress warmly that morning. Though they had experienced unseasonably pleasant weather that day, only a fool went out of doors without some sort of extra protection from unexpected chills.

Anne was exiting her own room at the same time Etta left hers. "It's a shame Miss Bates will be joining us. I do not harbor feelings of charity toward the woman."

"Maybe not charity, exactly," Etta agreed. "But she brings herself misery with her actions, so I cannot help but feel pity for her."

"We shall see if you're so generous by the end of today," Anne said with a laugh.

Anne's lovely sense of humor was a thing very few people knew of since she so seldom spoke with others outside her family.

They descended the stairs where Mr. Finch and Mr. Hartwell waited for them. Etta felt that sinking in her stomach as she thought of Anne's comment regarding Mr. Finch. "He laughed, Etta." Could the face smiling up at her with such genuine warmth be one that had laughed at her?

Perhaps Anne had been mistaken. Perhaps he had coughed or sniffled and the timing had made it seem as though he'd been laughing. Unsure of how much she might be fooling herself, she glanced away from Mr. Finch's smile and focused on Mr. Hartwell instead.

Mr. Hartwell also smiled at her, though his expression was not nearly so open. But then, why should it be? He was only pretending to admire her so that he might evade an association with a woman he didn't like and then perhaps wheedle his way into the good graces of Anne.

As they prepared to leave, Etta decided to stop analyzing everything and simply enjoy the day. After all, with her family leaving for London soon, she was unlikely to have many diversions to fill her time. "I do believe it will be a very good day," she said aloud.

Anne said nothing.

"We shall see," Mr. Finch said.

"Indeed," Mr. Hartwell said.

Once they were all settled in the carriage, Miss Bates seemed unhappy that Lucy had switched sides, scooting herself right next to Miss Bates, forcing her to slide closer to the window. Lucy then patted the seat next to her and said, "Anne, please do sit by me. I want to hear all about your plans for London. We must make time to see each other while we are there. I do hope we will be attending the same parties, for it puts one so much more at ease when there is a friend present."

Etta felt fairly certain Miss Bates would have also switched sides to avoid being trapped sitting between a window and Lucy, but before she could, Etta had moved in and seated herself across from Miss Bates, neatly pinning the woman in place.

Miss Bates glowered as Mr. Hartwell scooted next to Etta. She glowered ever more deeply when Mr. Hartwell leaned over to whisper, "I am glad you have joined us, Miss Etta. After last night, I worried you and your sister might not."

Etta did feel sorry for Miss Bates. But she did not feel sorry that the warmth of Mr. Hartwell's minted breath washed over her face. Had he eaten a mint leaf? Why had his whisper caused her stomach to twist and flutter and tighten all at once?

She immediately felt guilty since he was meant for her sister—even if Anne didn't know it yet.

"What a merry party we all make," Mr. Finch said loudly enough to include everyone in the carriage. "I do believe that before last night this particular set of people has not been together since we were twelve or some such age. A reunion is a grand thing, is it not, Miss Bates?"

The woman seemed surprised to be called out to answer his question. "Yes." Her agreement was quick. "Very grand for old friends to see each other again." She smiled warmly at Mr. Finch. Her gaze slipped to Mr. Hartwell, and she turned the full force of that smile on him.

The season hadn't even started yet, but here they all were, miles from London, and the games of unmarried women had begun. Well, Etta wanted nothing to do with those games. She wanted to avoid any more drinks flung in her face and women scorning her simply because she appeared to be competition. She was not in competition with any woman for the affections of any man. She was on a quest to retrieve her letter. That was all.

She repeated this statement to herself for nearly the whole of the ride.

Why did the statement require so much repetition, as if she were memorizing French conjugations in the schoolroom?

She glanced at Mr. Hartwell's leg, so close to her own that she need only shift to make them touch, and hurriedly glanced away, beginning her repetition once more.

Miss Bates pulled her from her thoughts. "Why so silent, Miss Stone? I've not heard you say anything regarding the London season."

"No. You would not have," Etta said. She almost left the statement at that, as what business of Miss Bates's was it what she did or did not do? But she did not want to be cold and unfriendly, no matter how the woman had behaved toward her in the past. "I'll not be going to London for the season."

Miss Bates laughed, which made no sense since Etta hadn't said anything humorous.

"Not going? Why ever not, when your sister and dearest friend are going?"

She said "dearest" with a sneer, as if calling Etta's friendship with Lucy into question. Etta could not think of how to answer, for to mention her attachment to Mr. Hartwell felt presumptuous and inappropriate to utter aloud in mixed company, but then Miss Bates added, "Surely your mama does not consider you on the shelf before you've even begun, does she?"

"Of course not!" Lucy declared, her voice forceful from the shock that Miss Bates could say such a thing. "Of course not. Etta has commitments that hold her here in Narborough."

"Commitments?" Miss Bates laughed. "What commitments can an unmarried young woman have?"

Etta squirmed under the scrutiny of this person, who seemed to understand Etta's real reason for missing her first season: her mother considered her marriage prospects to be poor.

Gerard sat up straighter, moving his leg to press against hers. "She stays because I asked her to stay. She is a good enough friend to humor me in this request."

He had, in one simple statement, announced a desire to court Etta. Not quietly, but boldly. He corroborated the lie she'd told his family without any hesitation.

If the claim came as a surprise to Miss Bates, it was nothing compared to what it had done to Etta. He seemed determined to rescue her from this woman who felt it necessary to attack again and again, even when rescuing her meant a deviation from his own hopes and plans.

Mr. Finch chuckled. "It is a lucky man who has a pretty woman willing to make such a sacrifice for him." His laugh sent a chill up Etta's spine as she recalled again her sister's words.

"It is no sacrifice." Etta wanted to explain that she didn't feel she was giving anything up by spending time with Mr. Hartwell, but to do so would be to imply she had feelings for him. Though she suspected she felt more than she ought, she did not want to lead people to believe that she felt even more than she truly did. The two of them were pretending at a courtship, and such an action could bruise her reputation and his. He did not deserve to be trapped in an engagement with her if they pretended with too much energy. She found herself unable to do more than whisper those four words and then look out the window. She was making a mess of everything. She was not sure if she was doing Mr. Hartwell or herself any favors when she spoke.

"Well." Miss Bates cast a rather chilly eye over the three people seated across from her. "That is a surprise. Though I suppose it should not be. You always did follow her around as if she'd tied a leash about your neck, Mr. Hartwell. I simply find it interesting that the leash is just as tight now as it was then."

Etta could not allow such an attack to be made against Mr. Hartwell's character. "If he has a leash about him, I have seen nothing of it. For as long as I have known him, he has always been entirely in possession of himself." She then turned away from addressing Miss Bates, afraid of becoming excessively curt and inappropriate. She instead addressed Mr. Hartwell. "Do you recall when, on one of the occasions you were visiting for the summer, we all wanted to build a raft to float on the lake, and we needed your suspenders to lash the branches together?"

"I remember," Mr. Finch said. "He was a selfish bore who refused to accommodate a great plan of adventure."

"Not a bore," Etta said, refusing to let anyone malign Mr. Hartwell. "But one who had made a choice and was willing to stand by it. No matter how we tried to convince you otherwise, you would not relent. You are your own man, Mr. Hartwell. There is much to respect in one who does not give way to his peers."

Mr. Finch scoffed. "And there is much to resent in one who does not give suspenders to a good cause."

Mr. Hartwell chuckled and shrugged. "It was more like a lost cause. If I recall correctly, your little vessel sank as soon as you shoved it into the water."

Lucy joined in the teasing since she had been a victim of the sinking raft due to her brother's insistence that she play the part of a fair maiden needing rescue in a vast and stormy sea. Anne smiled when Mr. Hartwell reminded her that she had been wise to refuse that role since she would have been the one nearly drowning instead of Lucy.

Miss Bates joined in only because she had also been present for several moments of Mr. Finch's poor judgment as a child.

When they arrived at the priory ruins, Miss Bates claimed Mr. Finch's arm. He raised his eyebrows but held out his other arm. "Miss Etta?"

She stepped forward to claim it. It was only fair since she'd promised to help Gerard get time to speak with Anne when they weren't surrounded by eavesdroppers, though she didn't particularly enjoy being so close to Miss Bates. As that lady let out a raucous laugh at something Frederick said, Etta could not help but feel that no letter was worth so much trouble.

"I must say," Mr. Finch began, "that never had I considered the merit of my cousin's exemplary taste before the last few days."

"His taste?" Etta asked.

Mr. Finch didn't answer but merely smiled at her.

Out of the corner of Etta's eye, she saw Miss Bates scowl.

Etta wondered if she understood the situation properly. Was he complimenting Mr. Hartwell's taste in choosing her? The thought warmed her.

Miss Bates said, "It is strange that you would leave Mr. Hartwell's side so readily."

Was it strange? It was hard to know when Etta was only pretending affection.

"I don't think it strange at all. He and I have no understanding. And it is good to give a man space to search his feelings, is it not?"

Mr. Finch laughed. "Well spoken, Miss Etta."

The harumph that came from Miss Bates showed she did not agree.

Etta chose to ignore her. The trio walked toward the southern end of the priory, where fragmentary remains of a wall crowned the banks. Etta took a deep breath of the fresh air. "How did you enjoy your time in France, Mr. Finch?" she asked.

"Exceedingly. I am considering a return sometime soon. I now consider myself quite a lover of all things French."

Miss Bates let out a laugh. "Hardly the words of a patriot."

"The war is over, Miss Bates, and we won. There is no reason to not play nice now."

"If you say so. Men can fight their battles and move on. Women are more complex." Neither party seemed too perturbed at their minor disagreement.

"You must tell me more about France someday." Etta slipped her hand out from where it had been tucked around Mr. Finch's arm since she felt silly clinging to him while Miss Bates stood just on the other side. "Excuse me; I think I'll go find Lucy." She walked back in the direction they had come. She could see Mr. Hartwell and Anne off in the distance and felt a twinge of . . . what? Displeasure at seeing them together? Perhaps.

They didn't appear to be talking, which was odd, and by the time she'd arrived at her sister's side, Anne was looking at the ruins around her with determination. Lucy appeared at the same time and suggested Anne go with her to see the gatehouse.

Anne readily agreed, and as the two ladies went to explore, Etta found herself briefly alone with Mr. Hartwell. Mr. Finch and Miss Bates were still visible but too far away to overhear them. "Did you enjoy speaking with Anne?"

He shrugged. "She's not much for conversation, is she?"

"She is more subdued than I, but that should suit your more even temperament."

Gerard stammered for a moment before saying, "I completely agree."

"Miss Bates is certainly interesting . . ." Etta glanced at him while trying to appear to admire the ruins.

"Yes," Mr. Hartwell said after a few moments.

"Yes?" she asked.

"Yes. Miss Bates is the woman on whom my mother has pinned her hopes for me. You can see for yourself that she would be ill-suited to my disposition and temper." He tapped his polished boot against a large stone and waited for her to respond to his confession.

"I didn't ask for such information regarding the woman you are meant to be courting."

Mr. Hartwell offered her a wry grin. "Yes. I know. But, Etta, you were not asking very loudly."

She laughed. "Why would your mother want such a woman for you?"

"She and Mrs. Bates have been planning this union since Miss Bates and I were both infants. You must think me absurd for not simply telling my mother no."

"I was not making commentary on your affairs with your mother either."

Mr. Hartwell removed his hat and squinted into the distance. "Again . . . you were not making commentary very loudly."

"Your keen sense of hearing must be such a burden to you."

"You have no idea."

Etta put her hand in the crook of Gerard's bent arm and they began to walk. "I do not blame you for needing to show your mother an alternative. I would hold letters hostage for such a reason as well."

"You are too generous. But she is not the only reason I made our arrangement."

"What other reasons are there?" Etta was glad he didn't walk quickly because she wanted this moment to speak to him without prying ears and eyes.

He stopped and turned to face her. With their arms linked as they were, they were altogether too close to one another. She could see a distinct white starburst pattern around his pupils that brightened the blue of his eyes. How had she not noticed such an intriguing detail before? He straightened. "The reasons are irrelevant, really. At least to you." The wind tousled Gerard's hair, reminding her that she had imagined he smelled like the wind, the crisp, clean fragrance of spring that now surrounded them.

"It's strange to hear you call me 'Mr. Hartwell,'" he said after a moment.

"You wish me to call you something else? Perhaps 'ghost'? Or perhaps 'prison warden of letters'?"

"Perhaps 'Gerard.'"

Those words filled Etta with an inexplicable burst of joy.

"After growing up together as practically cousins, it certainly feels more natural," he added.

The elation fled immediately. She stepped back from Gerard, letting the hand that had been tucked into the crook of his arm drop to her side. "Oh."

"I would like to find a moment to walk with Miss Stone again. Would you oblige me by engaging Lucy in conversation so that I might have another moment with her?"

Etta took another step back. "Of course."

"I am grateful to you, Etta. I know not what I would have done without you to conspire with." He stepped forward even as she stepped back again. To him, she was Etta, while her sister was Miss

Stone. She was the childhood friend, and her sister was the lady he wanted to court. It was a lucky reminder.

Etta didn't blame Mr. Hartwell. Anne was more deserving than anyone she knew. She would not let herself be swept into her romantic imagination.

Etta replaced her hand on his arm and said, "Let us go find Anne and Lucy."

His enthusiastic agreement made her frown, proving she had not entirely set aside the growing romantic notions she now harbored for Mr. Hartwell.

Chapter Twelve

Gerard turned the corner with Etta and passed under a large stone arch where Lucy and Miss Stone were surveying the crumbling tower to the side of them. They had not made it to the gatehouse.

"Lucy!" Etta called out. "There you are." She released Gerard's arm and hurried to Lucy's side, then pulled Lucy quickly toward the other archway as if intent to show her some interesting bit of history.

Gerard smiled. "Well done, Etta," he thought. He joined Miss Stone and squinted up at the tower remains. "Care to have a game of pretending we're monks?" he asked. He was determined to pull conversation from her this time.

Anne smiled. "Some might call that blasphemous."

He grinned. Though Miss Stone hadn't laughed at his joke like Etta might have, and she'd even given mild admonishment, he knew she wasn't cross with him, and any answer more than a "yes" or "no" from her felt like an accomplishment.

"You didn't mind playing that game when we were children. If I recall properly, it was one of your favorites when the governesses brought us here to play."

"It was far better than the reenactment of *The Tempest* when Lucy almost drowned."

"That's only because Freddie made such an abysmal Prospero."

Anne actually chuckled at this, a thing which made Gerard feel he'd accomplished something magnificent. "Do you imply that if he'd been a better Prospero, the raft would have floated?"

"Certainly."

She must have noted that Lucy and Etta had moved a fair distance because she began a leisurely walk in their direction. "Thank you, Mr. Hartwell."

"For what?" he asked as he offered her his arm.

Miss Stone took it and said, "For defending my sister at dinner. I know I am older than she and it should be my responsibility to stand up for her, yet I often feel she is the one watching out for me. She is my greatest champion."

"She is certainly a spirited friend."

"Only a friend?" She gave Gerard a sideways look, catching the sunlight in her hair as she tilted her head.

Well, that was certainly direct, and not at all the conversation he'd imagined having. "I must say yes. While she is a capital girl, I believe we might be destined for friendship alone. And one who counts Etta among his friends is lucky indeed."

"True," Anne agreed. "I wish she were going to London with me."

"Perhaps you should stay home as well." Gerard liked that Miss Stone didn't seem to be in any hurry to rejoin her sister. It made him think that perhaps she wanted this time with him.

Perhaps.

"Tempting. But Mama would not allow me to stay."

That was a disappointing fact. He would need to work faster to gain Miss Stone's favor, because he simply did not have time to go to London for the season. It was not ludicrous to think it could happen so quickly. Many marriage proposals were the result of a few weeks of courtship. Some came after mere days. The fact that he'd had years of friendship to recommend him should make his task easier. He spent his time with Miss Stone reminding her of their past together, hoping it inspired fondness for her in the way it did for him.

But for each memory Gerard brought to Anne's attention, it was

Etta's face he first pictured. Etta was at the heart of many of their childhood adventures. Every memory was encircled by her strength and compassion. It was a startling realization, one that made him scowl, a thing he wouldn't have realized he was doing except Miss Stone asked, "Are you all right?"

"Of course."

"I wouldn't ask, except you seem in distress."

"Oh. No. Not at all. How can I be in any distress when I am in such lovely company?"

At these words, *Miss Stone* seemed in distress. She quickened her pace, dropped her hand from his arm, and stepped away from him as soon as they'd caught up to Lucy and Etta.

Figuring it might be best to allow the ladies to have a moment on their own since Miss Stone was clearly trying to distance herself from his company, Gerard climbed the crumbling steps to where Freddie and Miss Bates were talking.

Freddie's recitation of historical facts buzzed in his ears as he wandered around. Had he offended Miss Stone in some way? Had she found his company irksome? What should he have done differently? He would have to ask Etta. His agitation and distraction were enough that he opened his mouth several times to tell Freddie to shut his, but he promptly closed his mouth again each time, realizing that his vexation wasn't Freddie's fault.

He noticed his cousin's lively explanations had come to a pause, and he looked up to see that Miss Bates stood off to the side, the wind blowing against her as she took in the view through one of the places where a window would have been if it hadn't crumbled away. She had posed herself in a place that showed her figure to advantage. Gerard had to give her credit; the woman played those sorts of games well.

Freddie was taking the moment to admire her physical form. "You don't even like her," Gerard whispered to him.

"No. Not really, but she amuses when there are no other amusements available. I'm sorry, Gerard."

"Sorry?"

"You have the sad demeanor of a man left in a daze after certain rejection. I am sorry."

He was about to deny any such daze or rejection when the tapping slippers on the steps called his attention in that direction.

Etta was there before him and breathless, as if she had been rushing to reach him. "Mr. Hartwell!" she called, which brought her to Miss Bates's and Freddie's attention as well. "Mr. Hartwell! I've been looking for you! Look what I found!" She held out her hand and unfolded her fingers, which had been wrapped around a bit of dirty, tarnished silver. The metal appeared to be lacking in anything to merit such excitement. But she flipped it over and revealed a rather impressive gemstone held fast to the silver.

"Is that a garnet?" Freddie asked. "Or perhaps it could be a ruby. That could be quite a valuable find, Miss Stone."

"Do you think this is a piece off of a crown or maybe a shield?" Etta asked.

"Possibly." Gerard smiled up at her, happy to be distracted.

When Etta smiled back up at him, he considered again how many of his happy memories involved her.

"That is a find." Miss Bates had joined them, likely realizing that she had been wasting her efforts, for no one was looking at her to admire her any longer. She was now peering over Gerard's shoulder in a proximity that made him uncomfortable. Did she have to stand so close? Her chin was practically resting on his shoulder. She moved closer still, as though there were room for her to politely do so, and stumbled. Her hand reached out and grabbed Gerard's arm to steady herself.

"Pray, forgive me," she said as her fingers tightened around his bicep.

He gently removed Miss Bates's hand from his arm. He moved so Etta was between Miss Bates and himself. Freddie noted the maneuvering and smirked.

"What's all the excitement?" Lucy ascended the last few stairs with Miss Stone directly behind her.

"Your dear friend found some buried treasure." Miss Bates flicked at the skirt of her dress as if some of the dirt on the bejeweled metal sheet had found its way to her person. "It seems she's feeling adventurous on this little outing and was digging in the earth." She laughed as if they all shared some delightful joke, though Gerard was certain she'd meant the comment as a cut and not at all as jovial camaraderie. Did she not see how unattractive her snide remarks made her?

She apparently didn't. He tried to form the same sort of compassion that Etta had shown and feel pity for her instead of irritation.

Etta ignored Miss Bates. "I'm going to the water to attempt to wash this."

"I'll go with you," Gerard offered, not wanting to stay with Miss Bates.

"I would like to see the lake as well," Miss Stone said, likely with the intent to act as chaperone.

Gerard sighed over that. How was he to shift this situation?

"Why don't we all go?" Lucy said. "And then we can open the baskets and eat in this lovely weather."

Gerard and Etta moved down the stairs first. When they were far enough ahead of the rest, he whispered, "What are some things your sister might like?"

"I might need you to elaborate. Do you wish to know what she likes to eat? To read?"

"Yes, and anything else you can tell me. I begin conversations with her, but they always gradually fail."

"She loves dogs," Etta said, coming to a place on the path where she had to step over a low wall of stones. Gerard decided further information could wait. He offered his hand for balance, which she took. When she was safely over and he had made it over as well, he continued, "How do I have a conversation about dogs?"

"If you haven't mastered the art of conversation as a grown man, then I really don't know that I am in a position to help you."

"I am in earnest."

"Anne also likes flowers and history. She enjoys gardening and watching animals. She's good at everything: art, music, singing, grow-ing. She likes long walks and the quiet of the country, but then almost anyone in Norfolk could be described as enjoying the quiet of the country."

"And you, Etta? Do you enjoy the country?" Gerard found that once he'd asked the polite question, he really did want to know.

"Very much. I'm glad you still call me Etta instead of Marietta. It is a pity we never gave you a nickname. Gerard sounds quite somber."

"If you will remember, you called me a somber young man a few years back. I suppose it is apt."

A small laugh bubbled out of her. "Did I say such a thing? Goodness, I am sorry. It was unkind."

"So, to be certain . . ." Gerard cleared his throat and soldiered forward. "To be clear, is Anne going to reject me because of our rather duplicitous beginning?"

Etta's shoulders slumped and her chin dropped. "I must apolo-gize, Gerard. I'm the one who bungled that up for you."

From this, he gathered that Anne just might refuse him. He felt himself panic. If Anne would not have him, how would Gerard re-cover from his current financial duress? He wished Freddie would give him a loan without the assurance of an upcoming wedding.

As if knowing Gerard had been thinking of him, Freddie called out from behind them, "What is the hurry you're all in? The lake isn't going anywhere, you know."

Gerard realized that he *had* been rushing them forward. He'd wanted to speak privately so he could learn more about Anne, and he'd wanted to keep Etta away from Miss Bates as much as possible so that he might shield Etta from cutting remarks. Those reasons were more than enough to merit moving quickly, but it hardly made them good companions to the rest of the party.

"True enough!" Gerard called back and then offered a shrug and a look of silent apology to Etta.

They slowed and allowed the others to catch up. Out of the corner of his eye, Gerard kept watch over Miss Bates. He had every intention of deflecting any cruelty she might feel necessary to fling in Etta's direction. Etta tended to defend others, but he noted that she seldom defended herself. Even when they were children, she managed to put herself between harm and others, but she never moved herself out of harm's way, even when there was no one else to protect.

Despite Gerard's determination to shield Etta from further insult or injury, Miss Bates had stopped abusing anyone in the party. She still laughed where no humor was meant, but it was as if the thought had finally occurred to her that perhaps her methods of husband hunting were more of a repellant than an attractant.

If she had always behaved so well, he might have come to like her long ago. As it was, her rather abrupt behavioral change made Gerard suspicious.

Once they were all gathered on the shores of the lake, Etta bent down to clean the treasure she'd found. Gerard handed her his hand-kerchief so she might dry it when she was through.

"I'd say your little bauble shines up quite nicely, Miss Stone," Freddie said. "It might be interesting to fashion it into a piece of jewelry for yourself. A necklace or a bracelet?"

"Yes, Etta," Gerard said. "If you would be willing to part with it for a period, Freddie and I could have something fashioned for you."

Etta blushed. "Pray do not trouble yourselves. I like it just for what it is and the reminder of a happy day spent together. Thank you, though, for your offer, gentlemen."

When the ladies had all begun a discussion on some sort of fashion that was all the rage in London but that the four of them agreed was unseemly, Freddie sidled up to him and whispered, "My, how she blushes when you speak to her."

Gerard looked at Anne and then realized Freddie was referring to Etta. "Does she?" He hadn't noticed Etta behaving any differently.

"You'll be a married man soon enough, and your worries will be over."

Gerard had always viewed Etta as his cousin Lucy's little playmate, but the more time he spent in her company, the less he thought of her that way. His regard for her had shifted so much that he felt a small flutter of joy at the idea of marrying Etta.

He stamped the feeling immediately. She would certainly never think of him in that same way. Not after everything that had happened between them recently.

"You think I'll be married soon, eh?" Gerard asked his cousin. He then lowered his voice. "Does this mean you want to give me that loan you offered? There is no time like the present to put my estate to rights."

Freddie laughed, and Miss Bates looked over to see what was happening. She lost interest again when she found the men were not welcoming her to their conversation.

"I don't believe I've ever seen you put yourself forward so boldly, Gerard. It's a refreshing look on you," Freddie said. "But I'd like to wait a little longer to see how things progress." Freddie then left to join Miss Bates.

Gerard sighed. He'd hoped Freddie would be more willing to give an immediate yes. He glanced to where Freddie had said something that made Miss Bates laugh. He'd likely told her that there were fish in the lake or that there were stones on the hills or something else equally mundane and not at all humorous.

As unhumorous as him saying, "I'd like to wait a little longer to see how things progress." Gerard couldn't explain why, but his instinct told him that Freddie would not be giving him the loan if he didn't become engaged soon.

This meant he had no choice but to get Anne to agree to marriage within the next two weeks.

Chapter Thirteen

Long into the night and the next day, Etta continually took out the bejeweled metal piece and stared at it. She did this not because it was beautiful—though, as Mr. Finch had said, it shined up quite nicely once cleaned off—but because it reminded her of Gerard's blue eyes staring at her with that white star pattern and him telling Miss Bates that he'd asked her to stay in Norfolk rather than go to London.

She wished he truly had asked that of her.

She glanced out the window from the drawing room and took a breath and held it, not like she did when her mother was berating her but in an entirely different way. As she slowly released that breath, she felt the warmth of Gerard's gaze, heard the gentle timbre of his voice, and saw the way he had decried Miss Bates's abuse toward her.

How had she never seen him so clearly before? During all those summers together, it had never once occurred to her to look at him as anything more than Lucy's cousin. She was surprised that Mr. Finch occupied less and less time in her thoughts while Gerard seemed to be taking up more and more.

Before Etta and Anne had returned home from the priory the previous day, Gerard and Mr. Finch had proposed a walk for the next morning. Their scheme was for Mr. Finch to spend time with Etta while Gerard spent time with Anne. When she learned of the outing,

Mrs. Stone had sniffed and smoothed her hands over her skirt. Etta wasn't sure if her mother was pleased that she had a man calling on her or if she was furious that the man was related to the Finch family.

All through dinner the night before, Mrs. Stone had spoken of the season and the musicales they would attend, the shops they would visit, and the ices they would eat. Of course, Etta was not included in those plans. Her mother's conversation felt designed to leave Etta out, but for the first time, she hadn't minded. Staying home with her father would be far better than going anywhere with her mother.

Etta heard the carriage pull up, startling her from her thoughts. Curious, she went downstairs to see who in her family was going somewhere.

It was Anne, who had a dress fitting in town.

"But Mr. Hartwell is coming to walk, Mama," Etta protested.

"What has that to do with your sister? But don't worry. I would never leave you unprotected. O'Brien will be here as your chaperone."

Anne flashed Etta an apologetic look before they were gone.

Etta hoped Gerard would not be too disappointed. She went to the drawing room to wait.

Greene, their butler, knocked on the door and opened it. "Miss Stone, Mr. Hartwell is here for you."

Greene stood to the side to allow Gerard entrance. Gerard was followed by O'Brien, her mother's maid, the chaperone her mother promised her.

"Are you ready to walk with me?" he asked.

"Yes. But . . ." She glanced behind him. "Where is Mr. Finch?"

"Freddie had some business or another and asked me to extend his apologies."

"It appears that he and Anne had similarly diverted paths. Our mother took Anne to a dress fitting in town." Etta hesitated. "Do you still want to go?"

"There is no reason not to. We are both here and in need of fresh air and exercise, are we not?"

"All right, then. I need only fetch my gloves. I'll return momentarily."

Once her gloves were on her hands and her bonnet ribbons tied under her chin, they set off. It was easier for her to feel at ease with O'Brien trailing behind them instead of Anne, since her one job in this whole affair was to place Anne beside Gerard while *she* trailed behind. O'Brien enjoyed walks, so this outing was as much to her advantage as it was to Etta's.

"How did you enjoy church on Sunday?" he asked her.

"Church?"

"Yes." Gerard placed his hand over hers as it rested in the crook of his arm. "I quite like our new clergyman. He is an upstanding, moderate sort of man who isn't as 'fire and brimstone' as some I've seen—especially while at Eton. But neither is he so lenient that he dilutes morality, as did a few I heard give sermons in London. I enjoyed his sermon on loving thy neighbor as thyself."

Etta laughed. "Do you think your aunt or my mother heard a word of that sermon? Are you of the opinion that they will extend an olive branch to one another?"

Gerard glanced at her, shook his head, and then laughed with her. "Much as I love her, I do not believe my aunt to be so easily swayed as that, though she has come around to the idea of you and your sister visiting us. It may be a while yet before she is ready to be on friendly terms with your dear mama."

The sun was bright and warm, and Etta's companion was perfect. She could not ask for anything more, except . . . except . . .

"Something is troubling you," she said. "And I can tell it has nothing to do with sermons and neighbors."

"What makes you say such a thing?"

"You have a small crease in your brow. It was there when we were washing my treasure at the lake, and I have not seen it leave your expression when I've seen you since then, not even when talking about sermons in church."

They continued their walk in silence but for their feet making soft thuds against the earth. Gerard finally said, "I have an abysmal career as a fraudster ahead of me if all you need is a little crease to discern my feelings."

"Did I do something displeasing?" Etta asked. "Well, aside from telling your relations we were courting?"

Gerard laughed again, and she was glad to be able to evoke that in him. "With you, Etta? How could anyone ever be displeased with you?"

She didn't bother telling him that her mother achieved such a feat several times in a day.

"The truth is . . ." Gerard plucked at a branch, snapping off a twig that he tapped against his thigh. "The truth is that I am thinking of frost on the fields."

"Frost on the fields? I'm afraid I don't exactly understand . . ."

"Last winter came early, if you recall. The frost was devastating to many of the farmers, especially those farmers who are my tenants. And truthfully, I must own that my father had not been good to them while he was alive. His neglect and then the frost left them with little choice in securing their futures. Many have left to find their fortunes in the mines or larger cities. Farming can no longer feed their families. They might have stayed if my father had been better to them. And they do not trust me to do better for them than my father."

"I am so sorry, Gerard."

He smiled and tightened his fingers around her hand on his arm. "I do not tell you all this to earn your boundless compassion. I tell you this because I am poor, Etta." He rushed to explain so quickly that he interrupted any response she may have had. "I believe you should be aware of this, because I want to make certain you know who I am and do not think I lied to you while trying to gain your sister's favor. I do not wish false pretenses to be between us."

Gerard stopped tapping the stick against his thigh. "I am not only marginally poor but immensely so. And at this moment, the crease in my forehead is due to worry that my only way to clear the debts my father left to me is to sell off land."

The news was certainly not what Etta had expected to hear. Since the crease in Gerard's brow had appeared while they were together, she had assumed that its presence had something to do with her. She wondered if that thought was hers or her mother's. Realizing her difficulties with her mother were nothing compared to the weightier matters Gerard wrestled with, she considered all he had said before asking, "What is the consequence of selling parcels of land? What will that do to your estate and to the people who live on your lands?"

"Leave it to you to ask such a reasonable question. Selling parts of the land that are generally profitable is bad because those profits support the rest of the estate. All the people who work in the manor, the stables, and the gardens—their livelihoods are supported by those profits. And though it pains me to admit this, I've already had to let go of so many of those who had depended on me for their employment, simply because I could not afford to continue paying them. But worse than all that, if I sell, the new owner is unlikely to honor my current arrangements with the tenants who are on the land." Gerard's frustration was evident as he swiped his stick at some low-hanging branches of the willow tree by the pond.

Etta did not respond but instead let him talk. She'd found that talking through troubles aloud sometimes untangled the snarls in her mind.

His shoulders slouched. "Those tenants would be faced with the prospect of having their rents raised. With last year's weather being so turbulent, many of the farmers had crops that barely yielded a profit. They can scarcely afford to reseed as it is. If the rents are raised, what will become of them?"

After Gerard was silent for a time, Etta felt certain he had retreated into his thoughts, and she said, "It seems to me that you have three tasks: You must find new tenants to replace the ones you have lost; you need to discover ways to make your current tenants profitable; and you wish to prove that you are not like your father."

"Yes. It all sounds simple when stated like that, does it not?

You listen well," Gerard said after a moment, "though this topic is probably uninteresting to a lady."

"Not at all! My father discusses such things with me often in his study."

"Your father speaks to you regarding business?"

Etta nodded. Her father took a great deal of pleasure in understanding the many facets of his managing of their properties, and he took even greater pleasure in explaining it all to Etta, not only because it annoyed Etta's mother but also because Etta's comprehension of it allowed her to help him untangle his own thoughts regarding his affairs.

"You might be surprised if you knew all my father dared say out loud."

"He must be the influence behind your daring letter writing."

Etta blanched at the inference.

"I am sorry, Etta. That was not meant unkindly. I am grateful for your letter writing, as it has led us here. I am glad to have your friendship. It has been a balm to have someone to discuss things with. And now that we are here, I would like to know your thoughts on all I have told you. I will free you from your obligations to help me with your sister if my circumstances are unforgivable in your eyes, and I will understand."

Etta smiled at his rather self-pitying theatrics. Though she did not laugh, she did feel it necessary to gently tease. "Stop moping about like some wounded thing. Unforgivable? When has poverty been a sin that requires absolution? The only thoughts on your circumstances that you will hear from me are possible solutions."

He stopped walking altogether and turned to face her. "What solutions?"

She set them to walking again. She had formulated some ideas that she felt certain would be helpful. "What do you think of sheep?" she asked.

"I don't know that I have ever considered them enough to gain an opinion."

"Well then. Perhaps after we talk, you shall find yourself unable to think of anything else. You could repurpose the unused portions of your land for ranching sheep. The textile industry is blossoming, and English wool has always been a desirable export. Our powered textile mills only make our wool that much more desirable. My uncle owns a few such mills, and my father has invested in his endeavors, which have been successful. Ranchers are expanding and looking for property. Your lands do not have to be used for farming just because they were in the past. I believe that supplying wool to the growing textile industry would be quite profitable."

The crease that had been Gerard's tell for distress stretched until it was nonexistent as his eyes widened while he considered the idea. But then the crease appeared again.

"It is a thought I've had before, but I've always dismissed it, as I know nothing about that sort of husbandry, and none of my current tenants seemed interested in trying something new. I have a few tenants who grow flax for linen, but mostly they grow grain. They don't keep large flocks of sheep."

Unable to hide her excitement, Etta tightened her hand on his arm. "That is where your current situation is lucky."

"You are the only one who would say so."

"You do not need to win over your current tenants to the idea of taking up something outside of their experience. You've lost several tenants already, which means you're in a position to attract new tenants, ones interested in an enterprise that is not wholly dependent on crops. You can advertise the land to ranchers looking to expand. My uncle has had quite a lot of success in this area."

Gerard was silent for a moment while they walked and he considered. "I am abashed at not having thought of advertising in such a manner. I've been so engaged in holding together what was already there that I haven't thought much about replacing what has been lost with something entirely different. You're right. This is a good plan to consider."

Etta suddenly felt unsure of herself. Was he merely placating her, or did he truly find value in her thoughts?

"Why do you look as though you don't believe me?" he asked. "It *is* a good plan. I believe I have become paralyzed in my ingenuity because the desperation is all consuming. I will send my steward after more information. He'll be able to discover whether any ranchers are looking to expand." Gerard placed his hand over the one she had nestled in the crook of his arm and tightened his fingers. "Thank you, Etta."

It warmed her to think she had possibly contributed a solution to his worry. At least that was to what she attributed the warmth flooding her cheeks at the moment his hand grasped hers.

They continued to walk slowly. When Etta glanced back, she saw that O'Brien was humming and staring out at the water and not exactly attending to Etta or Gerard. Etta took this to mean that O'Brien was content, so she didn't worry about hurrying along the walk.

She and Gerard were quite at their leisure as they discussed agriculture and planting seasons as well as the livestock his tenants currently raised. She happily offered her advice when she felt confident enough to have something intelligent to offer until he finally chuckled and put his hands up in front of him in a signal for her to stop—a thing she was very sorry for him to do since it meant he had dropped her hand.

Gerard seemed lighter than before. The crease in his forehead was gone. "How do you know all this? Does your father truly tell you so much?" He asked this after they'd had a rather animated discussion regarding the merits of planting seed in the late winter where they would stay dormant until spring to give a chance for an earlier spring harvest.

"My father is fairly informative when it's just the two of us. I also sometimes listen when he leaves his study door open."

"You eavesdrop on business conversations?" Gerard seemed confounded to consider that Etta would find any benefit to this.

At least he seemed so until she said, "My father leaves it open on purpose so that I *can* eavesdrop. I am not good for much in my household. I always hope that listening will help me discover a way in which

I can be useful. You confessed to me that you were poor; now you will hear my confession. I have no accomplishments."

When he laughed, she said, "I am in earnest! I cannot paint or draw or embroider. I make the pianoforte sound like a sickly and dying creature, and my singing voice is not much better. I cannot garden. I am abysmal at the many skills important to young ladies who want to make a good match. You may laugh, but I do assure you that I would make any man who married me the target of some fair amount of scorn due to these flaws. I'm not like Anne at all."

Gerard stopped laughing instantly.

They walked on in silence for a fair amount of time. Etta didn't fault him for his silence. Her confession was infinitely worse than his. Even a poor man wasn't useless in society. They had gone the whole circuit and were now nearing the house where, surely, her mother would be waiting to run her scornful eye over Gerard and sniff at him. Likely, Etta's mother believed that a disapproving glance inflicted some pain on him.

"You cannot say you have no talents, Etta." Gerard's voice startled her out of her thoughts.

"I can sing for you if you truly doubt me."

He smiled but shook his head. "No need to go to such extreme measures. But in earnest, you have the talent for bringing people together. You managed to forge a small bridge between our families—a bridge that grows stronger every minute."

"I do not want credit for that." Etta felt real alarm that Gerard would mention this. How could she explain that she had only mended things with Lucy so that she could retrieve her letters? But did he not already know that? He must understand the events preceding his stealing a letter from her.

"But it is credit that you deserve. I know what you're thinking. You worry that because your motives were not without a bit of desperation they do not count. But you're wrong on that score. I have seen you interact with Lucy, and in your eyes is true happiness to be friends again, as much as in hers. You might not have instigated the renewal of friendship without a little prodding, but the desire to do so was there."

It was a pretty speech. One that lifted her heart even as she saw, as expected, her mother standing at the door waiting for their return.

"I would ask to spend a moment with you and your sister, but I think your mother would not welcome that intrusion. I will have to try again later."

Etta felt a small pain that seemed to travel over all her nerves and into her toes.

Gerard wanted to see Anne. She didn't blame him. Anne was her favorite person too. But she worried that her romantic notions were getting away from her. Gerard had treated her with respect. He had listened to her thoughts. She worried she was showing a great vacillation of mind to have gone from writing love letters to Mr. Finch to dangling after Gerard. She worried because she felt fairly certain that if Gerard Hartwell asked *her* to marry him instead of her sister, she would have insisted the contract be written up and the banns be read immediately.

Chapter Fourteen

Gerard all but skipped back to his aunt's house, and he might have actually skipped if he didn't worry someone might see him. A grown man skipping would be a difficult thing to explain, especially to Freddie, who never let go of such things that could be used to torment others.

Gerard had worried a great deal when Freddie found excuse after excuse to avoid conversing with him alone. The promised loan had never seemed further away.

Also, he had not begun the day intending to tell Etta the truth regarding his financial situation.

What kind of person would let her sister marry a man who could not guarantee her comfort and support?

Not only had she not chastised him and banned him from her sister, but she had given some rather sound advice regarding actions he could take to salvage the situation. He felt hopeful for the first time in a very long time.

"Sheep," he said aloud. He laughed and made a bleating sound in celebration. He had previously tossed aside the idea of sheep as ludicrous when his steward had suggested it, but that had been when he was trying to stop tenants from leaving. Now that so many had already left, changing his tactics as Etta had suggested made sense. It was a reasonable opportunity now that his lands had vacant lots ready for such an endeavor.

He would set his steward on that trail as soon as he saw him. Gerard decided he would return to his own home within a day or two so that he might get work done on his lands. He had informed Etta of his plan before he bid her farewell after their walk. He needed to spend more time with Anne, but Anne seemed to rebuff his attempts to engage her in meaningful conversation at every turn. Etta had said she would try to resolve that situation for him. But they had been rushed when they were speaking, for Etta's mother had disrupted them.

"You've been gone for an age!" her mother had said. "You had promised to help your sister. Yet when we returned from her fitting, we found you were still gone. Your antics have left Anne in quite a lurch, for there is much to be done now. It is not kind to be so thoughtless toward others, Marietta."

Gerard was startled by the comment. It was as if Etta's mother wanted him to see Etta in a bad light, as though she wanted him to believe Etta to be inconsiderate and thoughtless.

Why would any mother want her daughter to be perceived in such a way? Wasn't it every society mother's goal to successfully marry her daughters off? What society mother would deliberately damage her daughter's prospects?

Etta's mother was a puzzle. But nothing the woman might orchestrate to make Etta look bad would work with him. To have unburdened himself and then to have received sound advice instead of censure had freed him in ways he had not thought possible. He counted himself lucky to have found such a friendship.

"You're late," his own mother said as he entered his cousins' home.

"Late?" How could she call him late when he'd arrived hours before dinner?

"I told you," his mother said, "that the young ladies would be delighting us before dinner with music."

"You said that they would be practicing their performances for the drawing rooms of London."

"Yes. Exactly." She said this as if, somehow, he was the most slow-witted man in all of England.

"How does that involve me?"

"They need an audience, obviously. Sometimes I think you never pay attention, my dear. And now you're late. Go get yourself ready. You're not at all dressed for dinner."

"That's because it isn't time for—oh, never mind." He went and did as he had been directed.

When he arrived back downstairs to play the part of the dutiful audience, everyone seemed annoyed by his apparent tardiness. Miss Bates went so far as to roll her eyes at him, which action, he was fairly certain, had not been part of her training when her mother had been preparing her for her season.

However, Gerard was glad to see that Miss Bates had finally given up her play for him. He thought he liked rather better the sincere, scowling version of her than the disingenuous, laughing one.

He found his seat on the chair nearest the door to avoid having to be too near the performers and did his best to appear attentive.

The performances weren't bad—as performances went. Lucy had always possessed a lovely voice, and her practice in preparing for this new season had only amplified her natural talent.

He thought Miss Bates could have done with a bit more practice on the pianoforte, but he was not in a position to be critical since he could not play the instrument at all. Men who criticized the abilities of young ladies made him sigh since he knew of very few men brave enough to be on display in such a manner.

Such thoughts brought to memory all that Etta had said earlier. She had called herself useless for not being able to perform as his cousin and Miss Bates were doing. She couldn't truly believe that this sort of thing made a person useful, could she?

Gerard's family began clapping vigorously, and his mother shot him a stern glance to remind him he should be doing the same.

Apparently, Miss Bates had finished her performance while he'd let his thoughts wander. She stood, smiled, and curtsied for them all. He applauded as well. Miss Bates might not have been a favorite of his, but he didn't want to make her feel insecure in her accomplishments.

Gerard was patient during the entire musical performance since both girls continued with several other songs. He really had no choice. If he had so much as considered yawning, his mother would have scolded him until her voice gave out.

Freddie seemed delighted by the performances, but more especially by the presentations of Miss Bates. Gerard wondered if Freddie had succumbed to that woman's charms or if he was merely toying with her because she happened to be in his vicinity. Freddie's affections were easily swayed when it came to temporary and convenient flirtations. With little else to entertain him, Miss Bates would do as well as anything. Etta had wanted Gerard to help her win Freddie, but the more he came to know Etta, the less inclined he was to help her in that endeavor. Freddie was not good enough for so good a woman.

Woman.

Not child.

When had he finally stopped thinking of her as merely Lucy's little friend?

Lucy finished her song. Gerard applauded with the rest. He even added a "Brava!" or two to make sure she knew how he approved.

"Did you truly like it?" Lucy asked Gerard once they had all stood with the intent to go in to dinner.

"You have the voice of an angel," he replied with a smile.

When Miss Bates looked at him expectantly, he turned his smile on her. "You both were delightful. I thank you for the entertainment this evening. The drawing rooms of London have much to look forward to."

"Such a shame you will not be in London," Miss Bates said.

"Yes. Well—"

Freddie interrupted them at that moment by clapping Gerard on the back. "Yes. Well, indeed. Gerard here has many responsibilities that will keep him away from town this season. Though I fear he is the greatest fool to think his plans are clever or even sound, for that matter."

"Courting a young woman will make a man foolish, I suppose." Miss Bates smirked as if she considered the idea of his courting Etta to be so preposterous that she could hardly contain her mirth.

Freddie smirked as well, as though he found the idea of Gerard and Etta together equally preposterous. Gerard shot his cousin a questioning look.

When Freddie shrugged and looked away to pluck at some imagined lint on the sleeve of his dinner jacket, Gerard decided that he hoped Freddie and Miss Bates *had* formed a connection. He halfway hoped it was a long-lasting one, because they clearly deserved one another. When had his cousin become so altered? Why would Freddie call him a fool, and in front of Miss Bates, of all people?

Dinner was announced, and they all made their way to the dining room in a rather uncomfortable sort of progression, uncomfortable for him anyway, because for the first time ever, Gerard felt animosity from his cousin.

Freddie maintained a rather cool distance for the rest of the evening. When the ladies left the men to their port, Freddie's attention stayed on Mr. Bates as he regaled the man with tales from his various travels. Freddie did everything in his power to rebuff any of Gerard's attempts to enter the conversation.

Gerard had already resigned himself to the fact that Freddie would not be giving him a loan, though he could not fathom why his cousin had retreated from his offer. But his treating Gerard like vermin struck a painful blow. Gerard and Freddie had been friends for their whole lives, and Gerard had counted on Freddie to be that friend always. He certainly expected Freddie to play the part of a gallivanting oaf from time to time, but underneath it all, it was only a part his cousin was playing.

Wasn't it?

When Mr. Bates suggested they join the ladies for cards, Freddie happily agreed and turned away from Gerard without a backward glance. Gerard could no longer stand it. He placed a hand on Freddie's arm. "Could I have a moment, cousin?" he asked, keeping his tone cheerful.

Freddie's face darkened as his eyes dropped to where Gerard's hand was still on his arm.

Gerard moved his hand as if it had been burned.

"I'm sorry, Gerard," Freddie said. "I don't much feel like dancing tonight."

Mr. Bates laughed heartily as if at a great joke. Perhaps he was the influence for his daughter's bizarre humor, or perhaps the man had simply had too much port. Either way, Freddie left with the laughing Mr. Bates, leaving Gerard wondering what could have possibly gone wrong with his cousin.

He steeled himself by straightening his shoulders the way he'd often seen Etta do—especially when her mother was around. Once he felt in control of himself, he followed the men to where the ladies waited with the card tables.

Freddie had already paired up with Miss Bates, and they had a game going. "We've been waiting for you!" his mother called out from the secondary table that had been set up. "Where have you been?"

Gerard glanced at Freddie, who was laughing along with Miss Bates and her parents about something absurd, he was sure. Freddie glanced in his direction briefly but looked away again immediately.

"Nowhere, Mother. I was nowhere important." Gerard sat down at the table with Lucy, his mother, and his aunt and felt the cut freeze through his core.

He had lost his best friend, and he could not think why.

Chapter Fifteen

"You should give him a chance," Etta said to Anne, who was dressing for breakfast.

"Don't you like him for yourself?"

"Well, certainly I like him, but I've been thinking that perhaps he is better suited to your personality than to mine. And he truly is wonderful, Anne. I do believe any woman lucky enough to catch his attention would never want for happiness."

Anne cast a sideways glance at Etta. "Then isn't it wonderful that *you* are so fortunate?"

"I believe he only cares for me as a friend or perhaps a potential sister-in-law."

Anne whirled in her seat. "Has he said such a thing? Regarding me?" She did not look pleased by the notion.

"Would it be so bad if he had?"

"Yes! I already have—" She clamped her mouth shut against whatever it was she had intended to say. Then she stood and said, "Mama will be waiting for us. We should go down."

Etta wanted to continue the conversation but followed her sister until they were both seated at the table with their mother and father.

Etta's mother tapped her spoon against her egg. "I've been thinking, Marietta."

Etta fixed her gaze on the gold design flowing through the turquoise of her plate as she braced herself for what would follow. Experience told her that any time her mother was "thinking" of her younger daughter, something unpleasant always followed.

"Yes, I have been thinking. It would be beneficial to have you join your sister and me when we travel to London."

Etta's head shot up. "Why?" She could not account for the sudden panic rising in her chest. Shouldn't her mother's wanting her presence bring her joy, not dread?

Her father's head also came up. He didn't look pleased either.

"Oh, Etta!" Anne looked truly happy for the first time in weeks. "It will be wonderful to have you at my side!" But then Anne's expression of joy seemed to melt into one of worry. "But what of Mr. Hartwell?"

"Oh, we needn't bother about him," her mother said with a wave, the motion wafting up the sharp odor of her beauty creams, making Etta's nose burn from the unpleasant smell.

Her mother's declaration solidified Etta's dread. Gerard was in Norfolk, not in London. She found she very much wanted to be wherever it was that he could be found. She knew he wasn't meant for her; he wanted to court her sister. But Etta could not help imagining him for herself. She wanted to accept her mother's olive branch for the relationship's sake. But for her own sake, she wanted to stay.

Etta reached into her pocket and felt the rough edges of the piece of metal with its ruby jewel that she'd found on her outing with Gerard. She'd been keeping it in her pocket of late as if it were some sort of talisman. She held her breath for the space of three seconds before she straightened her shoulders and responded. "I appreciate your kindness in including me, but there is no need for me to join you for the season. It is as you said, Mama; I would only be in the way. We would not want to hinder Anne's prospects." She felt terrible for saying such a thing. Didn't Anne have a prospect in Norfolk with Gerard?

But Anne didn't seem at all interested in Gerard, no matter what Etta said regarding the matter.

Mrs. Stone's lips puckered, making the fine lines around her mouth that much more distinct. "I was not requesting your presence, Marietta. I was insisting. Your sister needs a companion."

Anne leaned forward. "Mama, I don't—"

But her mother turned her sharp gaze on Anne, who immediately fell silent.

"No, ma'am," Etta said. The heat of that one word scoured her like a flashfire over her skin.

"No?" her mother said, the ice to Etta's fire.

The challenge in her tone made Etta grip her spoon all the tighter and meet her mother's gaze.

Her father's lip twisted up in pleased surprise.

"No. I will not be going to London," Etta continued. "You said I would be in Anne's way and asked me to stay, and I have agreed. My word is a valuable possession, one I shall not relinquish today." She stood, dropping her fork to her plate with a clatter that bolstered her confidence. "And speaking of today, I must finish dressing. Mr. Finch, Mr. Hartwell, Anne, and I are going for a ride."

"Marietta, you will sit down."

"It seems the discussion here is finished," her father said. "Leave her be."

"We shall see about that," her mother said, as Etta turned away.

The voice behind her was one Etta had curled inward at for the entirety of her life. But not today. Maybe it was that Gerard had listened to her the day before—that he had sought out her opinion and found value in her thoughts. Maybe it was that he had looked at her with eyes that made her feel as though he could truly see her. Maybe she was simply tired of holding her thoughts, her breath, and her words inside. She worried she might not survive with how crowded it was becoming inside her head. Maybe she was simply tired.

With that, she exited the room, leaving her mother's spluttering

fury, her father's impressed surprise, and Anne's stunned silence behind her.

Once in her room, Etta pressed her hand to her chest and
breathed deeply. As powerful as she had felt a moment ago, she now
felt that she should go back down and throw herself on her mother's
mercy, begging for forgiveness as she apologized for her insolence
again and again.

But she didn't do any of that. She rang for O'Brien.

When O'Brien arrived, Etta relaxed her death grip on the back of
the chair to her dressing table and calmly said, "I will be going riding
today with Mr. Hartwell and Mr. Finch and have a little less than an
hour until they arrive. Anne will be going as well and will also need
to get ready."

O'Brien then busied herself with preparing Etta for her outing.

Etta fully expected her mother to burst into her rooms and forbid her to leave now with Mr. Hartwell while demanding she go to
London, but no such outburst occurred.

Etta was dressed, pinned, and fully readied without any sort of
disturbance. She considered going to Anne's room but didn't want to
watch her prepare herself to see Gerard.

When she descended the stairs, it was with great care. She peeked
around every corner for fear of running into her mother. She stepped
lightly so that her footfalls could not be heard throughout the house.
She considered waiting in the drawing room for Gerard but decided it
very likely her mother was already there and waiting for her.

Etta informed Greene that she would be in the library and made
her way there as quickly and as quietly as possible.

She let out a sigh of relief when she closed the door with a click
that felt like a herald of refuge.

"Who are you hiding from?" the voice behind her asked.

Etta let out a squeal and whirled to see that it was not, in fact,
her mother with a set of keys to lock her in her room, but it was, instead, Anne, sitting on one of the red velvet chairs beside the statue of
Aphrodite. She held an open book in her hands.

"You gave me such a fright!" Etta said.

Anne smiled at the very notion that she could frighten someone. "You're hiding from Mama, aren't you?"

"After displaying such defiance to her, any intelligent, rational be-ing would hide," Etta said. "What did she say after I left?"

"She said . . . well, she said . . ." Anne looked down at the book and fiddled with the page edges. "She said I was not to fear because you would be going to London."

"Insufferable!" Etta almost howled. "I most certainly will *not* be going!"

"She said she would allow you your choice but that you would choose to go in the end."

Anne's big eyes conveyed how excessively sorry she was to have to repeat any of the conversation, but Etta was glad not to be in suspense over her mother's thoughts on the matter. She could not prepare for what she was not aware of.

"I, choose to go?" Etta scoffed as she slumped down into the other red chair. She thought them both rather ugly and wildly outdated, but her mother didn't spend enough time in the library to concern herself with its decor. "Why would I choose to go?"

Anne splayed out her hands.

"Well, she's wrong."

"Good. I hoped you would say that. Mama is not completely un-reasonable. She will come round if you do not bend to her wishes. I have seen you with Mr. Hartwell, Etta. There is a chance for true hap-piness there, and I do not want to see that squandered. We will change Mama's mind by degrees. You will see it come to rights."

That statement brought Etta to her senses. Gerard did not want her. He wanted Anne. She looked at her sister and realized Anne was not ready for riding. "Aren't you going with us?"

"I do not feel well enough to venture out today. I hope you will forgive me."

She would forgive her sister, but what about Gerard? How would Gerard feel about Anne staying behind yet again?

A knock at the door prompted both young ladies to straighten their spines and pull back their shoulders in preparation for their mother's entrance.

When it was only Greene and not their mother, Etta stood, and Anne relaxed back into her chair. Etta cast a worried glance out into the hallway.

"Don't worry, Miss Etta. Your mother is down with Cook discussing the coming week's menu. The only person in the hallway is Mr. Hartwell."

"Thank you, Greene. I'll see you when I come home, Anne." In spite of Greene's assurances, she still hurried to meet Gerard so that she could bustle him out the door before her mother could stop them.

Once outside, he looked concerned. "Is Miss Stone not coming?" he asked.

Etta sighed. "I'm sorry, no. She is feeling unwell today. I understand if you wish to postpone our outing."

Her horse had already been saddled and waited for her next to Gerard's horse.

"I see no reason not to venture out," said Gerard. "We're already situated to enjoy this fine day."

Relief flooded Etta. Then she realized she'd been missing someone whose absence she should instantly have noticed. After all, Gerard had immediately perceived that Anne wasn't there.

"Mr. Finch is not joining us?"

Gerard's worry crease appeared. "No. He is detained by business."

Her father's groom helped her into her saddle and then took the reins of the horse he would ride to accompany them.

Once they were comfortably situated in their saddles, they clicked their tongues and urged their horses to begin a leisurely walk. Etta imagined that her horse was unimpressed by the snail's pace, but she enjoyed being able to converse easily with Gerard.

Except they were *not* conversing.

"You're strangely quiet. Is there a reason?" she asked him.

"I apologize. I was thinking."

"Your thoughts must be terribly heavy," Etta observed.

When Gerard tilted his head in question, she motioned to him. "Your shoulders are slumped as if they carry a burden of some considerable weight. And there is that crease in your forehead again."

"You are perceptive. Not even my own family noticed my concern. But I feel foolish for mentioning it since it likely stems from my imagination."

"I have found that quite often when I imagine something to be a predicament, it is not usually as bad as I think, but it helps to talk it over. Anne has helped me with my own worry this morning. Perhaps you will let me do the same service for you."

She didn't add that Anne had also added to her worries. She did not want to tell him that Anne had exhibited no interest in him. Would he stop interacting with Etta if he realized Anne would never welcome his advances?

He sighed deeply, the noise as deep as the slump in his shoulders. "It's my cousin. Freddie and I have always been friends. Better even. We've been like brothers for most of our lives. But he's turned suddenly . . . cold toward me, and I cannot account for the change."

"Have you asked him what might be troubling him?"

Gerard's frown grew more severe. "That is not possible."

"Of course it's possible," Etta said as gently as she knew how. "If the friendship matters to you, surely you can set aside your pride to have a discussion."

He chuckled at that, though she didn't know what he found funny.

"I don't mean to imply that the impossibility is because I'm unwilling but that I'm unable. Freddie won't speak to me and will not hear me. If I approach him, he turns the other way. If I speak to him, he ignores me or directs his response to another in the room. He will not allow me to discover what is wrong between us."

Etta had never heard of anything so childish coming from a fullgrown man. She was grateful her feelings for Frederick Finch had dimmed, or this revelation would have been more alarming. "In all the time you've known him, is his disposition one that requires time alone to work things through before he will come to you? Or is he the sort of person who requires you to make the conciliatory move?"

Gerard grunted, a sound that made his horse's left ear twitch, while the creature released a noise that seemed to mimic its master's. "Freddie could never be described as having an easy manner," Gerard said after a pause. "Often when we were boys and my other cousin, William, was with us, William was quite an instigator of mischief, and Freddie held some rather epic grudges."

"William? The one with adorable curly locks who hid a frog in Lucy's wardrobe?"

"The very same. William was always pulling some prank or another. I recall the day of the frog vividly. We were all three punished rather acutely. Freddie wallowed in resentment for days."

Etta clucked her tongue. "It's a pity to hear that, since I'd taken such a fancy to William when we were all small."

"Goodness, Etta, did you fall in love with all my cousins?"

She couldn't help herself. She gave him her most innocent smile. "I couldn't say. How many cousins do you have?"

Gerard barked out a laugh. "You jest."

"You would like to think so, wouldn't you? I cannot help that there is such beauty in your family. In all seriousness though, I was probably six or seven when I thought William's golden curls were perfect beauty. And truthfully, a bit of my admiration might have stemmed from the envy of not having such lovely curls on my own head."

Gerard's brief mirth gave way to his silent brooding.

"You regard your cousin very highly, don't you?" Etta asked.

"Yes. As I said, he's like a brother to me."

"Then you must ask him what has caused such a divide. Do not let him slosh about in his displeasure for too long. The longer we hold our grievances, the harder they become to release."

"You are a wise woman, Etta, which reminds me that I've written to my steward regarding our discussion. When I return home, he and

I shall discuss it further. I've heard you've a knack for building design. I wondered if you might help me."

Her fingers felt suddenly too warm in her gloves. "Who told you that?"

"Lucy," he answered.

"Well, she's wrong. I can't sketch a rock, let alone a whole building."

"Lucy said that, too."

"Did she?" Etta felt that Lucy was becoming entirely too free with the information she supplied her cousin.

"She said you could do a rough sketch that was at least discernible, but that your true skill was an uncanny ability to see where things belonged and that you understood how to utilize a space more effectively. She said you reimagined a linen closet in my aunt's house. She said that though the sketches were rudimentary, the ideas in the designs were flawless."

All of that was true enough. Etta had come across the trouble with the linen closet when the boys had made sheets into ghosts. The closet had been an unwieldy mess, and the housekeeper experienced no small amount of displeasure from Mrs. Finch when it was discovered that it was kept in such disarray.

"Do you need a closet reworked?" Etta asked.

"No," Gerard responded. "Well, yes. Sort of. I have a tenant who needs more space because his wife is expecting another baby. Their home is full to the brim as it is. If I gave you a basic sketch of the layout, would you have a look at it and perhaps discover where space could be created?"

The novelty of his request filled Etta with joy. Gerard thought her to have something valuable to contribute. In all her life, only her father, Anne, and Lucy had seen anything of merit in her. According to her mother and the rest of the neighborhood, she was not very promising. She agreed immediately to Gerard's request.

He said he would have the plans delivered to her the following morning so that when he returned from his estate, they could discuss the possibilities.

Etta felt as though she might be glowing with the gratitude he bestowed on her. They rode on, discussing ideas for creating more space without building onto a home, laughing at the inadequacy of light in ballrooms where the ability to see a partner could be considered important, and debating which was better: pie or cake. It was in the middle of the debate when Gerard completely changed the subject and asked, "Is it hard to ride sidesaddle?"

"Excuse me?"

"Sidesaddle. I've always wondered. It looks uncomfortable and difficult. I would have asked Lucy, except she doesn't enjoy riding enough to have the experience to make her answer relevant."

Etta loved that Gerard had asked such a question. It signified that he felt comfortable enough with her to meander through the conversation much like the road meandered through the woods. It seemed that he trusted her with both the serious and the ridiculous.

Etta wondered if he would have asked Anne such a question. She gave him a look that showed she might be scandalized by the question.

He blushed, which was charming.

"I'm teasing. I don't mind questions of that sort. Of any sort, really. I've ridden astride before as a child. I can honestly say I don't think it any easier that way. I suppose my opinion might stem from being taught to ride sidesaddle from the beginning. But it's not difficult. The stablemaster says I can keep my seat better than most men, though I feel he's exaggerating, but I probably keep my seat better than that curly-haired cousin of yours."

Gerard laughed at the reference to his cousin and assured her he did not doubt her abilities.

However, she still felt a need to prove herself. Gerard had told her he had enjoyed listening to Lucy sing the night before, and she wanted to demonstrate her abilities somewhere. Though she might not have skills to show off in a drawing room, she did have skills she could show off on the trail.

"I'll race you back." She glanced behind her to where her groom still followed. The poor man looked bored and would likely benefit from a little livening to their outing.

"Etta, I hardly think that's necessary," Gerard said, looking slightly alarmed that she would suggest such a thing.

"You can keep talking and lose the race, or . . ." With that, Etta urged her mount forward. The horse happily complied, as he must have been as bored as the groom and was pleased with the new pace.

Gerard and Etta raced in and out of the light dappling the trail they traveled. She laughed out loud when she won. She wondered briefly if he had let her win and then realized that she didn't need to worry. Gerard had been honest with her in his every word and deed. He wouldn't cheat on anything, not even such a thing as a silly race.

When they arrived back at the stables, Gerard helped Etta down from her horse, his hands at her waist sending fluttering sensations through her whole body, and she wished the groom had found some work to do elsewhere, because she wanted nothing more than for Gerard to lower his head and press that perfectly formed mouth of his to hers.

But Gerard cleared his throat and stepped away. Etta felt instantly foolish. Of course he would not kiss her, chaperoned or not.

It wasn't until she was back in her room and changing out of her riding habit that she remembered wanting to talk to Gerard about her mother's announcement that morning. At first she hadn't told him because they were discussing Freddie and tenant housing, but then the pleasant silliness of the conversations that followed had driven any other thought from her mind. Etta admitted to herself that she wanted to see how Gerard would respond to the news. Would he be sad to know she might be leaving?

She considered going to her desk and writing her feelings out in a letter to him but refrained. She would not make that mistake again.

She stared into her mirror and raised her chin. The defiance she had shown her mother earlier still burned in her. She would not be going to London, and there was nothing her mother could do to make her.

Chapter Sixteen

"Are you all right?" Gerard had found Freddie in the library alone and decided he was through being ignored. He would do as Etta had advised.

"Why wouldn't I be? I'm perfectly fine. Though in truth, I cannot answer for you, as you've come to be so unpredictable of late."

"I?" Gerard almost made a scoffing noise in his throat but didn't want to antagonize his cousin. "You're calling me unpredictable? You must be joking."

"That's what I am to you, aren't I? A big joke? And that, cousin, is why I am *not* all right." Freddie snapped his book closed and stood abruptly.

Gerard raked his fingers through his hair in exasperation. "Look, I understand you don't want to give me the loan you promised. I begin to regret ever discussing my financial situation with you, as it feels that might be the reason for your sudden venom toward me. But blast it all, Freddie, I don't care about the loan. Forget I ever mentioned it. I do, however, care about you and whatever it is that is going on."

Freddie snorted. "Forget the loan, you say? I assure you I already have."

"Freddie . . . What is all this about? Why will you not talk to me? I want to—"

Freddie interrupted him. "That's just it, isn't it. *You* want." He tossed the book to the chair he'd occupied and left without another word.

Gerard stared after him a long while before picking up the book Freddie had abandoned and putting it back where it belonged on the shelf.

"Well, Etta, I tried to talk to him," he said to the now empty room. He could not account for the change in Freddie, but he could not allow himself to dwell on it. He was leaving for Hartwell Hall in the morning and had to make sure he was readied for the journey.

He made use of the library to prepare some paperwork for his steward and then found his valet to let him know of his plans. Wilson would have another few days off while Gerard was gone.

Even with Freddie's bizarre behavior, Gerard felt better about his prospects. He'd not been able to find time with Anne at all, which was disappointing. His every attempt had been rebuffed. She was always either unwell or otherwise engaged. But Etta had given him new ideas and hope for the future of his lands even without the loan and marriage he'd been so sure of needing not too long before.

Things were looking up. Freddie be hanged.

Gerard ran into Miss Bates on his way to dinner. She smirked at him, her lips curling into something that might have been an attempt at a smile. "Mr. Hartwell. I'm surprised to see you here."

"Where else should I be that my presence here is such a surprising occasion?"

She sniffed and lifted a slender shoulder. "I suppose your comings and goings are none of my concern. But have a care, Mr. Hartwell. Your ambitions might cost you more than you can afford to pay." She tilted her head in the slightest semblance of deference and continued on to meet the others.

First Freddie and now Miss Bates. What ambitions was he being accused of that could warrant her warning? "Everyone here is mad." He grumbled this under his breath, shook his head, and followed Miss Bates in to dinner.

He was relieved that Lucy still seemed glad of his presence. She chattered with enthusiasm about her hopes for her time in London. "Perhaps you should go to London as well, Gerard. Then Etta would come too, and I would want for nothing."

"Yes, Gerard," Freddie said. "Perhaps you will find a lovely heiress to ease your worries."

"Is Gerard worried over something?" Gerard's mother asked.

"Of course not, Mother," Gerard said, casting a glower at his cousin, who seemed not to notice. Freddie might be harboring ill feelings for Gerard, but surely those feelings did not extend to Gerard's mother.

Surely.

"What need would he have for an heiress when he seems so taken with the Stone girl?" Gerard's mother persisted.

Luckily, Freddie ate his venison without answering, and the conversation wandered to topics of greater interest to the others at the table. It seemed everyone was delighted by the prospect of the upcoming time in London. Gerard remained silent, offering only agreeable smiles when looked upon for input.

He would be glad when they were all gone to London.

Gerard made his excuses when the meal was over and vacated the company of his relations and their guests immediately. He didn't want to drink port with the gentlemen and put up with Freddie's continued insolence.

Instead, he retreated to his room, where he was assured privacy. He then stayed up half the night sketching out his tenant's house. He had a basic drawing of the establishment from when he'd visited last. He had hoped that by drawing it out, he might be struck with some sort of cleverness that would give his tenant and his wife the space they needed to welcome their new child. When he felt he'd made a faithful rendition of the abode, or as faithful as possible, he folded up the paper and sealed it. There could be nothing improper in sending such a missive to Etta, so he didn't fear her mother seeing it.

Gerard finally climbed into bed and allowed his mind to relax enough to sleep. He would get little enough sleep for the next couple of days, so he needed to take advantage of rest while the opportunity was available to him.

The next morning found him packed and gone before any other member of the family had awakened. He had intended to leave straightaway for home, but at the last moment, he decided to personally deliver his sketches to Etta.

He told himself he did so to allow her to begin working as soon as possible, but really, he just wanted to see her. "No. I want to see Anne," he reminded himself.

When he arrived at the Stones' home, he smiled at the good fortune of seeing Etta looking down from an upstairs window. He slid from his horse and raised a hand to her in greeting.

Her surprise was evident. She lifted a hand not so much in greeting as in a command that he stay where he was. Gerard took this to mean that she didn't want him knocking to alert the household.

He obeyed and secured his horse while he waited for her.

Several long moments passed even after this small task was done, but Gerard was rewarded for his patience when the door inched open and Etta slipped out, carefully closing the door behind her without making any noise.

"What are you doing here so early in the morning? Are you well? Is Lucy well?"

"Yes, yes," he said. "Everyone is well enough, but leave it to you to worry over their welfare. I only wished to give you this." He handed off the letter, his fingers brushing hers and making him regret his gloves for getting in the way.

Where had that thought come from?

Of course, Etta wore gloves too. A good thing, since the morning was another chilly one. Not a moment after the folded paper had exchanged hands, the door opened again, and Etta's maid joined them. Gerard realized that Etta had displayed the presence of mind to arrange a chaperone.

Etta broke the seal and unfolded the papers. "No letter?" she said in a teasing tone. "Only sketches?"

"Yes, well, when one is up against a rather prolific letter writer, one hates to feel that he might suffer in comparison."

She laughed. "Is that so? I don't recall you being so competitive in your youth. Is this some sort of bad habit you picked up while away at school?"

He stared at her with a happiness he could not account for. "It is good to see you this morning, Etta."

"It is good to see you as well." She hurried to turn her attention to his sketches. "This awkward little alcove here." She pointed at his drawing. "Is it really like this?"

"Yes. Well, maybe not precisely to scale, but quite close to it."

She smiled up at him. "You have a talent for sketches. I must say I'm surprised. I had no idea you were hiding such a skill."

"If you're impressed by that, you will be simply astonished to learn that I am an expert at embroidery."

She scoffed. "Embroidery indeed."

"Yes, indeed! I spent a good deal of time with my mother when I was a boy, and she taught me. I'll have you know I was an excellent pupil."

"I'll have you know that I was *not* an excellent pupil when it came to embroidery, but as I've already confessed to having no talents, this should not come as a surprise to you. Anne is very skilled with the needle."

Gerard wished she believed better about herself and wasn't always comparing herself to her sister. "I am here this morning to discuss your keen eye for space and design. That is a very desirable talent. I'll bet Anne is not skilled in this area."

"She probably would be if she set her hand to it." Etta turned her focus back to his sketches. "There is something you can do right away. See this awkward place I pointed to a moment ago?" She pointed again to the corner alcove. "This space could be fitted with shelving that would accommodate any number of necessities, from clothing to dishes to books. It will clear up clutter from the living spaces. And if you angle the shelves right, it would still allow for such items as brooms."

As if the one thought inspired more, Etta turned her attention to the children's room. "If you created a loft space for the beds here, the children would have more space to play when the weather is inclement or in the evenings when they have to be indoors. This will keep them from being so much underfoot. Also, as it tends to be warmer closer to the ceiling, the children will be able to sleep warmer—even in the winter."

These were good ideas. Gerard was sure Etta would have many other ideas the longer she looked at the sketches. "You must inform me of what they use for storage," Etta continued. "Pay close attention to everything while you're there and return a faithful report to me when you come back. In the meantime, I will review this and find more ways to work the space."

"I wish I could bring you with me. If you could see it in person, I am sure the task would be easier for you."

She let out a laugh. "To take me with you, you would have to marry me—" She cut off and her eyes widened in horror. "I mean . . . I did not mean to imply . . ." She pressed her lips together as if determined to keep any other word from falling from them.

Gerard frowned at the mention of marriage. Marriage to Etta?

While he conceded she was not a child, she was not someone he could marry. Was she?

His thoughts froze as he stared into her hazel eyes, the flecks of gold bright against the darker backdrop of amber. His gaze dropped to her pale pink lips. She bit her bottom lip as she looked up at him. He lowered his head slightly as she tilted her chin up.

He cleared his throat and hurried to step back. He tried to cover the fact that he'd almost blundered his way into *having* to marry Etta by laughing and saying, "Excuse me; I stumbled on a rock there."

"Of course." She stepped even further away. He couldn't say why, but her stepping back made him feel out of sorts.

"Yes," Gerard bumbled. "I think I shall ask Anne to go for a walk with me when I return. If you could put in a good word for me?"

"Of course. And perhaps you could put in a good word for me with Mr. Finch."

"You can do better than him, Etta."

Her jaw tightened. "Can I?" She was angry.

Oddly, he felt angry as well. "You know you can. Freddie is so in love with himself, he cannot see your value."

"That's the trouble, isn't it? No one sees my value. Goodbye, Mr. Hartwell. I'll work on your designs while you're gone." She turned on her heel and headed back to the house.

"Miss Stone," he called. "Etta!"

She swiveled just enough to look back. "What?"

"Are you angry?"

"Of course not. Why would I be angry? I'm merely recognizing my value." With that, she left with her maid trailing closely behind her.

He felt certain he'd missed something important.

Chapter Seventeen

Etta watched Gerard as he rode away from her, toward his duties at home. She hated that she'd begun imagining it was *their* home. Hadn't her silly romantic notions landed her in enough trouble?

She had at first considered herself fortunate to have been the first to rise this morning since it allowed her to see him, but now she wished she hadn't. She loved him. She was sure of it. But he did not love her. He only spent time with her because she had lied to his whole family and told them he was courting her. He only paid attention to her because they had formed a conspiracy out of a most inconvenient letter.

She was a fool.

She remembered once again that her mother's maid had been a witness to the whole affair, and she wondered what O'Brien had thought of the scene. Etta had almost kissed the man—would have, if he had only leaned a little closer. Perhaps O'Brien didn't know what her intentions had been in that moment, except that as she parted ways with O'Brien, the woman cut her such a look of reproof that it may as well have been a scolding.

Etta sighed. What would she give to have her future secured with a man like Gerard?

"Good morning, my heart," her father said, startling her out of her thoughts.

"Good morning, Papa."

"I see your young man is off quite early."

Her face warmed. "He's not really my young man, Papa."

Her father lifted an eyebrow and made a "hmph" sound. "I wouldn't be too sure of that. He looked like a man in love to me."

Etta wanted to tell her father that he was terribly, terribly wrong, but how could she without admitting her part in the ridiculous pact she'd made with Gerard?

"He's a good match for you," her father said.

She wanted to argue but simply asked, "How do you mean?"

"He's the reason you stood up to your mother—a thing that took quite a lot of fortitude on your part to accomplish. I was pleased to see it. And you have my blessing to stay home from London if you don't want to go. I was sad to think of you leaving me anyway, and it benefits me to have some company."

Etta gave her father a thin smile. "Is she very angry with me?"

"She was. Truth be told, I believe she was more surprised than anything. But I've calmed her."

Etta felt relieved to hear such news until she met up with her mother later in the day. Mrs. Stone was in the process of preparing for the sojourn to London and directing the household staff as to which rooms were to be shut up and which items must be packed and brought with her and Anne. The task of packing for the season seemed to recall to her memory the taint of the previous season's misfortune.

"We would have returned in glory were it not for that horrid Finch girl and her mother," Mrs. Stone said. "Your sister would be respectably married."

"Respectably?" Etta asked with no small amount of incredulity. "A title doesn't always mean respectable, Mama. Anne deserves so much more. We should be grateful for her fortune."

"Grateful?" Her mother matched her incredulity and added to it. "I should say not! Think of the whispers there will be as we move about town. I'll hardly be able to show my face anywhere without being chased by the memories of that ball and that family."

Her mother's fears were not unfounded. Society did not soon forget any morsel of gossip that might provide a reason to whisper behind people's backs. As Etta opened her mouth to ease her mother's worry, her mother's maid, O'Brien, caught her eye and said, "Your friend, Miss Lucy, sent a letter to you."

Her mother's back straightened. "I do not like that girl communicating with you, Marietta."

"It is a sign of her goodwill, Mama. I truly believe that if you go to London allied with the Finch household, it will give less fire to the whispers of society."

"She is right, Mama," Anne said.

Bless Anne for trying to help. Though it seemed to do little more than stoke more of her mother's fire.

It was some time before Etta was able to escape her mother's presence. When she did, she immediately went to collect the letter from Lucy.

She frowned at the envelope. She and Lucy had sent many letters to one another in the way of invitations and correspondence when one or the other had to leave for a time to visit family elsewhere in the country. They had certainly written enough to one another that Etta knew her friend's writing, and her name written in bold lettering was not in Lucy's hand.

Her heart fluttered. Had Gerard pretended to write a letter from Lucy to avoid accusations of impropriety from her mother? But why would he write to her?

He wouldn't.

Etta opened the letter to see the words, "Please meet me at the gate between our properties."

She'd received many notes in the past from her friend with these exact words, but she could not account for the handwriting. It did not appear to come from Gerard. And he was well on his way to Hartwell Hall, if he had not already arrived. It *must* be from Lucy. Perhaps she'd had one of her maids write the note for her. Worry jolted through Etta. Perhaps Miss Bates had written it and was using Etta's friendship with Lucy to lure her from the safety of her home to . . . what?

Such musings were silly. Etta felt ridiculous for ascribing the worst of intentions to the writer. Of course the message came from her friend. Etta fetched her pelisse and left the house, hoping she'd not kept Lucy waiting too long.

As she walked, her mind betrayed her by dwelling on what life would be like if Gerard would decide to love her. A wonderful side benefit to such a union was that she would be Lucy's cousin. Granted, she would be Frederick Finch's cousin too. That thought made her feel the need to twitch her shoulders in discomfort. She still had not reconciled her feelings on that score. She had thought her feelings for him were love, but now she had something to compare those feelings against.

As if pulled like a specter from her private thoughts, standing there next to the gate where she had anticipated seeing Lucy was Frederick Finch.

"Mr. Finch!" Etta could not keep the surprise from her voice. Why would he be standing near the gate where she was supposed to meet Lucy? "What are you doing here? Is Lucy unwell? Has something happened to her?"

Her thoughts turned in an entirely different direction. What if something *were* wrong with Lucy? How could she be so selfish as to worry about herself when her friend might be in trouble?

Mr. Finch's grim expression assured her that she did not err in feeling alarmed.

She was about to ask after Lucy again when she spied something in Mr. Finch's hand. A letter.

The letter.

Her letter.

The red wax seal had been broken on the familiar envelope. Her hands began trembling, and she rolled her fingers into her palm and pressed her hands to her sides to stop the violent tremors.

Mr. Finch followed her gaze to his hand. "I see you recognize this. That is one question answered. I wasn't entirely sure you'd written it, but now I know."

She tried to open her mouth to respond, but her lips felt like they had been frozen together.

"Your silence speaks volumes, madam."

"You were never meant to read that," she finally sputtered.

Freddie's eyes narrowed. All pinched and puckered as he was, she wondered how she had ever thought him handsome. He was angry, though she wasn't entirely sure why. She would have thought that possessing such a note would be excessively diverting to a man who could laugh when a lady had sherry flung into her face.

He held up her letter as if to hand it to Etta, but then he pulled it back again. A feeling beyond basic mortification overcame her. She wasn't immediately able to identify why the feeling of being shattered filled her every thought. She allowed the bone-deep ache and splintering to sit in her soul a moment before she was able to understand why she felt so broken.

If Mr. Finch had the letter that Gerard had promised to safeguard, there was only one way he could have obtained it.

Gerard must have given it to him.

Etta was not the sort of woman to swoon at every little thing. Indeed, she had never even come close. But spots flashed in her darkening vision, and she felt as though the trees and fields spun all around her instead of being perfectly still.

"What game are you playing at, Miss Stone? I need to fully understand where to direct my anger. I thought at first to despise my cousin and, in fact, have despised him these past days, but he seems so wholly ignorant of why I should be furious with him. I began to wonder if this plot to make me a fool was not his at all, but instead yours."

"How did you get that letter?" Etta asked instead of responding to anything he had said since she could hardly understand it.

"It came to me in the post." He almost snarled the words.

"But it couldn't have," she said. "Gerard promised me he would not allow you to see it. You were never, ever to see it. I am not so foolish as to believe that sending such a letter would bring me anything but the worst kind of mischief. He promised he would give it back when . . ."

She trailed off. Gerard had lied to her. He had mailed it or at least seen to it that the letter was found on the silver mail tray. And by so doing, he had fully betrayed her, after she had trusted him with her reputation and so much more.

She had trusted him with her heart. Time swirled until it was upside down, an hourglass with sand falling up. The world fragmented and came together again, but the parts were all garish and tilted and *wrong*.

Mr. Finch did not allow Etta time to mourn the loss of her heart. He continued speaking as if she had been the cause of terrible wrongs against him.

"Gerard promised he would give it back once he had secured a loan from me? Is that it? I should have guessed. To pretend to be courting to acquire a loan. It is most shocking that you two conspired against me in such a way. It is little better than blatant thievery. You can see he failed to keep his promise to you. He allowed this letter to fall into my hands. It appears he has failed to be dependable to either of us. Did Lucy know? Have you somehow drawn my own sister into your conspiracy of blackmail, or have you lied to her as well?"

Mr. Finch's questions pained Etta. She would never do anything to hurt Lucy.

"Of course Lucy does not know. There is no conspiracy. There is only a silly girl who wrote a silly letter when she was much younger. But that girl no longer exists. She has grown up. And that letter shouldn't exist either. I should have burned it. Mr. Finch, please believe that I have meant no harm to you, to your sister, or to any member of your family."

The tightness in his expression proved he did not believe her. His look had an unsettling edge to it, but she would not allow him to frighten her.

She drew in a breath that failed to fill the hollowed void now expanding inside her chest, squared her shoulders, and held out her hand. "Will you please return my letter to me? You must understand that the sentiments within are the ridiculous ramblings of a childish fantasy. I assure you they are no longer accurate and, indeed, mortifying to us both."

Etta stretched her hand out farther when Mr. Finch merely looked at her. What more could she do to damage her reputation than she already had? Were there degrees of damage? She shook herself out of her thoughts and said, "I will not be blackmailed by any member of your family. It is enough that you know how I once felt regarding you. You may speak of this wherever you wish. You may blacken my reputation, expound upon all my failings. You, as a man, are allowed to do as you wish. But I am done being manipulated. I must insist that my letter is returned to me."

His expression softened, if not entirely, then at least enough.

Mr. Finch didn't resist when Etta reached out and plucked the paper from his grasp.

She was surprised at herself for being so bold. If she had possessed this sort of nerve when she'd first been confronted about her letters by Gerard, she would never have been in this mess. She would have simply taken the letter from Gerard's hands. No. She would not think of him so informally. He did not deserve that familiarity. She would think of him as "Mr. Hartwell." She lifted her skirts so that she could take her leave without tripping over the hem when Mr. Finch spoke again.

"Did you mean any of it?" he asked softly. If taking back her own letter surprised her, the shock of such vulnerability in his question nearly knocked her over.

"I did when I wrote it," Etta admitted.

He grinned then. The cocky, satisfied smile darkened his handsome features into something less so.

"You think my eyes to be the color of the sky on a clear day?"

"I think your eyes are a lovely color, but they do you little good since you see nothing."

"I presume you mean that I do not see *you* clearly enough?"

Etta let out an exasperated breath. She had not meant to refer to herself. She had meant that Freddie did not understand his cousin, but wasn't *she* the one who did not see Mr. Hartwell properly?

"Mr. Finch, I no longer care how you see me or do not see me." She didn't intend to stay longer to debate the point with him. They both knew inconvenient truths, and neither was satisfied with the knowledge.

"Miss Stone?" Freddie said before she could stalk away and feel ridiculous and angry and hurt all by herself.

"Yes, Mr. Finch?"

"Dinner perhaps. Lucy would love you to join us for a family dinner. Gerard is not there to be boring and irritating. It would be good to have just you. We could talk and perhaps I may get to know you better."

Just her.

He was asking her, without any agenda, to spend time with him. There was a compliment to be had in that.

Etta heard Mr. Hartwell's voice in her head telling her that Mr. Finch wanted the toy in someone else's hand. She sighed inwardly. What did it matter whose voice hissed at her from inside her head? Mr. Hartwell was not here. Mr. Finch was not looking for something held by another. Mr. Finch was looking at *her*.

She wasn't sure if she wanted to hurt Mr. Hartwell as much as he'd hurt her or if she truly wanted to have dinner with Mr. Finch. "I thank you. I will not sit by Miss Bates at dinner, however."

Mr. Finch laughed. "Understood. If we are lucky, none of us will sit by her because she will declare herself too ill to dine with us. I doubt we will be so fortunate, however. I want to prepare you so you don't raise your hopes unnecessarily."

Etta shook her head at him and started to turn away again.

"Don't you want to know the time we will dine?"

She waited. He didn't provide the information. She held up her hands as if to say, "Out with it, then."

"I'll send a card."

"Very good." She turned then, not caring if he called her back, as she did not intend to stay in the absurd situation any longer.

Etta trudged the path back to her own home. Her legs felt like water beneath her, and she wondered at the fact that they continued to hold her up.

How could her feet keep moving and her legs continue to support her weight when her reputation hung from such a precarious perch? Frederick Finch knew the contents of her letter. Whether he owned the physical proof or not, his word would be enough. This meant that he held her reputation in his hands, and there was nothing she could do about it.

How could Etta trust her reputation to the sort of man who would laugh at her mistreatment? Would he truly destroy a woman's reputation merely because it entertained him?

She could hardly believe he would, but how well did she really know him? Worse, she'd agreed to dine with him. "I've lost my senses," she said to the trees. Fortunately, the trees did not prove her right by answering.

Taking her letter back from Mr. Finch had felt powerful for the briefest of moments. She had felt courage and strength, as if by taking the letter she had also taken control of the situation entirely. But this was false.

Gerard had *lied*.

The words tumbled over and over again in her thoughts.

Lied.

Gerard.

Gerard lied.

But why?

Etta tried to think of an explanation, some way to exonerate him from his crimes, because she thought she knew him too well to believe him capable of such treachery. Every explanation fell short of plausibility. She wanted to blame Miss Bates, but though she believed the woman to be a viper, Miss Bates could not have known the contents of the envelope if she had chanced upon it. She could not have known that delivering it into Frederick Finch's hands would condemn Etta. And Mr. Finch seemed sincerely hurt and angered by it, so this was no scheme of his.

Perhaps since Etta was unable to fulfill his request to coax Anne into liking him, Gerard had become fed up with the whole affair?

Perhaps.

Etta didn't go immediately home. Nervous energy kept her legs moving long enough that the light and shadow around her shifted as the sun moved through the sky.

She might have stayed out until well after dark if she hadn't remembered that Mr. Finch said he would send a card. It would take time to ready herself for dinner. She couldn't pace the woods and fret about Mr. Hartwell. She leaned against a tree, frustrated that everything had changed so much in only a few hours' time.

Something dug into Etta's side. She reached into her pocket and pulled out the bit of metal with the ruby jewel in it. She felt a fresh wave of sadness as she dropped it to the ground. The jewel was no talisman. It was only the reminder of a treasure that did not belong to her.

"Etta! Etta!" It was Anne's voice calling for her. She supposed the card had come and Anne wanted to make certain she was dressed in time.

She drew in a deep breath and was brushing off her skirts as best she could when Anne rounded the corner.

"There you are! Did you not hear me calling? I've been searching for you for quite some time. I thought you'd gone to the Finches' house. But then Mr. Finch sent an invitation for you to join his family for dinner, which could only mean you weren't with Lucy. Where have you been? Why is Mr. Finch sending you invitations and not Mr. Hartwell?" Anne then truly looked at Etta and blinked in what seemed to be surprise at what she saw. "What's happened? Are you hurt?"

"I've decided to go to London after all. And no, I'm not hurt."

Her sister could not have appeared more confused than she did at that moment. "But you and Mr. Hartwell . . . He will want you here, I am sure."

"He is not *my* Mr. Hartwell. And I do not want him."

"Etta, please talk to me. Are you all right? What happened?"

"I am perfectly fine. All is well."

She ground her foot over the top of the metal with the ruby jewel, sinking it deeper into the soft dirt.

As her mother had predicted, Etta had chosen to go to London of her own accord. She wondered if her mother had access to a fortune teller.

Chapter Eighteen

Gerard felt as though he had never worked so hard in his life in those days after leaving Etta and going to his property. But never before had he felt so accomplished either.

He had sketched out in greater detail the house he wanted Etta to help him design for greater space efficiency, and the family that occupied the home was excited by the ideas.

With every lowering of the hammer and with every fence post placed, things were coming together. The tenants who were already on the land seemed willing to stay.

"Things are looking better than they have in years," Grady said as the two men surveyed the property from the small rise where Hartwell Hall stood overlooking the rest of the land.

"They truly are. Even my mother will be pleased when she returns."

Grady ran a handkerchief over his forehead where sweat had beaded up just under his graying hairline. The land was being prepared for planting, and the smells of fresh dirt and manure hung in the air.

"Speaking of pleased, you'll be delighted to know that the advertisements are bearing fruit. You have a new tenant signed and contracted for five years. He'll be taking three of the south lots. He'll be moving his family and animals here in the next few weeks."

Gerard heaved out a relieved breath so large that he almost sagged with it. "A new tenant, and so quickly. Grady, no prettier words have ever been said to me."

Grady smiled knowingly. "How about these? *There will be more to come.* The interest was immediate. By this time next year, all will be well on the way to recovery."

"You cannot know how glad I am to hear it."

"I can, and do, know. If you would have taken my advice and considered wool sooner, we would not have gotten so out of sorts."

Gerard held up a hand. "I know."

"What changed your mind?"

"Would you believe me if I told you that a woman had advised me to do this?"

Grady's droopy jowls drooped even more as his scowl deepened. "You took a woman's advice before mine when you're paying me to help with these things?"

Gerard laughed. "What can I say? She is a very convincing woman."

"She must be. You should be smart about it. Snatch her up and make her your wife before someone else beats you to it. A companion of such good sense is a rare find."

"No. Marry her? No, no, no. It is not like that between us."

Grady eyed him and swiped the handkerchief over his brow again. "Is something wrong with her?"

"Certainly not."

"I won't ask the next logical question, since you are my employer and no matter how liberal you have been with me, I wish to keep my employment."

Gerard laughed. "There's nothing wrong with me either. The woman and I are childhood friends."

"She's a friend you're indebted to. We really needed those

vacancies filled to make the numbers work. She's given you hope that did not exist before."

Gerard thought about his steward's words long after the steward had gone. He thought about them into the night when he should have been sleeping. He thought of them when he awoke. His steward had told him to marry her.

Marry Etta.

Etta, who had given him hope.

Etta, who had listened to his woes and not judged him.

Etta, who laughed with him and teased him and conspired with him and made him feel less alone than he'd ever felt.

Etta, who was his friend.

Shouldn't his wife also be his friend?

He'd always thought so. It was one of the reasons he had thought Etta's sister, Anne, would be a good fit for him. Why had he never thought of Etta as being a good fit?

He didn't have a good answer.

What would Etta say if he came home and asked her to let him court her in reality and not for some concocted pretense?

Gerard didn't know. But he became suddenly determined to find out. He jumped out of bed so fast that he tangled in the bedclothes and tripped and fell. "Devil take me!" he cursed as he scrambled up again and made his way to his mother's rooms.

The housekeeper had kept his mother's belongings in meticulous order, as Gerard had emphasized. Though the rest of the house might fall around them, his mother's rooms must remain in good order. He was glad to see it. When his mother should return home, she would not feel as badly about the loss of income and staff if she could find peace in her own private space.

It was a space he now entered while feeling moderately guilty. He knew where she kept it.

The ring his father had given his mother as a wedding present was worth quite a lot. His mother had set it aside when his father had died. She said when it came time for Gerard to choose a wife, she expected him to give it with the promise of happiness. He had to swear to the woman he chose that he would live his life in such a manner that they would be happy until they died.

"I want my ring to have a better future than its past. Do you understand?"

At the time, Gerard had claimed he understood, but now he was sure he hadn't. He'd only just truly discovered what kind of future his mother expected for her ring.

He could have tried to make someone like Anne Stone happy, but ultimately he would have failed, because, much as he esteemed her, he did not love her. He could not have true conversations with her. As much as he thought well of Anne, she was not, nor could she ever be, like Etta.

Gerard found the ornate gold band in the wooden box in the bottom drawer of his mother's dressing table. Gerard knew a ring would not be expected or required by Etta, but he wanted to show her how sincere he was in asking for her permission to court her in earnest. If she seemed even remotely amenable, then he would have to restrain himself to keep from asking for her hand right then and there.

Gerard packed quickly for his return trip to Rosemary Manor. Once he'd wished the remaining staff farewell and settled on his horse, he glanced back at the house and felt a surge of pride in all he'd accomplished. He would save his home and lands. He'd be able to continue building up his estate and offering employment opportunities within his community. Gerard could be the man his mother had raised him to be. He looked forward to the day when he would return with Etta at his side.

With that thought, he turned his horse to the road. He did not want to wait a minute longer than necessary.

Immediately after arriving at Rosemary Manor, Gerard sought out his mother. He had the misfortune of passing Miss Bates in the hall, but, though she made some pretense at polite greeting, she didn't try to impede his aim of hurrying to the music room where his mother was practicing the pianoforte.

The melody floated down the hall, and Gerard inhaled deeply, as if he could breathe in every note. He loved listening to his mother play. She had stopped for a time before his father had died, and he'd felt she was truly on her way to healing when she'd started up again after Mr. Hartwell's death. When Gerard entered the music room, his mother glanced up, smiled at him, and continued playing. He rounded the instrument to see her fingers flying over the keys.

When she finished, he applauded. "Every time I think you could not possibly improve upon your skill at this instrument, you outdo yourself."

She beamed at the compliment. Her gaze then fell to the box in her son's hands.

"Do you flatter me because you have something to ask me and you fear my response?"

"I pay you the compliment because it is deserved. And I am more hopeful than I am fearful at this moment."

"Does the Stone girl play?"

"No. She does not."

Mrs. Hartwell grinned knowingly. "Yet you still want to ask for my ring so that you may give it to her?"

Gerard laughed at that. "Miss Etta creates a different sort of music. Hers is the music of a generous heart."

His mother stood and led him over to where they could sit together. "Have you already made your intentions known to her?"

"Not in so many words, but we have been spending a great deal of time together. I think she will be open to the arrangement."

She tsked at him and bumped his shoulder with her own. "She'd be a fool not to. You are handsome and well-connected, and you can provide a financially secure future. You are an enchanting catch, my son."

Gerard had to hold very still to keep from squirming at her belief that he could provide a financially secure future. He felt certain it would eventually become true, but at present, he was not exactly on sure footing. He would bring little to the union regarding financial stability. He would need to rely on Etta's dowry to keep them going for the immediate future.

Gerard could not tell his mother any of this, so he said nothing.

"No doubt," Mrs. Hartwell said, "you are silent because you tire of my keeping you in suspense of my answer, and you hope that by saying nothing, you will encourage me to get on with the business at hand."

Before he could protest, she patted his arm. "Well, since you are determined not to marry young Abigail, I shall have to content myself with the fact that you are choosing a woman who sings to your heart. I love you, Gerard, and I hope Miss Stone makes you as happy as you deserve. Can you promise my ring will have a happy future?"

"I can safely make that promise."

She heaved a long, drawn-out sigh. "Well then, my boy, you may present my ring to her and get to the business of happy futures."

He kissed her cheek. "Thank you, Mother. I know you will love Etta as much as I do."

Gerard stayed and talked with his mother for a while longer. She would be leaving the next morning with the rest of the party heading to London, and he wanted to take the chance to spend time with her while he had it. He only left her when she declared herself tired and desirous of rest for the afternoon.

Gerard was pleased that Freddie was nowhere to be seen. There was no one to hamper his current happiness. He'd had enough of his cousin's sour behavior to last him a lifetime.

While he hoped they would find their friendship again, he was not willing to allow Freddie to spoil what promised to be a perfect day.

Because Gerard could not wait another moment, he resolved to go to Etta's house and ask to court her in earnest.

He put on his best coat and left at the back of the house toward the trail that led to Etta.

He hurried along the path, but once he arrived at the Stone's manor, Gerard felt a great deal more nervous than he'd imagined he would be.

Gerard took a deep breath and lifted his hand to knock on the door but put it down again before he touched the brass ring. He took another deep breath, straightened his jacket, checked his cravat, and raised his hand to lift the knocker once again. This time, he actually let the knocker fall to the wood. He could not remember feeling so nervous in his entire life. Not during examination time at school; not even when he had first gone away for school, for that matter. Leaving home for the first time had felt like the most frightening thing in the world. But now, asking a woman to allow him to court her? Before Gerard's father's death, Gerard would have felt equal to the task of courting any man's daughter. But now? His poverty had diminished his value in his own eyes.

He could still not comprehend how it was that Etta was able to overlook his circumstances. She had not shunned him when he had told her the truth. She'd shown compassion.

He straightened his jacket again and waited for the door to open. When it did, the family butler raised his eyebrows as if astonished to see Gerard standing on the front step.

"I'd like to speak to Mr. Stone, please." In truth, he wanted to speak to Etta. But he felt her father to be the sort of man who would want to be involved from the beginning.

"I'm terribly sorry, sir, but the Stone family has gone to London for the season."

Gerard frowned. He had known they were leaving, but he had assumed, based on what Etta had told him, that he still had two or three days before the family went away for the season. And hadn't Etta said that her father would be staying in Norfolk with her?

"Oh, that is bad luck. Well, I will have to speak to Mr. Stone another time, then. But for now, may I speak to Miss Etta, please?"

"I do apologize, sir. But the *entire* family has gone to London, Miss Etta included. There is none here but household staff."

Gerard felt certain that his frown had reached comical proportions. "She went with them?" She'd given no indication that she planned to go with her family. In fact, she'd seemed entirely set against it. But perhaps she was trying to placate her mother or help her sister. "Did she leave any sort of correspondence for me?"

When the man appeared confused by such a suggestion, Gerard hurried to say, "For a Mr. Gerard Hartwell, that is."

When providing his name didn't add clarity to the confusion, Gerard gave up and headed back to his cousin's. He felt entirely dissatisfied with the turn of events. Etta had gone and had not left any word for him.

They had planned to discuss the renovations to his tenant's house. Of course, he'd also told her he hoped to spend more time with Anne when he returned.

A fear settled into the pit of his stomach. He thought back to their last conversation. He'd asked her to put in a good word for him with her sister, and she'd asked him to do the same with Freddie. What had happened after that?

Something was wrong. Gerard reviewed their parting words over and over as he walked slowly back to Rosemary Manor. "That's right," he said aloud. "I told her she could do better than Freddie." They'd both become cross then. Likely Etta was cross because she didn't like hearing that Freddie wasn't a good catch. He now admitted to himself that he'd been angry because he didn't want her to be with Freddie. He loved her himself. He just hadn't realized it yet.

Etta had said that no one saw her value. Her countenance had fallen. She was sad as well as angry.

He should have stayed. He should have talked with her rather than letting her turn back to her house in such an emotional state. He'd failed her.

What if that failure was enough to turn her away from him permanently?

Wouldn't the world be just a little worse now that he had known what joy could actually be?

Etta had already all but declared herself to Freddie by writing him those letters. Having a cousin like Freddie whose every movement was fashionable and correct in the eyes of society made Gerard feel inferior by comparison. Would he always feel himself to be just on the outside of acceptable?

But Etta was not the sort of woman who concerned herself with the silliness of society. Surely, she could not still prefer Freddie.

She had declared Gerard of value in spite of his poverty. Etta had likely gone to London because her mother had insisted. No other reason made any logical sense. Therefore, he would, of course, go to London as well, and there he would ask her father for permission to court her formally. He would make his intentions known. And he would beg her. She had to feel something for him as well, didn't she?

Gerard took a deep breath and strode down the lane heading back to his cousin's. Today had certainly not ended as the happiest day of his life. But he would not lose hope that the future had better things in store for him.

Along the path, something caught his eye. A glint of light flashed from the mossy dirt near the old tree where he and Freddie had once used a pulley system of ropes and buckets to create a tree house where Lucy and Etta were not allowed to go.

He smirked at the idea of ever wanting to stay apart from Etta and bent over to see what could shine so brightly in the moss.

Gerard felt his smile drop when he realized it was the bit of metal with the ruby jewel that Etta had found on their excursion a few weeks back.

His first thought was that Etta had left it for him to find as a clue that she was nearby. He glanced up, but no one else was around.

Not a clue. What a ridiculous notion. Why would she leave clues for him? She had simply dropped it.

He picked it up and tucked it into his pocket so that he could return it to her.

When Gerard arrived back at the house, he had the misfortune of running into Freddie, who practically impaled him with a glare.

"Well, well," he said. "If it isn't Brutus come to betray me."

"I truly do not know what you're talking about. You've been moping like a child for well over a week now. If you continue to refuse to tell me why, then I cannot help you, and I'm quite through with your unexplained tantrums, so I bid you good day." Gerard moved toward the stairs so that he could hurry to his rooms and instruct his valet to get him packed as quickly as possible when Freddie stopped him.

"You want an explanation? Does the letter from Miss Stone suffice?"

It suddenly seemed that though he was breathing, Gerard could not get enough oxygen to his lungs. He turned slowly. "What do you know about that letter?"

"It seems that your lady doesn't prefer you as much as you think. It seems she would rather have an honest man."

Gerard felt sick. Did Etta confess her feelings to Freddie? "What do you mean by that?"

"Nervous, are you? You should be, because I know all your secrets, cousin. And now . . . so does Miss Etta."

Gerard's breathing became erratic, almost frantic. He barely resisted the idea of clawing at his throat to force himself to breathe properly. "What did you say to her? What have you done?"

"You should be asking instead what it is that *you* have done. You sent a letter to me that was meant to be in your safekeeping. She was not happy to discover that you had deceived her in your attempt to blackmail her."

"You're a cad!" Gerard said. "You know I didn't mail that letter. How did you get it? Were you going through my things?"

"You feign innocence and then accuse me?"

They were both shouting now, calling the attention of anyone who might be in the household.

The butler popped his head out from where he'd been in the dining room, likely preparing it for dinner. When he saw that it was the gentlemen of the house, he immediately ducked back inside.

A maid peeked around a corner. She was likely heading to the dining room as well but apparently thought better of it and disappeared again from view.

"I need not feign anything because I did not send Etta's letter.

Why would I send a letter professing love to you from the woman I love? I would never be so stupid."

"Oh, do stop!" Freddie snarled and loosed his cravat from his neck, giving in to the action Gerard had wanted to do. "Are you going to pretend that you love her even now? We both know you do not love—and have not ever loved—that poor girl. That ruse was for a loan and the hope that she would speak well of you to her sister. How irritating it must be to you that I found you out so quickly. Now I find that it is within my power to grant the lady's wishes. We spent some time together while you were gone. I will be calling on her as soon as I arrive in London tomorrow. She and I shall be just the thing."

Gerard had spent a lifetime with his cousin and had wanted to hit him on many occasions, but these words finally unleashed his restraint. He let his fist fly.

Freddie, who had always been more physically agile, easily ducked the coming blow and lunged to plant a facer of his own. Gerard was not lucky enough to maneuver out of the way and felt the knuckles crack into his jaw. After a startled second when the two cousins locked furious gazes, they launched into one another, landing punches until their mothers found them.

Gerard heard Mrs. Finch shout, "Stop that this instant!" Her words were punctuated by her hands clapping together.

When Gerard felt he no longer needed to keep an eye on where his cousin's fists were aiming, he glanced over to see his mother and aunt standing side by side with Lucy, Miss Bates, and Mrs. Bates directly behind them. None of the five ladies looked terribly impressed by the display of the two young men fighting like little boys, though Lucy seemed curious as to what had preceded it.

Miss Bates laughed, a nervous, irrational sound that ground Gerard's nerves to dust. Mrs. Hartwell narrowed her gaze.

That gaze landed a punch of its own, making Gerard feel his shame for his childish behavior. He loosened his grip on Freddie's coat at the same time Freddie released the fistful of Gerard's shirt. They had to shove each other to extricate themselves from the tangle of their fight.

When Freddie drew breath to explain, his mother held up a hand. "No." She cast a meaningful glance toward the ladies behind her. She did not want his explanation to be overheard.

Being an adult and the head of the family did not exempt a man from his mother's ire when he succeeded in causing her any degree of embarrassment in front of her friends.

Gerard straightened his coat and raked his hair back with his fingers. "Forgive us, Mother," he said. "I'm afraid we let our sport go too far. Cousin." He bowed toward Freddie, turned on his heel, and left to his rooms. He had to pack for London. He didn't have time for this foolishness. He would not allow his traitorous cousin to delay him any further.

What must Etta think of him? She must believe he had betrayed her trust. Would she even allow him to come near enough to explain?

Wilson stood in his room with fresh clothes already laid out for him. "How did you know?" he asked his valet.

"Gibbs saw the display downstairs. He informed us upstairs to be prepared to receive the young men. Since it is almost time for dinner, I thought you might want to dress for that immediately, but if not, I have your other clothing here."

Gerard glanced where his secondary choice of clothing was laid out. He shook his head. "Actually, Wilson, we are to leave within the hour to London. I'll require clothing for hard travel. Pack all of my belongings, as we will not be returning here. You will come with me." If his hopes were dashed in London, he would tell his mother the truth about their financial state, and he would never again return to his cousin's house.

His mother could stay if she liked. She would certainly be more comfortable with her sister, but he had most certainly had enough of the flippant attitude and the games that Freddie played.

"Are you all right, sir?" Wilson said.

Gerard shrugged. What difference did it make if he confessed his situation? "My cousin received a letter from a young lady. I had been keeping it for her. It was addressed to him, but she did not want him to have it. When he did receive it, he assumed the worst about both her and me. And now, she feels I betrayed her trust."

The color drained from Wilson's face.

Gerard studied the man for only a moment before saying, "You gave it to him." All the oxygen left Gerard's lungs with the realization.

"I did not mean to," Wilson hurried to say. "I didn't know it wasn't meant for him. I found the envelope in the bottom of your wardrobe and thought it had fallen out of your coat pocket when I was returning it. It had his name on the front. Please accept my apologies, sir."

Gerard wanted to be furious with the man, but how was this Wilson's fault? He wouldn't have known not to give the envelope to the person it was addressed to. Gerard had placed it at the bottom of his wardrobe between the slats, thinking it was too obscure a space to be noticed.

"I understand how such an error could have been made," he told his valet. I won't pretend I'm not disappointed, but neither can I hold you accountable."

He didn't add that it was all Freddie's fault—his fault for being the congenial one. His fault for being more eligible. His fault for going to Etta and ruining everything. Even after Freddie had the missive, he hadn't needed to go to Etta with it. He could have waited for Gerard. He could have respected Gerard enough to allow him to explain himself.

All the venom he felt toward his cousin reminded him that he needed to speak to his mother.

He knocked on the door in a way that almost felt like pounding. "Mother! I must speak with you immediately," he called.

Her maid answered the door with surprise in her eyes that he would dare attack the door in such a manner.

He ignored her and swept past her into the room.

"One would think I had not raised you to be a gentleman," his mother said as she appraised him from where she sat at a small writing desk by the window.

He waved away her comment and pressed ahead with his message. "Urgent matters take me to London. I will require the carriage. I hope that will be all right since you were planning to travel with Aunt Lucinda in her carriage. I leave within the hour, I hope."

Her eyes lit up. "So you will be there for the season after all! I am so pleased."

"No, Mother. Not for the season. Miss Stone's family had gone before I could speak to her father . . . before I could speak to her. I must get there before is too late."

"Too late?" Mrs. Hartwell tilted her head as if trying to view him better. "Does this have something to do with your performance downstairs?"

Gerard shifted on the white rug under his feet. He considered hiding the truth, but he had already hidden too many horrible truths. He did not have the capacity to hide another. "Yes."

"What happened?"

"Freddie happened. I need to speak with Etta. I need to tell her that he was wrong."

"Wrong about what? And are you sure none of the blame falls on you? What is it I always say?"

"It takes two to fight," Gerard replied sullenly. He opened his mouth to deny ownership of any culpability in the matter, but when he considered further. . . wasn't a good deal of the current situation his fault? He began stammering as he tried to clarify.

His mother held out a hand to stop him from saying more. "Don't let's waste time here with lengthy explanations. Go and tell Miss Etta that you are sorry for whatever blame is yours, and then admit to her that your cousin is a bit of an over-indulged buffoon. I love my sister, but sometimes she has a blind spot where that boy is concerned. Not that I blame her. I believe I have a blind spot where you are concerned. It's the way of mothers. Apologize for your cousin and tell Miss Etta you love her."

Gerard felt a piece of his anger melt into sadness at the realization that there was a chance Etta would not let him give her such a message, but he crossed to his mother and kissed her cheek to thank her for understanding.

She would likely be understanding about their financial difficulties as well. Perhaps he had been wrong not to confide in his mother regarding their situation.

By the time Gerard returned to his rooms, he found that everything was packed and had been carted off to the waiting carriage. He would ride his own horse ahead of the carriage so that he could hurry faster. The carriage would deliver his belongings to Hartwell Hall and then catch up with him in London.

He tugged on his gloves and climbed up on his horse. Before he could encourage his horse to take the first step forward, Freddie appeared. Gerard wanted to run him down but managed to refrain from the impulse.

"Leaving so soon?" Freddie asked.

Gerard did not respond but neither could he leave as he wanted since Freddie planted himself directly in front of Gerard's horse. He could have turned to the side and gone around his cousin, but he would not give Freddie the satisfaction. After years of playing games like "blink first" or "flinch first," Gerard was tired of being the one to step aside or be run over by his cousin.

Freddie viewed the loaded carriage. "This looks ominous. Have you finally decided to stop eating off the generosity of your relations and figure out how to stand on your own?"

"You really are a wretch of a cad, Freddie. You have my word that I will not return here to take another morsel of your barbed generosity. You have no idea what that generosity has cost me." Gerard's horse stepped in agitation, likely feeling Gerard's fury.

"It cost you a loan, that's for certain."

"Why is everything about money for you? Is your life so vacuous that you can think no further than finances? I would rather drink swill than take any amount of money you might offer me."

Freddie's face darkened like a sky about to drop a deluge. "Is that why you've decided to take it from Miss Stone instead? How can you pretend to be so high and mighty, even now? 'I would never consider marrying a woman for money, Freddie,' you said. But you have no issue with bribing a woman and skulking your way into her sister's life. You are nothing better than a fraud, cousin.

"And to think . . . all of these years, I've felt inferior due to how steady you made our mothers believe you to be. Now you've revealed yourself to be the worst sort of fraudster any of us could have ever imagined. I've not cost you a thing. I've only saved Miss Stone from a lie."

Gerard was stabbed with unexpected guilt as well as unexpected pity. What had his cousin said that was wrong? None of it, really. And Freddie felt inferior to him? How? He let his gaze linger over his cousin, taking in the way the man stood, always with his chest puffed out—like a child trying to prove his strength by making himself seem larger.

He felt a thickness in his voice when he said, "If you need to believe that to feel any value in yourself, then you have my sincerest sympathy. We have never been rivals, cousin."

Gerard heeled his horse and turned to the side. Who cared if he flinched first?

He had his future happiness to save.

Chapter Nineteen

"I'm sorry Mama has you wearing that gown, Etta," Anne whispered. "I know how much you hate it." Anne's anxious face peered out from under her silk bonnet. Her blonde ringlets were caught up in the ribbon in a way that looked charming instead of accidental. They were walking along the path in Hyde Park with their mother trailing directly behind them, nodding at people and asking after family members of her particular friends, or at least of those people she felt held sway over her reputation and who were willing to talk with her.

In truth, Etta was surprised that her mother had allowed Anne out of the house with her hair caught in her bonnet ribbons. She was even more surprised to find herself invited to join Anne and her mother for their morning walk.

On occasion, she felt the weight of a curious stare following them.

Honestly, did society believe that a little incident with punch was of such importance that it stayed in their memories for so many months? Had they really nothing better to think about?

More than her profound astonishment that people still remembered or cared about the punch was her distrust of her mother's motives for wanting Etta out on the walk.

"You must truly hate that dress to look so fretful," Anne said.

"What?" Etta hated that she continually had to ask people to repeat themselves when they addressed her. The ache of Gerard's betrayal drowned out every other thought, every sound, *everything*.

"Etta, I am worried about you."

"Don't be. I'm fine."

"You have not been fine since before we left home, no matter how much you insist otherwise."

Their mother's voice broke into their conversation, sparing Etta from having to respond. "Well look at this, girls. It is Mrs. Seagram and her son."

Anne seemed startled and flustered, though Etta could not think why, since her sister had never mentioned these people, and they usually confided everything in each other. Etta looked away from Anne to see the mother and son coming toward them with the obvious intention of stopping to talk.

They all bowed and curtsied for one another. Etta was introduced. Then there was talk between the mothers about getting the families together for dinner, though Etta allowed herself to wander mentally after a moment as she turned to take in the way the wind gently flowed through the trees.

"Don't you agree, Miss Stone?"

Mr. Seagram had been addressing her. Not wanting to be rude by telling him he was not enough to command her attention, she simply repeated, "Do I agree . . ." and trailed off as if contemplating.

He laughed. "I did not know the weather to require such consideration."

"Yes, well . . . a thing that is always changing and which has no regard for the shoes a lady chooses for the day should be treated with care, Mr. Seagram."

"Yes. I do see your point."

Etta stared into his brown eyes and decided that he was a reserved and kind young man. "Are you looking forward to the musicale tonight?" he asked of both her and Anne. Anne blushed and murmured something that might have been a response. He continued the conversation with determination. "I am fond of quiet, meditative music. I hope we shall hear some of that sort."

"I'm sure we shall," Etta said, wishing Anne would do some of the talking.

"Yes. My mother assured me your family would be in town again this season. I was glad to hear it, as I feel we have things to say to each other." His gaze was fixed on Anne.

Etta felt as though her eyes might pop out of her head. What was this?

"I wonder if you ladies might want to see the fowls on the water," Mr. Seagram said. "There are some charming little ducklings."

Etta and Anne walked with him to the water's edge.

They were admiring the fuzzy new ducklings when Mr. Seagram lowered his voice and said to Anne, "Do you recall when we met?"

Mr. Seagram had met Anne? The confusion must have been plainly etched on Etta's face. Anne said, "Yes." She turned to her sister. "Mr. Seagram was traveling in Norfolk and stopped in to visit his aunt, Mrs. Pritchard." Anne's eyes were glowing, and a heightened color was in her cheeks.

Etta glanced back toward the walk, where the two mothers had their heads bent together, casting covert gazes in the direction of the group in a way that could only mean they were conspiring.

Quiet, reserved Mr. Seagram and her quiet, reserved sister. She now understood Anne's earlier anxiety.

"Exactly," Mr. Seagram said. "We met at my aunt's house. Your sister was there playing the pianoforte and I was quite drawn in. I decided to extend my stay for many weeks to allow myself the privilege of hearing her play for my aunt."

Etta watched the exchange of polite conversation, small smiles, and brief nods between the pair. With such a blush on her cheeks and a smile of contentment, Anne had never looked lovelier.

After a time, the ladies and gentleman made their way back to the walk. Mr. Seagram and his mother moved on after promising to join the Stones for a family dinner later that week.

Etta's mother seemed most pleased with herself as she watched them walk away. "Last season was not the rain cloud on your prospects that we feared. If Mr. Seagram is so enamored, others will be too. We might even find you a duke, Anne. Just think of it."

Mrs. Stone had stepped in close enough that there was no escaping the sharp smell of her creams, even though they were out of doors. Mrs. Stone smiled, twirled her pale pink parasol, and continued walking.

"Etta?" Anne whispered, the alarm evident in that one tremoring word.

"Do not worry, Anne," Etta whispered back.

"But there is something you do not know . . ."

Etta slid her sister a look that conveyed she knew exactly what she ought to know. "You are not so sly as you think. Well, that is not true. You are incredibly sly. You haven't let slip even one hint of this young man before. I owe all of my information to my own deductions. He wants to call on you, Anne."

"I do not want a duke. I only want Mr. Seagram."

As their mother sighed in satisfaction ahead of them and greeted people as though there was nothing wrong in the world at all, Anne's world crumbled more and more.

"You're her favorite, dearest," Etta murmured. "She will want your happiness—especially when he is so agreeable. But how is it you never said a word these many months?"

Anne looked guilty. "I wanted to tell you. I almost did several times, but it was all so uncertain. I half-wondered if it was only me imagining it. And then with Mama planning the trip to London and all of her schemes, it seemed impossible." Anne's lips quickly clamped together as their mother shot back a look that indicated the girls needed to keep up.

"I'm sorry I didn't tell you about Mr. Seagram," Anne said softly. "It is not as though I didn't trust you with the information. It is more that I didn't trust myself that the information was true. I worried it was all on my side and none on his."

"Judging from the way he looked at you, he's clearly smitten."

"If his look holds even half of the adoration of Mr. Hartwell when he looks at you, it would be enough."

Etta's heart shoved away the small rush of hope that swept over it. Perhaps Anne knew something about Mr. Hartwell that she didn't. But no. He had promised to keep the letter safe.

He had not delivered on that promise. He could not care for her.

Chapter Twenty

Gerard was vexed when he first arrived in London. The three days of travel had left him cross and despairing. He'd stopped at Hartwell Hall along the route and left the carriage there for the household staff to unload and unpack. He and Wilson had then continued to London on horseback.

The fact that it took hours to locate the Stone family's address once he'd arrived only further perturbed him.

He reached into his pocket and felt the edges of the metal with the ruby jewel. He'd seen Etta with the small treasure a few times after she'd found it that day at the priory ruins.

She'd confessed that she had come to think of it as her good luck charm. She'd even commented that it reminded her of the happy day they and their friends had all spent together.

When Gerard had first found it on her property, he'd believed that she'd dropped it by accident, but as he had made the journey into town, he'd had time to ponder. Etta had not lost it by some mischance. The bit of metal had been discarded by design. Why would she want to keep something when it no longer made her happy?

"Freddie, if you could only see what destruction you've wrought," Gerard whispered. He had intended to reverse the damage by chasing Etta down and telling her everything. But after much thought, he was no longer sure that telling her he cared would be enough. He'd need to show her.

Gerard's fingers tightened around the bit of metal. He stared into the street busy with horses and carriages. He almost didn't hear the sound of thumping hooves and gentlemen talking as they admired a coat in the shop window next door. He usually enjoyed being in town during its busy times. He liked the bustle, movement, and myriad entertainments found at every turn. At that moment, however, it was all just noise. His gaze landed on a shop down the street, its wooden sign swaying gently in the breeze, and an idea struck him.

He needed to act quickly.

He hurried down the street, threading himself between the crowds of people to reach that sign. He stepped through the door and crossed to the man at the front of the shop. He pulled the metal out of his pocket and set it on the counter. "I'd like to see what can be done to fashion this into a necklace."

It might have been a foolish expense, but his urgency to show Etta his feelings persuaded him of its necessity. The jeweler had been willing to take the snuffbox that had belonged to his father in trade.

When Gerard left the jeweler, he felt better, as though he were moving on the right path. His next destination was the front step of the Stones' London home in Mayfair. He stood and stared at the door for several moments. Was Etta home? Would she be willing to talk to him if he were to ask to see her?

He knocked on the door. When the butler answered, Gerard asked to speak with Mr. Stone.

"He is not at home," the butler said.

"I see. Would you see that he receives this?" Gerard handed over an envelope that he'd prepared beforehand.

The butler bowed his head and took the envelope. "I'll see that he gets it, sir." The butler moved as if to close the door again, but Gerard said, "Is Miss Etta home and accepting callers at this time?"

"I'm sorry, sir. She's gone with her mother and sister for the afternoon. Do you have a message for her?"

"No. No, thank you." Gerard left feeling slightly disheartened. He had hoped for some sort of resolution. He returned to his own house because he had nothing better to do than wait for Etta's father to answer his letter. He knew he was not exactly a promising prospect, especially since Mr. Stone had been so generous with his daughters' dowries. It made Gerard look mercenary to be pursuing Etta when his own fortune had been squandered. He hoped to explain to Etta's father his plans and prove his worth, but the man had already seemed less than likely to be impressed by anything Gerard might have to say.

Gerard ate a meager meal and felt guilty since Wilson and the remaining staff in his London home were likely stuck eating worse. The limited funds to purchase necessities meant that any meal more luxurious than the one they'd received that night would have to come from an exterior source. He knew he should be grateful that he had a meal at all. He'd worked closely enough with a few of his tenants to understand that sometimes there was no food of any kind to be had for days. He should have traded his father's snuffbox for food and household supplies, but he could not regret his choice. Etta deserved the gift being prepared for her. He had other things of his father's that he could sell to bring the townhome to a respectable condition when his mother arrived. Gerard went to bed still hungry and more than a little discouraged, though not because of his stomach.

If Etta chose never to forgive him, what would he do? He tried to put the thought out of his mind so that he could sleep.

But when the morning light found him still staring at his ceiling, he considered all the things he could have done instead of trying to sleep. He could have caught up on reviewing paperwork from the estate. However, doing so would have meant using up a candle.

Gerard arose and dressed for the day. He waited for any sort of response from Etta's father. Surely the man had received his letter and would try to set up an appointment to meet. Gerard stayed close to home the whole of the day waiting.

The three days that followed were spent similarly. No word came.

Gerard's time was not wasted, however. Since he knew his mother would soon be in London and would want to stay in her own home, he had much to prepare for, including a better-stocked larder. He would not expect his mother to eat as conservatively as he did.

Mrs. Hartwell arrived on the fourth day after Gerard had delivered his message to Mr. Stone. "Hello, Mother," Gerard said when she entered the house. "I have a confession." It was perhaps not the best way to begin a conversation with one's mother, but he was well past due making a clean breast of it with her.

She shook her head. "I do not believe you have much to tell me that I do not already know, but I am willing to humor you." Mrs. Hartwell settled herself in her favorite chair by the fireplace. "Tell me, then. What is this all about?"

Gerard sat across from her and began at the beginning. From the state of their finances to his dealings with both Freddie and Etta, he confessed his part in the whole of it all.

His mother's silence hung heavy in the air.

Even after he'd stopped talking, she made no move to speak any opinion, thought, or consideration of her own regarding the whole of his dealings.

"Well?" Gerard asked, finally unable to bear her silence any further.

"Well, what?"

"Do you not have anything to say? You cannot tell me you have no views on all of this."

Mrs. Hartwell leveled her penetrating gaze on him. "Oh, believe you me, I have opinions enough. Let's start with the most important one."

He steeled himself to hear her disappointment regarding the fact that he could not fix their financial situation.

"You mean to say to me that you are guilty of blackmailing that poor girl?"

That was not exactly what Gerard had expected her to say. "Out of everything I told you, that's your chief concern?" he asked.

"What else shows you lacking in even the smallest amount of

decency? The finances are not your fault. They are the fault of your father. Freddie is responsible for his own actions. The only thing you bear fault for is the fact that you treated a lady like a bargaining chip."

Gerard scratched the back of his neck and scowled at his mother. He had no right to feel vexed with her, but she spoke as though Gerard had done something truly dreadful, and it hadn't been like that at all.

Had it? "Mother, I—"

"No, my dear. I won't hear your excuses. You could have given the letter back immediately and then asked the girl to allow you to call on her like a proper gentleman. Or you could have decided to court her sister, if she was your aim, *like an honest man*. Instead, you created all this chaos and then have the nerve to feel offended when it descends into the chaos you created in the first place."

Gerard hung his head. How could he argue with that?

"But, Mother," he said quietly, "she had written a love letter to Freddie. Why would she ever be my aim when she had already chosen him in her heart? To be honest, I cannot be sorry for my actions, because holding that letter in my hand and refusing to give it back brought Etta vividly to my attention. She has helped me solve problems. She has made me feel valued and capable."

Mrs. Hartwell finally had the decency to show signs of sympathy. "You and Freddie have long been locked in a cruel competition created by your fathers. Such competition breeds insecurities that have no real foundation. You are both fine men."

Gerard scoffed at that. "You say this of the man who refused to give me aid when I needed it and who then purposely confronted a woman for whom I had feelings? And now she has fled from me, and her father remains stubbornly silent regarding my request to meet with him. Freddie did this. How does that make him a fine man?"

Mrs. Hartwell leaned forward and put her hand on his knee. "You are rather unperceptive sometimes, Gerard. It pains me to say so, but it is true. Try seeing this from Freddie's point of view, without the luxury of knowing your true feelings and intentions. Your cousin sees this as you trying to use him, deceive him, and make a fool of him."

Gerard leaned forward as well. He took his mother's hand. "When you put it like that, I come across as quite the villain."

"Oh stop." She removed her hand from his so that she could lightly cuff the side of his head. "No one likes a man who acts pitiful." Her lip twitched as if to tell him she was teasing. Mrs. Hartwell leaned back. "I think perhaps it is time I pay the Stones a call while we are all here in London. Perhaps we could end the feud between the families, and then Mr. Stone might find his time freed up enough to see you."

"Do you think it will help?"

"Well, it can't hurt things more than they are. And since I am going in armed with all the information, I can attempt to see where things are with these young ladies."

"She hates me. I'm sure of it."

Mrs. Hartwell rolled her eyes. "Darling boy, you should have taken to the theater with all your dramatics. Let me go see what I can discover."

Gerard agreed. He felt the first spark of real hope: he had a spy on his side. His mother glanced around the back parlor. "So, we're penniless, are we?"

"Yes. Very."

"And you've been keeping this secret all this time?"

"Yes."

She stood and crouched in front of him, peering into his eyes. He suddenly felt like a small boy. "You do not have to carry burdens on your own. Never again assume that I am too weak to share in a difficulty merely because I sometimes act silly."

"I'm sorry, Mother. I tried to fix it. Truly I did. And the estate is doing better. If I can pay off this first load of debt, it will recover well enough."

"Dear, I believe in your ability to manage it all."

"Even though I sold the curricle?"

Mrs. Hartwell stood and brushed her skirts to smooth them back into place. "Yes, that *was* a silly thing. With all my jewelry available, you chose to sell the curricle?"

"I never really drive it," Gerard said, feeling defensive of his position.

"But *I* do."

They shared a smile, understanding one another perhaps better than ever before.

Chapter Twenty-One

"He's coming tonight." Etta waggled her eyebrows at her sister, who was sitting in the courtyard sketching the cherry trees with their blossoms. "Now that Mama understands the situation—at least as well as Mama can understand such things—I predict the evening will be perfect." Etta plopped down rather unceremoniously onto the bench near her sister's art table.

Anne set aside her pencils and reached for Etta to embrace her. "Goodness. What is all this fuss?" Etta asked.

"I am so anxious, Etta." Anne pulled back and peered into Etta's face. "But let us not worry about my emotions for a moment. What are we to do with yours?"

"Mine?"

"You are unhappy."

Etta straightened and arranged her skirts so they hung properly. "I am perfectly happy."

"You are perfectly lying. Well . . . not perfectly, else I would not be able to discern the truth under your words. You have been unhappy since we left home. What can I do?"

Etta focused on the pale pink blossoms. "There is nothing to be done."

"It is because of Mr. Hartwell. I am sure of it."

Etta didn't deny the fact. She had confessed most of her dealings with Mr. Hartwell. Anne did not judge her, even though Etta admitted to agreeing to contrive ways for Anne and Mr. Hartwell to spend time together. Anne was shocked, certainly, but not unkind regarding the whole awful production. And when Etta told Anne that Mr. Finch had returned the very letter Mr. Hartwell had promised to keep safe, Anne had not spoken unkindly regarding Mr. Hartwell either. She'd gone so far as to give him the benefit of the doubt.

Despite everything she'd heard, Anne did not change her view that Mr. Finch was not to be trusted with Etta's heart. She cited, again and again, the situation with the sherry and how Mr. Finch had laughed while Mr. Hartwell had leaped to Etta's protection.

"Perhaps we should find a way to talk to him," Anne said, referring to Mr. Hartwell, "and ask him what happened."

"Oh, Anne, how would I even begin such a conversation?" Etta reached up and plucked one of the blossoms from a branch. "I can't ask a man why he betrayed me when we had both conspired to deceive all our relations. There are some levels of ridiculousness even I will not endure."

"You cannot really believe that."

"What? That I refuse to give in to complete ridiculousness?"

"No." Anne reached out and pulled the blossom from Etta's fingers, where she'd started shredding the petals. "I mean you cannot believe that he betrayed you. There has to be another explanation. A man so in love could not so easily betray the object of that love."

Tears blurred Etta's vision. "He does not love me, Anne. Perhaps I am not lovable."

"How can you say that?" Anne took Etta's hands in her own. "Look at me."

Etta met her sister's gaze. Anne tightened her grip on Etta's hands. "*I* love you. I know that Lucy loves you. And sincerely, Etta, I feel that Mr. Hartwell does as well. I think he needs to be allowed to explain himself. He owes you that much. You owe it to yourself."

"That is all impossible now. I am here. He is there. There is no opportunity for explanations or reconciliations. We must, both of us, move forward in our separate lives."

Anne opened her mouth probably to argue, but she closed it again. She then pulled Etta close and embraced her tightly for a long time.

This was how they were when the butler interrupted them. "A Mr. Finch is here to see you, Miss Etta," he said. "Would you like me to show him to the drawing room?"

"Mr. Finch!" Etta exclaimed.

"Mr. Finch?" Anne did not sound nearly as enthusiastic.

"Please show him to the drawing room. I'll be in immediately."

The butler left to do as asked.

"Better to have him told you weren't home."

"Anne! He has been nothing but a gentleman to me since he informed me he'd received my letter. I don't want to be rude to him."

"You should not encourage him." Anne picked up her pencil and scowled at her drawing.

Etta shook her head at her sister and pulled her up to meet Mr. Finch. "Why must I go?" Anne asked.

"Because I need someone else there. What if O'Brien isn't available?"

Anne groaned but went.

Once they were all together in the drawing room, Mr. Finch handed Etta a small posy and bowed over her hand. Etta had once imagined him doing this very thing in London. Hadn't she written to him about this hope in one of her letters? Granted, that was not the letter he'd received. That information had been in one of the letters she'd retrieved and subsequently burned. But still . . . she'd imagined it, and now it was happening.

"Would you care to take a stroll with me in the park? It's a lovely day for walking. Of course, you are also welcome, Miss Stone," he said to Anne.

Anne's thin smile almost made it appear that she was grinding her teeth, but she didn't argue when Etta agreed to the scheme. Once they were walking in the direction of Hyde Park and Anne trailed behind them, Etta said, "I hope this not rude to observe. You look slightly disheveled, Mr. Finch. Where are you coming from that you are in such a state?"

"Honestly?" he said with a jubilant tone. "I've come directly from traveling. I rode all the way here with barely a stop because I could not wait to see you."

When she didn't respond to his announcement right away, he said, "You don't believe me?"

Her sister's warnings of him not being trustworthy rang in her ears. "I don't disbelieve you. It's that I don't understand why."

"Etta, can't you see how utterly transfixed I am by you?"

Again, she didn't respond right away because his interest in her felt strangely sudden. Happily, she was saved from responding when they were hailed by Mr. Seagram, who was walking toward them and who, apparently, knew Mr. Finch. Anne quickened her pace to catch up to Etta and Mr. Finch.

"I'm so looking forward to dinner tonight," Mr. Seagram said, his gaze decidedly on Anne's face in a way that made Etta think of the word "transfixed." Mr. Finch might have just said the word, but it was Mr. Seagram who showed Etta what it could mean.

"Dinner tonight?" Mr. Finch asked.

"It's a family dinner," Anne said quickly, clearly intending to indicate that an extra person was not to be invited.

"Seagram here is family?" Mr. Finch asked.

"His family and ours are sharing an intimate meal. But I don't see why we cannot increase our party by one should you be amenable to coming, Mr. Finch." Etta purposely did not meet Anne's spearing gaze.

"If you think I would be welcome, I should be delighted." Mr. Finch grinned amiably at everyone present. Etta smiled in return to make up for the fact that Anne did not. Mr. Seagram seemed perfectly unruffled by the invitation of another, though Etta wasn't certain he was paying attention to anything except her sister.

For Etta's part, she was glad to have Mr. Finch to dinner. She had questions regarding him and her feelings for him. How was she to discern what those feelings were if she did not allow herself to examine them closely?

Mr. Seagram turned back with the group, and he and Mr. Finch walked the ladies home to dress for dinner.

"Why would you invite him?" Anne asked Etta when they were behind closed doors.

"I don't know. I suppose I'm curious as to how I feel about him. I need more time with him to determine it. And now that Mama has found that society is not nearly as concerned as she had imagined about the dispute between her and Mrs. Finch, she won't be unhappy that he's coming. His presence will even out the numbers. And you know how Mama loves that."

"Please be careful, dearest. I don't want to see you hurt."

Etta didn't remind her sister that the only one who had inflicted any pain had been Mr. Hartwell— the one Anne kept trying to convince Etta to forgive.

Mama, once informed about the addition to the party, didn't seem concerned at all that Mr. Finch was joining them. Etta suspected it was only because her mother was too preoccupied with making certain all the preparations were made and giving instructions to their staff. As much as Mrs. Stone had said she wanted a duke for Anne, the Seagram family were highly respectable, and their son was a fine match for her daughter. The fact that Anne had convinced her mother that she really liked him meant that their mother was resolute in making the evening successful.

Mr. and Mrs. Seagram arrived with their son at almost the exact moment Mr. Finch arrived. Conversations were easy and comfortable. Anne's attention was completely consumed by Mr. Seagram, and his was likewise engaged. Etta took satisfaction in seeing the two of them together. They were a good match in both temperament and fortune and would do well together.

Mr. and Mrs. Seagram apparently thought so too. They smiled at one another as they gazed at the blossoming friendship between their son and Anne.

The conversation turned to Mr. Seagram's love for dancing, since they were to all attend a ball the next night. Mr. Finch whispered, "I do hope you'll save me a dance tomorrow night."

"You'll be in attendance?" Etta asked.

"Now that I know you will, I wouldn't dream of missing it."

"Sometimes I feel you're teasing me," Etta said.

"We would be brilliant together?" Freddie said. "Would we not?"

Etta's heart leaped into her throat, and she stared at him goggle-eyed. No.

No.

Freddie could not wish to pay that particular attention to her. This was moving too quickly.

Last year, she might have welcomed it, but now, her heart was broken, her soul emptied.

She finally recognized the danger of the marriage mart. This was not always a game wherein the winner walked away with the prize of a home and loving husband.

Futures were fragile things.

The relationship of husband and wife should come from something more than a few dances in candlelit ballrooms, where one could scarcely see what one is about. How could a couple truly understand one another when all they were allowed were walks in the garden and conversations which seemed to always stay on the weather?

A man and a woman should have shared experiences.

But then . . . she and Mr. Hartwell had shared experiences, and what good had it done them? Perhaps not knowing the particulars of one another was the better path after all.

She should have felt something more than confusion. Shouldn't there have been elation, delight, a thrill?

She could only describe her emotional state at that moment as slightly unwell, as if she'd eaten something that did not quite get on with her stomach.

Etta realized she'd left Freddie waiting for a response of some sort.

She stammered to come up with something when he said, "You'll save me a dance tomorrow night, won't you?"

"Certainly." She offered a smile that she hoped didn't reflect her relief to have the conversation take a different turn. "I can promise that."

As they all parted from one another for the evening, Anne blushed and promised the dinner dance to Mr. Seagram. The agreement was made where everyone could hear, and there seemed to be satisfaction on all sides.

Mr. Finch said nothing regarding Etta's promised dance nor hinted as to his earlier statement regarding them.

He'd suggested they would be brilliant together. She had always wanted a husband who was resplendent.

Could Mr. Finch be described as a resplendent husband? He might *look* the part, but could he *be* the part?

The answer eluded Etta.

Except it didn't . . . not really.

If someone had placed the same question before her regarding Mr. Hartwell, the answer would have been immediate.

Yes.

Etta frowned at her reflection after Jillian had finished pulling out the pins from her hair and brushing out the reddish-brown curls. She stayed at the dressing table even after Jillian had left. "I'm not resplendent either," she told the glass. "Perhaps that is why Mr. Finch is a better match for me. We can be less shining together."

Such a speech hardly encouraged her. No matter how she looked at the situation before her, she didn't find it to her liking. She abandoned the quest for answers and went to bed.

The next morning found her just as confused as the previous night had left her.

The ball was the big event of the day, and preparing for it was all Mama wanted out of her daughters.

Etta expected to receive no special regard as she readied herself for the ball, so when her mother entered her bedchamber with a smile and small flowers for Etta's hair, she could not account for it.

"Is that what you're wearing?" her mother asked.

Etta didn't respond, since it should have been apparent that the dress she had already been buttoned into was her choice for the night.

"We should try something else. Don't you think?"

Etta did not think so; she liked the gown she wore.

Attempting to keep her mother from selecting a different gown that she probably wouldn't like as much, Etta said, "This is fine, Mama. We are to leave soon, and I would not wish to be the one to delay us."

Her mother wrapped a finger around a curl that framed Etta's face and held it tight to coil it even more. "Your father has asked me to talk to you. I know you think I'm hard on you, Marietta. I don't mean to be. You are so much like me when I was your age, with your romantic notions. I worry you will be disappointed to learn that life is not what it is in our imaginations. I have probably been overzealous to quell some of your more fanciful leanings. I'm sorry if that means you believe I don't care."

Her mother could have sprouted wings and flown to the treetops to roost and surprised Etta less than she did with this unveiling of emotion. She didn't know what to say, so she murmured an awkward "Thank you."

Mrs. Stone straightened, and the moment was over.

Etta stayed silent while her mother directed Jillian as to the best placement for the flowers in Etta's hair. She smiled at Etta's reflection, then swept out of the room as if she had not done any such thing.

Etta thought of the baby bird from so many years ago and smiled as well.

Chapter Twenty-Two

Gerard had been pacing the floor waiting for the post to come in the hopes that he would receive some response to his letter to Mr. Stone. Aunt Lucinda and Lucy had been in the drawing room visiting with his mother. The women exited the drawing room to inform him they'd decided to take a stroll in the park. His mother muttered something about having to walk since they had no curricle, but no one except him heard her. It was on account of their excellent persuasion skills that they were able to pull him from his pacing and convince him to accompany them on their walk.

He and Lucy kept a brisker pace than their mothers and were able to talk about Lucy's expectations for the ball that evening. "Will you come?" she asked Gerard.

"I do not wish to dance."

"Do not be so unobliging, Gerard. It's a ball. You must dance. Besides I will need another person to talk to. Anne will have Mr. Seagram, and Etta will be—" Lucy stopped and widened her eyes at him as if horrified by what she'd said.

"Etta will be there?"

Lucy looked away from him and quickened her step as if trying to outrun him. "You are right. You shouldn't go if you don't want to dance. It would be silly to attend a ball and refuse to participate in the intended amusement."

"Lucy, will Etta be there?"

"I haven't spoken to her myself. I assume so, yes. Freddie said she would be. Gerard, I'm sorry. I didn't think when I asked you to come. I don't want you to be uncomfortable."

"Why would I be uncomfortable with Etta?"

Lucy squinted at him as if trying to see him better. "Do you not know?"

He raised his hands to show he might know if she'd simply say what she was thinking.

"Well, because Freddie has been courting Etta. I do not know the exact nature of their courtship, but it does seem as though it is progressing."

It was as if Lucy's words had punched the air out of his lungs. Nothing could have prepared Gerard for that information. He'd known Freddie had pushed his horse far too hard and made it to London ahead of Gerard, but he hadn't known his cousin had managed to obtain time with Etta, not time enough to—

"She can't be serious. Not about Freddie." Had his voice ever sounded so flat?

"I don't mean to uninvite you to the ball. After everything that has happened between you and Etta, I worry you might not be comfortable at the dance. But perhaps I am misunderstanding. I would like for you and Freddie and Etta to be friends." Lucy looked hopeful.

"Certainly. I will always be Etta's friend."

Only her friend. But in truth, not even that. If her courtship was progressing as Lucy believed, then Etta was lost to him. Freddie was lost to him as well. There was nothing left for Gerard in London. He needed to return to Hartwell Hall and focus on repairing his life. His mother would understand.

"—dance with me?" Lucy had asked him a question.

"Yes. I'll go to the ball and dance with you," Gerard said, inferring her petition.

She stopped and looked at him, her eyes swimming with sympathy. "Are you sure you won't be uncomfortable?"

"I can manage. There is nothing I want more than Etta's happiness. If she is happy, then I shall be happy as well."

He was telling the truth. Her happiness meant more to him than his comfort. It meant more than anything. That was why he had to see her again. He needed to tell her as much.

He returned Lucy to her mother and made his apologies to the ladies. "I have some business that must be attended to before the ball tonight."

"You're going?" his mother asked.

"Of course. I thought you could all benefit from an upstanding gentleman to accompany you." He didn't add that they needed him because Freddie wasn't upstanding. He didn't say it because it wasn't true. Freddie was a gentleman who was admired far and wide. Gerard also didn't say it because he knew he was being petty.

The truth was that he loved his cousin too. If Freddie and Etta truly would be happy together, then he would endeavor to be happy for them, or at least as happy as he knew how to be. But if there was a chance that Etta would accept him, he owed it to everyone involved to take that chance.

With that in mind, Gerard made an important stop on the way home. "It turned out beautifully," the jeweler said. He removed something wrapped in velvet from a strong box behind the counter. He untied the strings, and the velvet fell away to reveal the contents.

Gerard could only stare. The jeweler had turned Etta's treasure into an exquisite necklace. He'd cut the metal in half, then rounded out the two halves before connecting them by a hinge and a clasp. The ruby jewel decorated the center of the locket and was surrounded by fine filigree work and etchings created from the bits of metal left over. When Gerard had seen the finished product, he knew that no matter how Etta might feel about him now, this was a locket she deserved to own.

"It's perfect," Gerard said.

He felt his father's snuffbox to be a fair trade for the craftsman-ship but he also felt the financial pain of the gift. He could not afford this extravagance. The snuffbox could have been traded for any num-ber of necessities, but he would not allow himself to regret his choice. Etta deserved this treasure. Whether she was his or not, she deserved this beautiful thing to remind her of her own perfect, exquisite beauty, both body and soul.

Once back at his home, he leveled a look at Wilson. "I need to appear my absolute best tonight, Wilson. Whatever magic you might have, please use it with generosity." If he was going to be rejected, he would do it with the dignity of a man who had fought the good fight bravely and died trying.

Wilson went to work.

Gerard arrived at the ball with his mother on his arm. She was genuinely pleased to be there with him, and he realized he should have been willing to go for her sake alone. "I'm going to be a better son to you," he said in her ear above the noise of the musicians and people talking.

"Don't be ridiculous. You're the very best son." She patted his cheek. "I heard from Lucy that your cousin beat you to London, but your lady is not his yet. So don't be foolish by thinking I want you to stay here with me. I absolutely do not. Go find her."

He kissed her forehead. "As soon as the estate is recovered, I am buying you the best curricle available."

"True, right, you will!"

The Eddings were a wealthy, well-liked family, and no one hosted a ball as they did. Gerard could not take two steps without tripping over people and flowers and candles. The floral scent mingling with the smoke from the candles created something oddly comforting. He recalled that he and Etta had joked over the impracticality of candles at a ball, where seeing one's partner might be considered important. He smiled with this memory, knowing she would smile too if he men-tioned it to her.

As Gerard searched for any sign of Etta, he began to wonder

whether she'd arrived yet. Or perhaps she'd decided not to come at all, and he'd missed his chance to speak to her while she was home.

Suddenly, there she was, set aglow by the surrounding candle-light. Beads and embroidery embellished her white silk gown. He felt his breath leave but could not seem to recall how to draw in another one as he watched her lean over and whisper something in an elderly woman's ear. The elderly woman laughed and seemed pleased by what-ever Etta had said to her.

"Smitten," Gerard whispered to himself.

He moved to approach her, to ask her to dance, to ask her to stay with him always, when he heard a laugh he recognized come from a side room.

Miss Bates.

Gerard shook his head, determined to ignore that woman's noise, but when he glanced up again to see Etta, she'd vanished like some ethereal being. He scowled. Curse Miss Bates and her terribly timed laughter. It was then he noticed the other laughter. It was an under-current of sound easily masked by the much louder Miss Bates. But he still recognized it.

Freddie.

Unable to help himself even as he scolded himself for not having greater restraint, he followed the sound to a room. The door stood slightly ajar. Gerard toed it open farther.

Freddie and Miss Bates both jumped and parted, their expres-sions showing mirrored surprise to have been caught together in the intimate setting such as they were. Though they were not exactly to be considered alone with the ballroom bustling with people and the door to the study ajar as it was, still their presence together was shock-ing. Miss Bates wiped at her mouth as if she could smooth away the indiscretion.

No. He could *not* have been kissing Miss Bates. Certainly not. Gerard refused to believe it.

"Why are you in here?" Gerard demanded to know. "Freddie! Etta is here! What if she'd been the one to come upon you?" Though

Gerard couldn't prove anything had happened, disgust twisted his insides. "Miss Bates, may I suggest you leave at once."

For perhaps the first time, Miss Bates promptly did as directed. She ran for the door as if she could not get away fast enough. She hesitated slightly when she passed Gerard and looked as though she might say something to him, but whether to defend herself or ask him to stay silent, he didn't know, because she said nothing and instead continued away.

"Freddie, I cannot bring myself to speak to you right now, because, frankly, I am too bewildered and horrified, but be assured we *will* talk." Gerard left, making certain to leave the door wide open so that any guests passing by could easily view the room.

Gerard's urgency to find Etta overpowered him. He had to tell her. She deserved to know that Freddie was trifling with Miss Bates.

Whether she chose Gerard or not, he would not allow her to be with someone who did not appreciate her enough to have eyes for her alone.

When he saw the flash of her white gown, he followed and was dismayed to realize that he followed some other young lady. He'd been introduced to her once before but could not recall her name. She smiled at him expectantly, as if she thought he'd come to ask her to dance in the next set. "Please excuse me," he said. He smiled back and turned awkwardly away, feeling like a cad.

Another flash of white. He was more careful this time as he approached so as not to give the wrong idea to a lady who was not Etta.

But it was Etta.

His Etta.

"Will you do me the honor of dancing with me?" he asked when he was close enough.

Another young woman was with her, and she put a hand on Etta's arm, nudging her in Gerard's direction as if to encourage someone she thought might be too shy to accept without prodding.

Etta raised her chin and stepped forward to take the arm he held out to her. She didn't speak.

After Gerard led her to the dance floor, they moved into the waltz position. She wouldn't look at him.

"Etta—"

"Do not use my name. You deserve no such privilege." Her hand rested on his arm so lightly, she might not have been touching him at all. It was as if the idea of touching him repulsed her.

"I did not give your letter to Freddie. Freddie is a liar. You cannot trust a thing he says—"

"A liar?" she spat the word. "He had the letter in his hand. Don't tell me whom I can trust when you are the one who broke your word."

"Please just listen. I must warn you against Freddie. I saw him just now. He's—"

"No. Stop. I will *not* listen to you. Not ever again." She pulled away from him, and his hand slipped from where it had been on her waist. He wanted to pull her back, but there was no way to do so without drawing attention. Etta slipped through the edge of the crowd and disappeared into it. He followed but couldn't find her.

Gerard would have left the ball if his mother hadn't been with him.

He sat at a table, worried for Etta. Even if she didn't want Gerard, she deserved to be with someone who cared only for her.

"You look miserable."

He looked up to see Lucy. She'd settled in the chair across from him. "You promised me a dance, Gerard."

"So I did." He didn't move to his feet.

Lucy tilted her head and eyed him. "Why are you so put out?"

"It hardly matters, Lucy. Shall we dance?"

"It appears you are not in spirits. We'd be tripping over your gloomy disposition."

He would have argued that his skill on the dance floor would overcome his despair, except a young man asked for Lucy's next dance.

Gerard then saw the young lady he'd encountered earlier, the one who thought he'd come to claim her next dance. She was with a small group of friends. He still could not recall her name. She must think him a clod. Gerard lumbered to his feet. He could do nothing regarding his situation with Etta, but he could repair to some degree his management of the situation with this young woman. He begged pardon for forgetting her name, was reminded that it was Miss Julianna Kessler, and asked her to dance.

Miss Kessler seemed glad to be given the chance to join the set, and Gerard was glad to take his mind off himself for a moment. After thanking her and escorting her back to her friends, he kept his promise and danced with Lucy.

"She's gone," Gerard told Lucy while they danced. "Your rotten brother does not deserve her."

"Freddie is not rotten," Lucy said.

Gerard snorted. He considered telling Lucy about what he'd seen, but, truly, what had he seen? He hadn't caught Freddie and Miss Bates locked in any kind of embrace. Was it possible he was mistaken? Could he slander the young lady in question and his cousin if he wasn't entirely positive?

Lucy was claimed again for the next dance by the same young man as before and seemed delighted to see him again. Gerard leaned against the wall and watched.

He felt someone at his arm and turned, expecting to see his mother or aunt commenting on how happy Lucy seemed. He did not at all expect to see Etta's sister, Miss Stone. She was peering up at him with open curiosity. "Are you a villain, Mr. Hartwell?" she asked.

"I suppose that would depend upon whom you are asking."

"I'm asking you."

The lively, happy tune of "Auretti's Dutch Skipper" and the tapping of feet felt wrong as a backdrop to their conversation.

"I try not to be. May I speak openly?"

Miss Stone nodded her permission.

"I love your sister. I don't deserve her—I know that. I don't know what she has told you, but I can assume she has told you everything, or you wouldn't inquire after my level of villainy. I can with honesty say that I bear both more and not nearly as much guilt as you may think."

"Did you give her letter to your cousin?"

"No. My valet found the letter, saw to whom it was addressed, and did the only correct thing a man in his position could do."

Anne nodded, her blonde ringlets swaying. "You should tell her the truth."

"I attempted to. She doesn't want to hear from me."

Anne scoffed. "So I suppose that's it, then. Giving up is probably for the best for both of you. After all, why be happy together when you can be so pathetic individually?"

It was the least kind thing he'd ever heard Anne say. He'd had no idea she could be so derisive. "You cannot let her marry Freddie," Gerard told her.

"You mean *you* can't let her marry him. Though I doubt she would either way. My sister is not stupid. She knows he is not at all right for her."

Gerard considered her words before nodding in agreement. Compassionate and willing to love with her whole soul Etta might be, but this certainly did not mean she was foolish.

"Miss Stone, please indulge me. Would you be willing to help me?"

Anne raised an eyebrow at him.

"Wait here a moment. I'll return quickly." Gerard hurried to the room where he'd found Freddie and Miss Bates and spied the desk supplied with writing material. He took a sheet of paper, dipped a pen, and began to write.

He explained everything: the letter, his feelings for Etta, his gratitude for the woman she was and the man she had taught him to be. He briefly mentioned that he had witnessed a moment of indiscretion in his cousin that made him worry for her welfare, but that he had then realized that she didn't require him to save her because she was clever enough to do that for herself.

He filled one sheet.

Then two.

He had started on a third when Gerard heard the music shift. He worried that Miss Stone might not have waited and hurried to sign his name.

He sealed the letter and returned to Miss Stone, who was still standing where he had left her.

She gave him an incredulous smile. "You cannot be serious," she said as she eyed the missive.

"I understand the impropriety, but I count on your love for your sister to give you discretion. She can burn it after she reads it if she likes."

"I will see that she gets it."

"Another favor before you leave, Miss Stone?" He pulled out the small, velvet-wrapped package from his pocket. He'd meant to give it to Etta earlier but hadn't been given the chance. "I want her to have this. With no obligation or expectation."

Anne's eyes were sympathetic as she accepted the package and promised Etta would get it as well. Gerard bowed and walked away. He'd done what he could do, and, short of disrespecting Etta's wishes and forcing her to talk to him, there was nothing left but to leave and hope just a little.

Chapter Twenty-Three

"Hiding in the Eddings' library is childish, Etta. No one hides at a ball." Anne had her hands on her hips and stared down at where Etta had curled up on a gold-embroidered sofa in the small alcove that was mostly hidden from the view of the door.

"You might be surprised to learn that I was joined by several others who were also hiding. I met a lovely young lady, Miss Alison Howarth, who was avoiding the matchmaking meddling of mothers. She invited me to tea the morning after next. You'll like her when you meet her."

"I'm sure I will. Speaking of friendships, I came across Mr. Hartwell. He had the look of a man desperately disappointed."

"You must have told him Mr. Seagram already has a claim on you and that now he won't have your dowry to help save his estate." Etta sounded like a bitter harpy.

"Do not make a cake of yourself. He spoke only of you. And he gave me some things to give to you." Anne pulled a letter and a small package from her beaded reticule.

A letter.

Of all the foolish things.

Did he not know what that letter—another one—could do to her reputation? For him to hand it off to her sister in a public place was beyond comprehension. Etta cast a worried glance at the door.

"No one saw him give it to me, and Mama is with Mrs. Seagram. They're planning another dinner, at the Seagrams' home this time. Take it. Wait until we're at home to read it."

Etta took the letter and package and placed them into her own bag. She hated how much she loved the intrigue of it all.

Never had a ball seemed so interminable, nor the ride home so long. Etta had to wait even after she was freed from the carriage and back in her bedchamber since she had to wash her face and have her hair taken down. Once she'd been readied for bed, she set the beeswax candle on the table near her bed, curled up under her blankets, and opened the letter.

She almost put it away again immediately as she thought she heard someone out in the hall. Etta did not want to be caught with another letter scandal on her hands. But no one entered her room. She looked down again.

> *My Dearest Miss Etta,*
>
> *I don't expect anything from you, Miss Etta. I do not blame you for being angry with me. I know what you believe happened, but if you will give me a moment to explain, you will, I hope, find that this is all a misunderstanding.*
>
> *We renewed our friendship on rather shaky ground. I take all the blame for that. But I will not lie to you by saying I regret my actions. I do not regret them at all.*

Etta snorted and shook her head. Of all the arrogant, insolent non-apologies he could have given!

> *I do not regret my actions because they allowed me to really know you, to understand you, to find myself wanting to improve my behavior based on the generosity I found in your soul. When we last parted in*

Norfolk, you were upset. My behavior at that time is regrettable. You walked away, and I allowed it. I did not see clearly. You mentioned your value, and I should have explained that you are priceless in every particular. But I failed you. If I could go back and do that moment over, I would tell you how valuable you are.

You are the woman who stands guard over the dignity of others so that no one may assault them. You are the woman who loves other people, whether they deserve it or not. I've heard you say you have no talent, no skill, but what is love if not a skill that must be practiced regularly? It is a thankless talent to be sure, receiving neither applause nor accolades in drawing rooms, but it is a talent so few possess. It allows you to frankly forgive all those who wound you. To want to protect those of your acquaintance. You are of immeasurable value.

Tears blurred Etta's vision. She wiped them away on her sleeve.

While at Hartwell Hall, I had time to contemplate our friendship. When I received good news from my steward, you were the one person I wanted to tell. When I hit my hand with a hammer, I wished you near for comfort—though, in truth, you'd have probably laughed at me and reminded me not to be so clumsy in the future.

I love that we laugh together. That we share ideas. What I realized at Hartwell Hall was that I love you. What good is it for me to make such efforts to repair my home if I do not bring love to it? How is Hartwell Hall ever to recover itself if genuine love is not part of its healing process? It cannot.

I cannot heal my home without you.

I returned immediately to tell you, to shout my love from the hilltops. You and your family had already gone.

At first, I felt no alarm. I could declare my love and in-
tentions in London as easily as I could in Norfolk. But
then I found something abandoned in the woods be-
tween your home and Rosemary Manor. I'm returning it
to you. It is in this package that accompanied my letter
to you. Please open it.

Etta wrinkled her brow. She put down her letter, glanced again at
the door, and covered the letter with her bedclothes. She picked up
the velvet-wrapped package and opened it, gasping as she saw what it
concealed. Her talisman was now a stunning necklace. How had he
managed such a creation?

"Oh, Gerard," Etta murmured. She breathed deeply to calm her
racing heart, the faint sweet scent of her candle filling her nostrils. She
breathed deeply like that for a moment, admiring her treasure, before
having the ability to think clearly enough to return to her letter.

When I first found your treasure, I thought you had
left it by accident, perhaps dropped it. When Freddie
confronted me upon my return to Rosemary Manor, I
knew you had given it up in the same way I believe
you want to give me up, but if I could, I would be on
my knees begging you to believe me when I say I did
not betray your trust in me. I never gave your letter to
Freddie. My valet found the envelope in my wardrobe.
He had no reason to know why it was in my possession.
He only saw that it had Freddie's name on it and deliv-
ered it to him.

I am sorry for that. I should have hidden it better
. . . No, I should have given it back to you immediately.
What I did was wrong. Forcing you to pretend was un-
forgivable—even for your forgiving heart. I know that.
My cousin advised me to marry for the money I
needed to ease my financial distress, and he suggested
your sister specifically. I told him I could never do such

a thing. When I saw you again, it felt like fate. I had been friends with Anne. I believed a marriage based on friendship is almost as good as one based on love. Finding love in you proved to me just how foolish I was. With you, I would have it all: love, friendship, and happiness.

I know you likely believe that my actions are all the desperate maneuvering of an impoverished man. But I assure you that they are the desperate attempts of a man who has fallen irrevocably in love with you.

I am so very sorry to have put you in a situation that gave you distress. If I could do it over, I would hand you back your letter and simply ask you to allow me to call on you, but that moment is gone now. But if you would consider me as an option for your future, nothing would make me happier, and I would spend all my days striving for your happiness as well. I believe that with you by my side, we can save my estate without any inoculation from your dowry, and I will be able to provide you a life you deserve. You are the song of my soul, Etta. I will love you to my last breath. I will love you forever.

Yours, Gerard

Etta read the letter again and then a third and fourth time. Gerard loved her.

Truly loved her.

She believed him and felt a fool for not having guessed the reason for Mr. Finch having her other letter. Now what could she do about it?

She wanted to jump up, get dressed, and bang on Gerard's door, pleading entrance to his home and heart.

Etta stayed where she was until long after the candle had guttered out. She wasn't sure she slept much, if at all. By the time the sun had come up, she knew what she had to do. She dressed quickly and ventured to Anne's room.

Anne was still in bed, burrowed deeply in her blankets so that only the ends of her sunshine hair were visible.

Etta sat next to her sister and pulled the covers down enough to reveal Anne's face. Her lips were slightly parted, and her deep breaths came out in long peaceful puffs. Even while sleeping, Anne was lovely. Etta woke up tangled and puffy.

She hated to disrupt her sister but believed Anne would forgive her given the news. "Anne!" She shook her shoulder gently. "Anne, wake up."

Anne's mouth closed and her brow creased with irritation. She rolled over and murmured, "I'm sleeping, Etta."

"You're not anymore, because you don't talk in your sleep."

With a grunt of frustration, Anne opened her eyes. The crease in her brow deepened into a full scowl. "What could possibly have you smiling so deliriously?"

"Happiness." Just saying the word made Etta smile even more widely.

Anne studied her for a moment. "I do believe you are serious."

"I've never been more so."

Anne sat up, propping herself against the pillows. "Well? What are you waiting for? Tell me what has you smiling as though you've drunk yourself silly on Mother's ratafia."

"I've decided to get married."

Anne's eyes widened in alarm. "No, Etta. No. You cannot marry him. He's all wrong for you. You know he is."

"I thought you liked him."

Anne threw her hands up in exasperation. "I don't dislike him, but I think he will break your heart before the first month of marriage is out."

"Wait." Understanding dawned on Etta. "Do you think I mean Mr. Finch?"

Understanding then came to Anne as well, for she suddenly smiled. "Do you mean Mr. Hartwell?"

"Yes."

Anne threw her arms around her sister. "That *is* excellent news! When did this happen? Did he come by this morning?"

"That's the tricky bit. No. He did not come by. No. I read his letter. Now I must go see him. Will you come with me? He's not far. I can't go alone, and having a chaperone feels a burden at present."

Instead of responding, Anne threw off her bedclothes so fast and with such energy that she nearly knocked Etta off the bed. If anything, Anne dressed faster than Etta had. In short order, they were both brushed, buttoned, and headed to Gerard's house.

"How do you know where he lives?" Anne asked as they turned off their street and headed west.

At this, Etta felt slightly abashed. "I might have made a few discreet inquiries around the neighborhood."

Anne only laughed. They arrived at the house in question. While it was not as nice as their home, no observer would guess at the owner's current poverty.

The butler answered the door, greeted the ladies politely, and waited expectantly for one of them to speak. Etta felt silly. What sort of young woman called on a man? If her mother only knew what she was doing, Etta would have been able to hear her fuming from several streets over.

"Hello," Anne said when she realized Etta was unable to speak. "We've come to call on Mrs. Hartwell. Is she home at present?"

Of course. While calling on Gerard was entirely inappropriate, surely nothing would be wrong in visiting his mother.

The butler showed the sisters to the drawing room. They waited only a moment before Mrs. Hartwell joined them. She didn't seem too surprised to see them sitting on her sofa. She seated herself across from them and rang for some tea. "It may take a moment for the tea to come. I do apologize."

Etta and Anne assured her that no apology was necessary.

They made small talk for a moment, remarking on the weather and the variances from life in Norfolk to life in London. Finally, Mrs. Hartwell put an end to polite conversation. "Why don't you tell me why you've come to visit? Surely it's not to reminisce over Norfolk."

"Well, no. I did not come to discuss Norfolk." Etta searched for a way to respond without the woman thinking ill of her but was saved when Gerard's voice came from the doorway. "Miss Stone? Miss Marietta? What an unexpected surprise!"

His shirtsleeves were rolled up to his elbows, and dirt smudged his left cheekbone and one side of his shirt. The shirt was also open at the neck and clung to his perspiring form, and Etta had to look away to avoid staring.

"You're clearly in the middle of something," Etta said, unable to think what else to say.

His mother waved at Gerard. "He has been making some repairs. With circumstances being what they are, he's become quite adept at handling any number of things. He was sanding down some doors that had swollen since we were last here. They'd become difficult for me to open and close. He's a dear that way.

Gerard, why don't you show Miss Etta your work?" Mrs. Hartwell looked at Anne. "Miss Stone? I've a lovely kitchen garden that might interest you." Anne was up on her feet before Etta could reply.

As Mrs. Hartwell and Anne left the room, the former turned back to Etta. "In case I don't have the opportunity to see you later, I do thank you for the lovely visit and hope you will call on me again." Then they were gone, leaving Etta alone with Gerard.

"You don't need to see the sanded doors," Gerard said slowly. "The floors are dusty and dirty. I would not want your dress to be soiled."

His eyes trailed over her face and to the ribbon at her neck and the locket that now hung from it. "It looks well on you."

She placed her hand over the cool surface of the metal. "Thank you for such a wonderful gift."

Had any conversation between them ever been so stilted and awkward?

She took a step close to Gerard. "Did you mean it?" she said in a rush. "Did you mean it when you said you loved me? Because I don't think I could bear it if I were a means to solve financial distress."

He took a step closer as well. "The first time I truly became aware of you was when I was seven. Your hair seemed always to be hanging in your face. And it was always filled with leaves, no matter how much your governess tried to keep you from the fields and trees. You challenged me to a race. You won, might I add. I don't know if you remember that."

"I do remember that race," Etta said. "You laughed when I beat you and said, 'Well done.' I thought it very brave for you to admit defeat to a girl in front of your cousin."

She took another step. So did he.

He continued. "Brave? No. Losing vexed me at the time. The next time I saw you, I was eight. You were saving a baby bird, and all I could think was that there was no one else I would rather lose a race to than you. Every time I saw you after that, you challenged me in some way. Miss Stone, I have loved every interaction, every challenge, even as I stumble to keep up with you."

Another step. How many more would she have to take before reaching him? Four? Five?

But if he stepped with her, they would come together in two and a half.

He took another. "I came to London to ask your father permission to formally court you. But now all I can think is how I wish to ask him for your hand, Et—Miss Stone. I know you must think me mercenary in some way after all of our dealings together, but I wrote him a letter. I confessed to him my poverty, and I also told him I would not touch your dowry to save my circumstances; I wanted only you, and with your ingenuity and support, we would save my estate together."

They both moved at the same time.

"He never responded." Gerard looked pained by this. "I don't blame him. I offer nothing but ask for everything in desiring the hand of his acknowledged favorite daughter."

Etta stared at him. He had gone to her father. He had declined the use of her dowry—not that she believed her father would ever let her enter the marriage state without assurances that all was well financially—especially if he knew her intended had no material means of his own, the dowry would absolutely be required to make her situation secure, but Gerard would not have known that.

"I . . ." Did she dare say the words aloud? "I love you too," she said. "I'm sorry for doubting you. I should have known you would not have betrayed me on purpose. I was wrong to tell you that you had no right to my name. So wrong. You are never allowed to call me Miss Stone again. You may call me Etta, or Mrs. Hartwell, if you're feeling flirtatious. Yes. I will marry you. Not because you're holding a letter captive, but because you are holding my heart. May you never set it free."

She took the last step.

So did Gerard.

They came together.

He pulled her into his arms and lowered his face to hers but hesitated, as if unsure.

Etta was not unsure. She pushed up on her tiptoes and pulled him in by his shirt, not caring that it was covered with dust. Their lips were barely a breath apart when she whispered, "And I apologize in advance for any odd treatment you may receive from my mother."

Gerard seemed startled by such a comment and laughed, but she cut short his mirth when she pressed her lips to his. He stumbled in his surprise. If she hadn't been steady on her feet, he would have pulled them both to the ground.

His hand went up to cradle her face as he gently traced another kiss on her lips. His fingers slowly wrapped around a curl of her hair.

"I love you, Etta."

"And I love you."

He kissed her again and deepened the kiss until they were tied together as one, not by an errant letter, but by truth and the future. Each shared a breath in and out and collided against the other in a tangle of love that seemed to spiral into eternity.

Chapter Twenty-Four

Etta's mother was delighted by the announcement that her eldest daughter, Anne, was to marry Mr. Seagram.

She had not been exactly pleased with the information that Etta was to be married to Gerard Hartwell, cousin to the wretched neighbors who seemed to always outdo her in some way. But neither was she displeased.

And with both of her daughters marrying before Lucy Finch, Etta's mother felt as though she had triumphed over her neighbors at last.

Etta decided this was the best she could hope for.

Her father had not received the letter Gerard had sent him. They surmised that it had been caught in the breeze coming from an open window and blown behind his desk. They didn't find the letter until after her father had passed away and the desk had been moved.

Once things were settled between her and Gerard and the banns had been read, Etta convinced him to talk things over with his cousin. He had fought the idea until she insisted she wanted Freddie at her wedding.

"Whatever for?" he'd asked.

"We owe our thanks to him for all our happiness. Had it not been for him, I would never have written the letter. You would never have tried to use it to blackmail me. And we would never have found ourselves so lucky in love."

Gerard finally agreed, a thing which relieved Etta from a great burden.

She remembered the pain in Gerard's eyes when he'd spoken of his cousin shutting him out. She wanted to heal that pain in any way she could, because she knew the friendship mattered to Gerard and that he would never be completely happy without it.

She was glad when Gerard returned from his cousin's house to inform her that they had reconciled and that Freddie would come to their wedding.

And Freddie kept his word.

Certainly, he flirted with the bride, which irritated Gerard. He told Gerard that she had loved him first, which irritated Etta. And he scowled fiercely at the young man who had been calling on Lucy, which irritated Lucy.

Gerard had told Etta about finding Freddie with Miss Bates, and she advised him to not report on the incident unless Miss Bates decided to make it known. A lapse in judgment in the form of an assumed kiss was not worth the future happiness of both.

After they were married and Gerard took Etta home to Hartwell Hall, she fell in love all over again. For as much as he'd said the place was crumbling into disarray, she found it all charming and perfect.

She told him so as they sat in front of the fire late one night.

"Its only resemblance to perfection, darling," he said, "is that you are now in it. There is still much that needs to be worked on."

"Certainly," she agreed. "And now you have my help."

"Will you wield a hammer, then?"

She shrugged. "I think I might be good at that."

Gerard laughed. "I think you might be as well. Considering the balance of our skills, our marriage will require a secret pact."

She narrowed her eyes at him. "I'm going to regret asking what sort of pact you might require of me, aren't I?"

He smirked. "It's nothing too sinister, darling. It's only that, since

I am an expert at embroidery and you've already declared you despise the activity but you might like hammering, how would you feel if I plan to do all the embroidery and for you to do any hammering you might wish? We would spare our reputations by your taking the credit for the embroidery and my taking the credit for the hammering."

Etta lightly shoved at her husband's shoulder. "Embroidery indeed." She sniffed as if the idea were preposterous, but she'd actually seen his embroidery, and it was nothing short of exquisite.

He caught her hand in his and leaned in close so that there was barely a space between them. "I love you. You saved me from the despair of a lifetime of loneliness, Etta. Like that bird all those years ago, you saved me. I need you to know that."

She did know.

She had thought she understood love when she'd written those letters to Frederick Finch. But she now knew the difference between a candle flame and the blaze of the sun. She tilted her chin up to kiss him. "And I love you."

"How do I know you love me?"

She smiled against his lips. "If you don't believe me, I suppose I could always write you a letter."

Acknowledgments

Confession: I've totally written love letters and not sent them. So if you think I might have once been in love with you . . . Well, you'll never know, will you? This book would not be possible without my real-life, contemporary romance and love, Scott Wright, who supports my every dream (except the one of him wearing a Regency costume) and who makes me laugh as often as he makes me roll my eyes. Thanks for holding my hand through the good and the bad. I love you more than Mr. Darcy.

To my kids and grandkids: I love our family group chats with the gifs, memes, and jokes. You all make me so proud. I know I've always had a career, but you all are my greatest work. You are my joy.

Several years ago, I was approached by the project manager of a much-sought-after publishing company. Heidi Gordon asked me to go to lunch with her to talk about a career with them. I am so grateful for that encounter. I appreciate her, Chris Schoebinger, Troy Butcher, Callie Hansen, Lisa Mangum, and everyone else at Shadow Mountain who put so much of your hearts into my projects. Thank you for the wonderful edit, Maddie Senator. I appreciate the fact checking and insightful information. You are a wonderful editor.

I recently got back from a writing conference—one I started with several close writing friends twenty years ago. It reminded me of the fact that I would not be where I am today without those friends encouraging me and driving me to improve. There is not enough paper and ink to name you all, but you know who you are. Thank you.

I owe a lot to my parents. Hi, Mom and Dad! You did a good job. We all turned out great—even Gary. (Okay, okay, *especially* Gary.)

Also, thanks, Heavenly Father. It rained last night, and you know my favorite scent is petrichor. It smelled, well . . . *heavenly*.

Finally, thank you, dear reader. Without you, I would be entirely unnecessary.

Discussion Questions

1. How would you react if your secret love letters to your crush were accidentally mailed?

2. What could Etta have done differently so she didn't have to pretend anything? Or were the falsehoods necessary to save her reputation?

3. Etta makes the observation, "The longer we hold our grievances, the harder they become to release." In what ways is this true for the characters in the book? In what ways might it be true in your own life?

4. Like letters, truth and understanding are not always convenient, but when love hangs in the balance, they are always worth it. In what ways do truth and understanding bring about the real emotions of love for Etta and Gerard?

5. Gerard's mother tells him, "Secrets are damaging little demons." Would Etta and Gerard have found love with one another had it not been for their secrets? In what ways were their secrets damaging?

6. Gerard makes the observation that he had "grown tired of people more committed to easy solutions than to correct solutions." In what ways did he choose the easy solution? In what ways did he choose the correct solution?

7. Gerard asks the question, "How was it so many people managed to botch up the whole business of being family so thoroughly?" From Miss Bates to the various mothers and cousins, in what ways did the characters manage to botch up the business of being family? How could they have handled things better in order to show greater respect and understanding for one another?

About the Author

JULIE WRIGHT was born in Salt Lake City, Utah. She wrote her first book when she was fifteen after an English teacher told her she would never be a writer. Since then, she's written twenty-six novels and ten novellas. Julie is a two-time winner of the Whitney Award for best romance with her books *Cross My Heart* and *Lies Jane Austen Told Me* and is a Crown Heart recipient. Her book *Death Thieves* was a Whitney finalist. Her books have received several starred reviews and have been listed in the American Library Association's top ten romances of the year.

She's a sucker for almost all things nerdy: *Doctor Who*, Disneyland, the Marvel Universe, *Harry Potter*, *The Lord of the Rings*, fairy tales, and Jane Austen. She believes in second chances, getting up and trying again, and the power of generosity and compassion.

She is surrounded by a loving and supportive family, one dog, and a varying number of houseplants (depending on attrition).

She loves writing, reading, traveling, hiking, snorkeling, playing with her family on the beach, and watching her husband make dinner.